CROCODILE ON THE SANDBANK

Also by Elizabeth Peters

CROCODILE

ON THE SANDBANK
by Elizabeth Peters

DODD, MEAD & COMPANY, New York

Library of Congress Cataloging in Publication Data

Peters, Elizabeth.
   Crocodile on the sandbank.

   I. Title.
PZ4.P4816Cr   [PS3566.E755]   813'.5'5   74–31490
ISBN 0–396–07080–9

to my son Peter

The love of my beloved is on yonder side
A width of water is between us
And a crocodile waiteth on the sandbank.
Ancient Egyptian Love Poem

Author's Note

ALTHOUGH my major characters are wholly fictitious, certain historic personages make brief appearances in these pages. Maspero, Brugsch and Grebaut were associated with the Egyptian Department of Antiquities in the 1880's, and William Flinders Petrie was then beginning his great career in Egyptology. Petrie was the first professional archaeologist to excavate at Tell el Amarna and I have taken the liberty of attributing some of his discoveries—and his "advanced" ideas about methodology—to my fictitious archaeologists. The painted pavement found by Petrie was given the treatment I have described by Petrie himself. Except for discrepancies of this nature I have attempted to depict the Egypt of that era, and the state of archaeological research in the late nineteenth century, as accurately as possible, relying on contemporary travel books for details. In order to add verisimilitude to the narrative, I have used the contemporary spelling of names of places and pharaohs, as well as certain words like "dahabeeyah." For example, the name of the heretic pharaoh was formerly read as "Khuenaten." Modern scholars prefer the reading "Akhenaten." Similarly, "Usertsen" is the modern "Senusert."

CROCODILE ON THE SANDBANK

1

When I first set eyes on Evelyn Barton-Forbes she was walking the streets of Rome—

(I am informed, by the self-appointed Critic who reads over my shoulder as I write, that I have already committed an error. If those seemingly simple English words do indeed imply that which I am told they imply to the vulgar, I must in justice to Evelyn find other phrasing.)

In justice to myself, however, I must insist that Evelyn was doing precisely what I have said she was doing, but with no ulterior purpose in mind. Indeed, the poor girl had no purpose and no means of carrying it out if she had. Our meeting was fortuitous, but fortunate. I had, as I have always had, purpose enough for two.

I had left my hotel that morning in considerable irritation of spirits. My plans had gone awry. I am not accustomed to having my plans go awry. Sensing my mood, my small Italian guide trailed behind me in silence. Piero was not silent when I first encountered him, in the lobby of the hotel, where, in common with others of his kind, he awaited the arrival of helpless foreign visitors in need of a translator and guide. I selected him from amid the throng because his appearance was a trifle less villainous than that of the others.

I was well aware of the propensity of these fellows to bully, cheat, and otherwise take advantage of the victims who employ them, but I had no intention of being victimized. It did not take me long to make this clear to Piero. My first act was to bargain ruthlessly with the shopkeeper to whom Piero took me to buy silk. The final price was so low that Piero's commission was reduced to a negligible sum. He expressed his chagrin to his compatriot in his native tongue, and included in his tirade several personal comments on my appearance and manner. I let him go on for some time and then interrupted with a comment on *his* manners. I speak Italian, and understand it, quite well. After that Piero and I got on admirably. I had not employed him because I required an interpreter, but because I wanted someone to carry parcels and run errands.

My knowledge of languages, and the means which enabled me to travel abroad, had been acquired from my late father, who was a scholar and antiquarian. There was little else to do but study, in the small country town where Papa preferred to live, and I have an aptitude for languages, dead and alive. Papa preferred his languages dead. He was a devoted student of the past, and emerged from it only occasionally, when he would blink at me and express surprise at how I had grown since he last noticed my existence. I found our life together quite congenial; I am the youngest of six, and my brothers, being considerably older, had left the nest some time before. My brothers were successful merchants and professional men; one and all they rejected Father's studies. I was left, then, to be the prop of my father's declining years. As I have said, the life suited me. It allowed me to develop my talents for scholarship. But let not the Gentle Reader suppose that I was ill equipped for the practical necessities of life. My father was disinclined toward practicalities. It was left to me to bully the baker and badger the butcher, which I did, if I may say so, quite effectively. After Mr. Hodgkins the butcher, Piero gave me no trouble.

My father died, eventually—if one may use so precise a word for the process that took place. One might say that he gradually shriveled up and ran down. The rumor, put about by a pert housemaid, that he had actually been dead for two days before anyone noticed, is a complete exaggeration. I must admit, however, that he might have passed away at any point during the five hours I spent with him in his study on that particular afternoon. He was leaning back in his big leather chair, meditating, as I assumed; and when, warned by some premonition, I hurried to his side, his wide-open eyes held the same expression of mild inquiry with which they had always regarded me. It seemed to me quite a respectable and comfortable way in which to pass on.

It came as no surprise to anyone to discover that he had left his property to me, the aforesaid prop, and the only one of his children who had not an income of its own. My brothers accepted this tolerantly, as they had accepted my devoted service to Papa. They did not explode until they learned that the property was not a paltry sum, but a fortune of half a million pounds. They had made a common mistake in assuming that an absentminded scholar is necessarily a fool. My father's disinclination to argue with Mr. Hodgkins the butcher was due, not to lack of ability, but to disinterest. He was very much interested in investments, " 'change," and those other mysterious matters that produce wealth. He had conducted his business affairs with the same reticence that marked his habits in general; and he died, to the surprise of all, a wealthy man.

When this fact became known, the explosion occurred. My eldest brother James went so far as to threaten legal proceedings, on the basis of unsound mind and undue influence. This ill-considered burst of temper, which was characteristic of James, was easily stopped by Mr. Fletcher, Papa's excellent solicitor. Other attempts ensued. I was visited by streams of attentive nieces and nephews assuring me of their devotion—which had been demonstrated, over the past years, by their absence. Sisters-in-law invited me, in the most affectionate phrases, to share their homes. I was warned in the strongest terms against fortune hunters.

The warnings were not unselfish; they were, however, unnecessary. A middle-aged spinster—for I was at that time thirty-two years of age, and I scorned to disguise the fact—who has never received a proposal of marriage must be a simpleton if she fails to recognize the sudden acquisition of a fortune as a factor in her new popularity. I was not a simpleton. I had always known myself to be plain.

The transparent attempts of my kin, and of various unemployed gentlemen, to win my regard, aroused in me a grim amusement. I did not put them off; quite the contrary, I encouraged them to visit, and laughed up my sleeve at their clumsy efforts. Then it occurred to me that I was enjoying them too much. I was becoming cynical; and it was this character development that made me decide to leave England—not, as some malicious persons have intimated, a fear of being overborne. I had always wanted to travel. Now, I decided, I would see all the places Father had studied—the glory that was Greece and the grandeur that was Rome; Babylon and hundred-gated Thebes.

Once I had made this decision, it did not take me long to prepare for the journey. I made my arrangements with Mr.

Fletcher, and received from him a proposal of marriage which I refused with the same good humor that had characterized the offer. At least he was honest.

"I thought it worth a try," he remarked calmly.

"Nothing ventured, nothing gained," I agreed.

Mr. Fletcher studied me thoughtfully for a moment.

"Miss Amelia, may I ask—in my professional capacity now—whether you have any inclinations toward matrimony?"

"None. I disapprove of matrimony as a matter of principle." Mr. Fletcher's pepper-and-salt eyebrows lifted. I added, "For myself, that is. I suppose it is well enough for some women; what else can the poor things do? But why should any independent, intelligent female choose to subject herself to the whims and tyrannies of a husband? I assure you, I have yet to meet a man as sensible as myself!"

"I can well believe that," said Mr. Fletcher. He hesitated for a moment; I fancied I could see him struggle with the desire to make an unprofessional statement. He lost the struggle.

"Why do you wear such frightful clothes?" he burst out. "If it is to discourage suitors—"

"Really, Mr. Fletcher!" I exclaimed.

"I beg your pardon," said the lawyer, wiping his brow. "I cannot think what came over me."

"Nor can I. As for my clothes, they suit the life I lead. The current fashions are impractical for an active person. Skirts so tight one must toddle like an infant, bodices boned so firmly it is impossible to draw a deep breath. . . . And bustles! Of all the idiotic contrivances foisted upon helpless womankind, the bustle is certainly the worst. I wear them, since it is impossible to have a gown made without them, but at least I can insist on sensible dark fabrics and a minimum of ornament. What a fool I should look in puffs and frills and crimson satin—or a gown trimmed with dead birds, like one I saw!"

5

"And yet," said Mr. Fletcher, smiling, "I have always thought you would look rather well in puffs and frills and crimson satin."

The opportunity to lecture had restored my good humor. I returned his smile, but I shook my head.

"Give it up, Mr. Fletcher. You cannot flatter me; I know the catalogue of my faults too accurately. I am too tall, I am too lean in some regions and too amply endowed in others. My nose is too large, my mouth is too wide, and the shape of my chin is positively masculine. Sallow complexions and jetty black hair are not in fashion this season; and I have been informed that eyes of so deep a gray, set under such forbidding black brows, strike terror into the beholder even when they are beaming with benevolence—which my eyes seldom do. Now, I think I have dealt with that subject. Shall we turn to business?"

At Fletcher's suggestion I made my will. I had no intention of dying for a good many years, but I realized the hazards of travel in such unhealthy regions as I proposed to visit. I left my entire fortune to the British Museum, where Papa had spent so many happy hours. I felt rather sentimental about it; Papa might just as well have passed on in the Reading Room, and it would possibly have taken the attendants more than two days to realize he was no longer breathing.

My last act before departing was to engage a companion. I did not do this for the sake of propriety. Oppressed as my sex is in this supposedly enlightened decade of 1880, a woman of my age and station in life can travel abroad alone without offending any but the overly prudish. I engaged a companion because—in short, because I was lonely. All my life I had taken care of Papa. I needed someone, not to look after me, but the reverse. Miss Pritchett was a perfect companion. She was a few years my senior, but one never would have supposed it from her dress and manner. She affected dainty frilled gowns of thin muslin which hung awkwardly on her bony frame, and her voice was a preposterous high-pitched squeal.

She was clumsy; her stupidity was so intense it verged on simplemindedness; she had a habit of fainting, or, at least, of collapsing into a chair with her hand pressed to her heart, whenever the slightest difficulty occurred. I looked forward to my association with Miss Pritchett. Prodding her through the malodorous streets of Cairo and the deserts of Palestine would provide my active mind with the distraction it needed.

After all, Miss Pritchett failed me. People of that sort seldom fall ill; they are too busy pretending to be ill. Yet no sooner had we reached Rome than Miss Pritchett succumbed to the typhoid, like the weak-minded female she was. Though she recovered, she delayed my departure for Egypt for two weeks, and it was manifest that she would not be able to keep up with my pace until after a long convalescence. I therefore dispatched her back to England in the care of a clergyman and his wife, who were leaving Rome. Naturally I felt obliged to pay her salary until she was able to secure another post. She left weeping, and trying, as the carriage left, to kiss my hand.

She left a vacuum in my carefully laid plans, and she was the cause of my ill humor when I left the hotel that fateful day. I was already two weeks behind schedule, and all the accommodations had been arranged for two persons. Should I try to find another companion, or resign myself to solitary travel? I must make my decision soon, and I was musing about it as I went for a final visit to the desolate Cow Pasture which was the seat of the ancient Forum of Rome.

It was a brisk December afternoon; the sun was intermittently obscured by clouds. Piero looked like a cold dog, despite the warm jacket I had purchased for him. I do not feel the cold. The breezy day, with its alternating shadow and sunshine, was quite appropriate to the scene. Broken columns and fallen stones were obscured by tumbled masses of weeds, now brown and brittle. There were other visitors rambling about. I avoided them. After reading a few of the broken inscriptions, and identifying, to my satisfaction, the spots where Caesar fell and where the senators awaited the arrival of the Goths, I seated myself on a fallen column.

Piero huddled at my feet with his knees drawn up and his arms wrapped around the basket he had been carrying. I found the hard, cold seat comfortable enough; there is something to be said for a bustle, in fact. It was compassion for Piero that made me order him to open the basket the hotel kitchen had provided. However, he refused my offer of hot tea with a pitiful look. I presume he would have accepted brandy.

I was drinking my tea when I noticed that there was a cluster of people some distance away, who seemed to be gathered around an object that was concealed from me by their bodies. I sent Piero to see what it was, and went on drinking my tea.

After an interval he came bounding back with his black eyes gleaming. Nothing delights these gentry quite so much as misfortune; I was therefore not surprised when he reported that the "turisti" were gathered around a young English lady who had fallen down dead upon the ground.

"How do you know that she is English?" I inquired.

Piero did not reply in words; he went through an extraordinary series of grimaces to indicate a certainty so profound it requires no evidence. His eyes rolled, his hands flew about, his shoulders rose and fell. What else should the lady be but English.

English or not, I doubted that the lady was dead. That was only Piero's Latin love of the dramatic. But so far as I could see, no one in the crowd was doing anything except stare. I rose to my feet, therefore, and after brushing off my bustle, I approached the group. My parasol proved useful in passing through it; I had to apply the ferrule quite sharply to the backs of several gentlemen before they would move. Eventually I penetrated to the center of the circle. As I had surmised, no one was behaving with sense or compassion. Indeed, several of the ladies were pulling their escorts away, with comments about infection and criticism of the fallen lady's probable character.

She was so pitiful as she lay there on the cold, damp ground that only a heart of stone could have been unmoved. There are many hearts of that composition, however.

I sat down upon the ground and lifted the girl's head onto my knee. I regretted very much that I had not worn a cloak or mantle. However, that was easily remedied.

"Your coat, sir," I said to the nearest gentleman.

He was a stout, red-faced person whose extra layers of flesh should have been enough to keep him warm, without the fur-lined greatcoat he wore. He carried a handsome gold-headed stick, which he had been using to poke at the fallen girl as a lecturer in a waxworks indicates the exhibits. When I addressed him, he turned from his companion, to whom he had been speaking in an undertone, and stared at me.

"What—what?" he snorted.

"Your coat," I said impatiently. "Give it to me at once." Then, as he continued to stare, his face getting redder and redder, I raised my voice. "Sir—your coat, at once!"

I put the coat over the girl. Having assured myself that she was only in a faint, I was at leisure to look at her more closely. I was not a whit distracted by the whalelike sputterings of the red-faced gentleman whose coat I had appropriated.

I have said that I am a plain woman. For this reason I have a quite disinterested love of beauty in all its forms. I could therefore disinterestedly admire the girl who lay unconscious before me.

She was English, surely; that flawless white skin and pale-golden hair could belong to no other nation. She was naturally fair of complexion; now, in her fainting state, her face was as pallid and pure as marble. The features might have been those of an antique Venus or young Diana. Her lashes were several shades darker than her hair, forming a pleasing contrast. She was dressed, quite inappropriately for the chilly weather, in a summer frock and thin blue cloak; both cloak and gown were sadly worn, but had once been expensive—they were of costly material and showed good workmanship. The gloves on her small hands had been neatly mended. The girl presented a picture of poverty and abandonment that excited my curiosity as much as it aroused my compassion; I wondered what had reduced a young woman of obvious refinement to this state. I surmised that she suffered chiefly from cold and hunger; the thin white face was pinched and sunken.

As I watched, her dark-gold lashes fluttered and lifted, disclosing eyes of an exquisite deep blue. They stared dreamily about for a time, and then fixed themselves on my face. The girl's expression changed; a touch of color came to her thin cheeks, and she struggled to sit up.

"Be still," I said, putting her down with one hand and beckoning Piero with the other. "You have fainted and are still weak. Partake of some nourishment, if you please, before we proceed to further measures to relieve you."

She tried to protest; her helpless state and the circle of staring, unfriendly eyes clearly distressed her. I was perfectly indifferent to the observers, but since she seemed embarrassed, I decided to rid myself of them. I told them to go. They did so, except for the indignant gentleman whose coat was over the girl.

"Your name and hotel, sir," I said, cutting short a loud protest. "Your coat will be returned later this evening. A person of your excessive bulk should not wear such heavy clothing in any case."

The lady by his side, who had the same rotund outlines and hard red face, exclaimed aloud.

"How dare you, madame! I have never heard of such a thing!"

"I daresay you have not," I agreed, giving her a look that made her step back. "I do not doubt that it is too late to awaken in you any faint sense of Christian compassion or normal human emotion, so I shan't try. Take yourself away, madame, and this—I can hardly say 'gentleman'—this male person with you."

As I spoke I was administering bits of food from my basket to the fallen girl. The fastidious manner in which she ate, despite her obvious hunger, confirmed my assumption that she was a lady. She seemed better when she had finished a piece of bread and the remainder of my tea; and since the crowd had retired to a distance I was able, with Piero's assistance, to raise her to her feet. We then proceeded, by carriage, to my hotel.

II

The doctor I summoned assured me that my diagnosis had been correct. The young lady was suffering from starvation and cold only. There was no sign of infection, and she was recovering quickly.

A plan had taken shape in my mind, and I considered it, striding up and down the drawing room of my suite, as is my habit when engaged in thought. It did not take me long to reach a decision. Frail as the girl appeared, she must have a stout constitution in order to have resisted, in her weakened state, the putrid air and water of Rome. Clearly she had no friends or relatives to whom she could look for relief, or she would not have sunk to such a state. Equally clearly, she could not be left in that state.

Having made up my mind, I went to tell the young lady what was to be done.

She was sitting up in bed, taking soup from the hand of my maid, Travers. Neither of them appeared to be enjoying the process. Travers is a living contradiction to the theories of the physiognomists, for her face and shape do not at all reflect her personality. She is a round, cheery-faced little person with the soul of a dried-up old spinster. She did not approve of my taking in a "stray," as she would have said, and her sour look expressed her

11

feelings. To be fair, that was the only way in which Travers *could* express her feelings. I do not permit verbal complaints.

"That will do," I said. "Too much food might be ill advised at present. Go away, Travers, and be sure you close the door tightly."

When she had obeyed, I studied my patient and was pleased at what I saw. My flannel nightdress was considerably too large for the girl. She would need clothing—dainty, delicate things, to suit her fairness—garments of the sort I had never been able to wear. She would look charming in pale shades, blue and pink and lavender. There was color in her face now, a delicate rose flush that made her even prettier. How on earth, I wondered, had such a girl come to her present pass?

My stare must have been more intent than I realized. The girl's eyes dropped. Then she raised her head and spoke, with a firmness I had not expected. Her voice settled any lingering doubts as to her class; it was that of a well-bred young lady.

"I am more indebted than I can say," she began. "But be assured, ma'am, I shall not take advantage of your charity. I am quite recovered now; if you will direct your maid to return my clothing, I will rid you of my presence."

"Your clothing has been thrown away," I said absently. "It was not worth the trouble of laundering. You must remain in bed for the rest of the day in any case. I will order a seamstress to come tomorrow. There is a boat leaving for Alexandria on Friday next. A week should be sufficient. You will need to do some shopping, of course, but first I had better see what you have with you. If you will tell me where you have been staying, I will send a man around for your boxes."

Her face was very expressive. It had registered a variety of emotions as I spoke; the blue eyes had flashed with indignation and then narrowed with suspicion. But the ultimate emotion was openmouthed bewilderment. I waited for her to speak, but she merely opened and closed her mouth, so I said impatiently, "I am taking you to Egypt with me, as my companion. Miss Pritchett failed me; she took the typhoid. I had agreed to pay her ten pounds a year. Naturally I will be responsible for equipping you for the journey. You can hardly travel in a flannel nightdress!"

"No," the girl agreed, looking dazed. "But—but—"

"My name is Amelia Peabody. You will call me Amelia. I am a spinster of independent means, traveling for pleasure. Is there anything else you wish to know about me?"

"I know all I need to know," the girl said quietly. "I was not entirely unconscious when you came to my rescue, and I hope I am able to recognize true kindness of heart. But my dear Miss Peabody—very well, Amelia—you know nothing about *me!*"

"Is there something I should know?"

"I might be a criminal! I might be vicious—unprincipled!"

"No, no," I said calmly. "I have been accused of being some-what abrupt in my actions and decisions, but I never act without thought; it is simply that I think more quickly and more intelligently than most people. I am an excellent judge of character. I could not be deceived about yours."

A dimple appeared at the corner of the girl's mouth. It trembled, and was gone. The blue eyes fell.

"You *are* deceived," she said, so softly I could hardly hear. "I am not what you think. I owe it to you to tell you my story; and when you have heard it, then—then you will be justified in ordering me out of your sight."

"Proceed," I said. "I will be the judge of *that.*"

"I am sure you will!" The dimple reappeared, but did not linger. Her face pale, her eyes steady, the girl began to speak.

THE GIRL'S STORY

My name is Evelyn Barton-Forbes. My parents having died when I was an infant, I was brought up by my grandfather, the Earl of Ellesmere. I see you recognize the name. It is an ancient

13

name and an honorable one—although many of the holders of the title have not been men of honor. My grandfather . . . well, I cannot speak fairly of him. I know he is regarded by many as miserly and selfish; though he possesses one of the greatest fortunes in England, he has never been known as a philanthropist. But he was always good to me. I was his pet, his little lamb, as he called me. I think perhaps I was the only human being to whom he never spoke harshly. He even forgave me for being a girl and not the heir he so ardently desired.

I suspect you are a feminist, Miss—Amelia? Then you will be indignant, but not surprised, to know that although I am the only child of my grandfather's eldest son, I cannot inherit his title or estates. There are few exceptions to the rule that only male descendants may inherit. When my father died prematurely, the next male heir was my cousin, Lucas Hayes.

Poor Lucas! I have not seen a great deal of him, but I always liked him, and I cannot help but pity him because Grandfather was so cruelly unfair to him. Of course Grandfather would never admit to prejudice. He claims to dislike Lucas because of his extravagance and wild habits. But I feel sure such tales are only rumors. Grandfather really hates my unfortunate cousin for the sin of being his father's son. You see, his mother, Grandfather's eldest daughter, ran away with—with an Italian gentleman. . . . (Excuse my emotion, Amelia, you will understand its cause presently. There; I am better now.)

My grandfather is British to the core. He despises all foreigners, but especially those of Latin descent. He considers them sly, slippery—oh, I cannot repeat all the terrible things he says! When my aunt eloped with the Conte d'Imbroglio d'Annunciata, Grandfather disowned her and struck her name from the family Bible. Even when she lay dying he sent no word of comfort or forgiveness. He said the Conte was no nobleman, but a fraud and a fortune hunter. I am sure that is untrue. The Conte had very little money, to be sure, but that does not mean his title was not genuine. However, Lucas, on reaching maturity, felt it wise to change his name, since his true one maddened Grandfather. He calls himself Lucas Elliot Hayes now, and he has abandoned his Italian title.

For a time it seemed that Lucas had succeeded in winning Grandfather by his assiduous attentions. I even wondered whether Grandfather was considering a marriage between us. It would have been a happy solution in a sense, for, the estate and title being entailed, Lucas would eventually inherit them. But without my grandfather's private fortune, which was his to dispose of, the earldom would be a burden rather than a privilege; and Grandfather made no secret of his intention of leaving that money to me.

Yet if there was such a scheme, it came to nothing. Hearing of some new misbehavior, Grandfather flew into a rage and sent Lucas away. I am ashamed to admit I was relieved. Fond as I was of Lucas, I did not love him; and being a foolish, sentimental girl, I fancied love must precede marriage. I see you frown, Amelia, to hear me use such terms of myself. They are too mild, as you will soon learn.

For love came, as I thought; and it proved my utter undoing.

While Lucas was with us I had become interested in drawing. Lucas said I had considerable natural skill, and before he left he taught me what he knew. Afterward, I was desirous of continuing, so Grandfather, who indulged me more than I deserved, advertised for a drawing master. Thus Alberto came into my life.

I cannot speak of him calmly. The handsome features and shining dark hair, which seemed to me angelic, now take on a diabolical aspect. His soft voice, with its tender broken accents—for he spoke English rather badly—come back to me, in retrospect, as the sly whispers of a fiend. He—he. . . . Let me be short and succinct. He seduced me, in short, and persuaded me into an

15

elopement. At his instigation I fled my home; I abandoned the old man who had loved and sheltered me; I flung away every consideration of religion, moral training, and natural affection. I cannot speak of Alberto without loathing; but, believe me, dear Amelia, when I say that I blame myself even more. How true are the old sayings, that evil brings its own punishment! I deserve my wretched fate; I brought it on myself, and I cannot blame those who would shun me. . . .

Forgive me. I will not give way again.

The end of the story is soon told. I had taken with me the few jewels, suitable for a young girl, which Grandfather's generosity had bestowed upon me. The money procured from the sale of these jewels did not last long as we made our way across Europe toward Rome. Alberto insisted that we live in a style that was worthy of me. The lodgings we took in Rome were *not* worthy of me, but by then my money had run out. When I asked Alberto what we were to do, he was evasive. He was also evasive about marriage. As a good Catholic he could not entertain the idea of a civil ceremony. But I was not a Catholic. . . . Oh, his excuses were feeble, I see that now, but I was so naïve. . . .

The blow finally came a week ago. Alberto had been increasingly elusive; he was out a good part of the day, and when he returned he would be intoxicated and sullen. I awoke one morning, in the shabby, freezing attic room to which our poverty had reduced us, to find myself alone. He had had the courtesy to leave me a gown and cloak and a pair of shoes. Every other object I possessed had gone with him, from my ivory brushes to my hair ornaments. He had also left a note.

The sight of this ill-spelled, badly written document was the final blow; its crudities stung me even more than the message it contained, though this was blunt enough. Alberto had selected me as his prey because I was a wealthy heiress. He had expected that my grandfather would react to our elopement by cutting me

16

out of his will; and through communication with the British authorities in Rome he had learned that this had in fact happened. He had believed, however, that with time the old man, as he disrespectfully called him, would relent. His most recent visit to the consul—whom he had always refused to let me visit—had destroyed this hope. My poor grandfather had suffered a most violent stroke, as a result of my cruel abandonment. He had retained his senses only long enough to make a new will, cutting me off with a shilling, and had then fallen into a coma that was expected to end in death. Finding his expectations frustrated, Alberto saw no reason to waste any more time with me. There were, as he explained, more enticing prospects.

You may only faintly imagine my state of mind, Amelia. I was ill for several days, grudgingly nursed by the horrid old woman who owned the lodging house. She did not want a corpse on her hands, I suppose, for charity had no part in her actions. As soon as I was well enough to speak, she discovered that I was penniless. This very day she evicted me from the last refuge I had, poor as it was. I went out, fully determined to end a life which had become unbearable. What other option had I? I had no money and no means of procuring employment. For all I knew, my darling grandfather might already be dead. If some miracle had spared him, the dear old gentleman would rightfully refuse to take me back, even if I could communicate with him; and I would rather die than admit to anyone that I had been so cruelly betrayed. My wrongdoing was bad enough; my folly I would admit to no man. No, I had no choice, or so it seemed then; but you need not fear, your kindness has saved me from that ultimate crime. I will not take my own life. But I can no longer stay here. Your countenance is as benevolent as your mind; it betrays no sign of the loathing and disgust you must feel, but you need not spare me. Indeed, I would welcome words of contempt, for punishment relieves some of my feelings of guilt. Speak, Amelia—Miss Peabody—speak, I beg you. Chastise me, and I will welcome your reproaches in the spirit of Christian humility in which I hope to end my miserable existence.

III

When she had finished, Evelyn's blue eyes were swimming with tears, and her voice was unsteady; but she had kept her promise to remain calm. She had spoken with vigor and decision throughout the last part of this shameful narrative.

I was silent, trying to decide which of many things I should say first. My silence was painful to the girl; she drew a long, shuddering breath. Her hands were clasped so tightly that the knuckles showed white; the slender shoulders under my flannel nightdress were braced as if for a blow. I was in a state of some mental confusion. The words that finally came from my lips were not at all those I had meant to say.

"Tell me, Evelyn—what is it like? Is it pleasant?"

Evelyn's astonishment was hardly greater than my own; but having once begun, I had to explain more fully. I hurried on.

"You will forgive me for probing into what must be a source of pain for you; but I have never before had the opportunity of inquiring. . . . One hears such conflicting stories. My sisters-in-law whisper and shake their heads and speak of the cross a wife must bear. But I have seen the village girls in the meadows with their sweethearts and they seem—they look—in short, they do not seem to find. . . . Dear me! How strange, I seem to be at a loss for words. That does not often occur. Do you understand what I am trying to ask?"

For a moment longer Evelyn stared at me, her wide eyes brimming. Then an extraordinary grimace crossed her face. She covered it with her hands; her shoulders shook convulsively.

"I must apologize," I said resignedly. "Now I suppose I will never know. I did not intend—"

A choked sound from Evelyn interrupted me. She lowered her hands. Her face was flushed and tear-streaked. She was gasping —with laughter.

I took it for hysteria, of course, and moved alertly forward. She caught my lifted hand.

"No, no, you needn't slap me; I am not at all hysterical. But, Amelia, you are—you are so—Is that really all you can think of to ask me, after such a story as mine?"

I considered the matter.

"Why, I really do not think there is anything else to ask. The shameful behavior of your abominable old grandfather and your villain of a lover require no comment. I presume your other family connections are equally cold-hearted, or you would have appealed to them."

"And you are not repelled by my ruined character?"

"I do not consider that it is ruined. Indeed, the experience has probably strengthened your character."

Evelyn shook her head. "I can't believe you are real!"

"There is nothing extraordinary about me. However, I suppose —yes, I am sure that it would be wise for you to make certain I am what I claim to be before you accept the position I offer. My father had friends in academic circles; I can give you references to a clergyman here in Rome, and the consul knows of my—"

"No. I do not need to make such inquiries." With a gesture, Evelyn indicated that I should take a seat on the bed beside her. I did so. She studied me earnestly for a few moments. Then she said,

"Before I answer your question, Amelia, perhaps you will answer one for me. Why did you say, 'I will never know'? Referring, of course, to the question—"

"Well, it is unlikely that I shall ever have firsthand experience. I am fully acquainted with the use of the mirror and the calendar.

19

The latter tells me that I am thirty-two years old; the former reproduces my plain features without flattery. Moreover, my nature does not lend itself to the meekness required of a wife in our society. I could not endure a man who would let himself be ruled by me, and I would not endure a man who tried to rule me. However, I am curious. I had thought. . . . But no doubt I spoke out of place. My brothers assure me that I constantly do so."

"If I have not answered your question," Evelyn said, "it is not because I consider it unfair, but because I find it difficult to give a balanced answer. At this time, my recollection of the hours I spent—shall we say in Alberto's arms?—makes a shudder of disgust pass through me. But at the time—at the time. . . ." She leaned forward. Her eyes were brilliant. "Oh, Amelia, under the right circumstances, it is—in a word—perfectly splendid!"

"Ah. I suspected as much. Well, my dear Evelyn, I am indebted to you for the information. And now shall we consider a more pressing question? No doubt you will wish to inquire of those references I mentioned before making a decision as to—"

"No." Evelyn shook her head vigorously. Her golden curls danced. "I need no references, and no time to consider. I would love to be your companion, Amelia. Indeed—I think we will get on very well together."

With a quick, graceful movement she leaned forward and kissed me lightly on the cheek. The gesture took me quite by surprise. I mumbled something and left the room. I never had a sister. I began to think that perhaps a gesture that had begun as an act of charity might benefit me as much as it helped its object.

IV

I may say, without undue egotism, that when I make up my mind to do something, it is done quickly. The lethargic old city of the Popes fairly quaked under my ruthless hand during the following week.

20

The week brought several surprises to me. I had looked forward to adopting Evelyn and dressing her, rather as if she had been a pretty, living doll. I wanted to buy for her all the dainty, impractical garments I could not wear myself. But she was not a doll, and she soon made that fact apparent. I don't know quite how she accomplished it, for she never openly countermanded an order or contradicted me; but she eventually acquired a wardrobe that was charming and simple and astonishingly inexpensive. And, in the process, I somehow acquired half a dozen new frocks of my own, which I had had no intention of buying. They were not the kind of frocks I would have chosen for myself. One evening dress, which I certainly did not need, was of the most astonishing shade of crimson, with a square neckline cut several inches lower than anything I had ever worn. The skirts were draped back over a bustle, displaying a sequined underskirt. Evelyn chose the fabric and bullied the dressmaker quite as effectively, and much more quietly, than I would have done. I thought the gown quite absurd; it squeezed my waist down to nothing and made my bosom look even more ample than it unfortunately is. But when Evelyn said, "Wear it"; I wore it. She was an amazing girl. She also discovered a weakness, so secret I was not aware of it myself, for embroidered batiste; the dozens of fine undergarments and nightgowns I had meant to get for her ended being made to my measurements.

I was in something of a daze during that week. I felt as if I had picked up a pathetic, half-drowned kitten from a pond and then had seen it turn into a full-grown tiger. Enough of my natural instincts remained, however, to allow me to take certain practical steps.

I am not at all a man-hater, despite the innuendos of a certain person whose name has not yet entered into this narrative. I had found, however, that few persons of the male sex were to be trusted, and Evelyn's story had merely confirmed this theory. It was obvious that Alberto was an untruthful person. The story he had written to Evelyn about her grandfather was not to be believed without investigation. I therefore went to our consul in Rome and made inquiries.

I was disappointed for several reasons to learn that on this account, if no other, Alberto had spoken the truth. The Earl of Ellesmere was personally known to our consul; and of course the health of a peer of such rank was a matter of general concern. The elderly earl was not yet dead, but word of his demise was expected at any moment. He had been in a deep coma for days.

I proceeded to tell the consul about Evelyn. He had heard rumors of this affair; that was clear, from the way his face changed to its blank diplomatic mask. He had the temerity to remonstrate with me when I explained my intentions with regard to the girl. I cut him short, naturally. I had only two reasons for mentioning Evelyn at all. Firstly, to ascertain whether or not any of her kin had made inquiries about her. Secondly, to inform someone in authority of her future whereabouts in case such inquiries should be made in the future. The answer to the first question was negative. The diplomatic mask notwithstanding, I could see by the consul's expression that he did not expect any such inquiries; he knew the old Earl too well. I therefore gave him my address in Cairo and departed, leaving him shaking his head and mumbling to himself.

On the twenty-eight of the month we boarded the ship at Brindisi and set sail for Alexandria.

2

I WILL spare the Gentle Reader descriptions of the journey and of the picturesque dirt of Alexandria. Every European traveler who can write his name feels obliged to publish his memoirs; the reader may refer to "Miss Smith's Egyptian Journals" or "Mr. Jones's Winter in Egypt" if he feels cheated of local color, for all the descriptions are the same. The sea voyage was abominable, but I was happy to see that Evelyn was a good traveler. We made our way to Cairo without incident and settled down at Shepheard's Hotel.

Everyone stays at Shepheard's. Among the travelers who meet daily in its magnificent dining room one may eventually, it is said, encounter all one's acquaintances; and from the terrace before the hotel the indolent tourist may watch a panorama of eastern life pass before his eyes as he sips his lemonade. Stiff English travelers ride past, on donkeys so small that the riders' feet trail in the dust; followed by Janissaries in their gorgeous gold-embroidered uniforms, armed to the teeth; by native women swathed to the eyebrows in dusty black, by stately Arabs in flowing blue-and-white robes, dervishes with matted hair and fantastic headdresses, sweetmeat vendors with trays of Turkish delight, water sellers with their goatskin containers bloated with liquid and looking horridly lifelike. . . . But I see I am succumbing to the temptation of the traveler, and will stop; the procession is unending and fascinating.

There were not many English travelers in Cairo that winter. The fighting in the Sudan had apparently alarmed them. The mad Mahdi was still besieging the gallant Gordon at Khartoum. However, Sir Garnet Wolseley's relief expedition had reached Wadi Halfa, and the gentlemen we met at Shepheard's reassured us—or rather, reassured Evelyn—when she expressed doubts as to the wisdom of traveling south. The fighting was still hundreds of miles below Assuan, and by the time we arrived there the war would surely be over—the Mahdi taken and his barbaric army crushed, the gallant Gordon relieved.

I was not so sanguine as the gentlemen. The mad carpenter of the Sudan had proved himself an extremely potent general, as our losses in that area proved. However, I said nothing to Evelyn, for I had no intention of changing my plans to suit the Mahdi or anyone else. I planned to spend the winter sailing up the Nile, and sail I would.

Travel by water is the only comfortable method of seeing Egypt, and the narrow length of the country means that all the antiquities are within easy reach of the river. I had heard of the pleasure of travel by dahabeeyah, and was anxious to try it. To call these conveyances houseboats is to give a poor idea of their luxury. They can be fitted up with any convenience the traveler chooses to supply, and the services available depend solely on his ability

24

to pay. I intended to go to Boulaq, where the boats are moored, and decide on one the day after our arrival. We could then inspect some of the sights of Cairo and be on our way in a few days.

When I expressed this intention to some of our fellow guests in the lounge of the hotel after dinner, a burst of hilarity greeted my remarks. I was informed that my hopes were vain. Choosing a dahabeeyah was a frustrating, time-consuming process; the native Egyptian was a lazy fellow who could not be hurried.

I had my own opinions on that score, but I caught Evelyn's eye and remained silent. She was having an astonishing effect on me, that girl; I thought that if I continued in her company much longer, I might become mellow.

She was looking very pretty that night, in a frock of pale-blue silk, and she attracted considerable attention. We had agreed that her real name was not to be mentioned, since it was well known to many Englishmen; she was therefore introduced as Evelyn Forbes. Tiring, finally, of the clumsy efforts of some of the ladies in the group to discover her antecedents, I used fatigue as an excuse for early retirement.

I awoke early next morning. An ethereal, rose-tinted light filled the room, and I could see Evelyn kneeling by the window. I thought she was brooding over past events; there had been moments of depression, quickly overcome, but not unnoticed by me. I therefore tried to remain motionless, but an inadvertent rustle of the bedclothes caused her to turn, and I saw that her face was shining with pleasure.

"Come and look, Amelia. It is so beautiful!"

To obey was not as simple as it sounds. I had first to fight my way through the muffling folds of fine white mosquito netting that encircled the bed. When I joined Evelyn, I shared her pleasure. Our rooms overlooked the garden of the hotel; stately palms, dark silhouettes in the pale dawn, rose up against a sky filled with translucent azure and pink streaks. Birds fluttered singing from tree to tree; the lacy minarets of mosques shone like mother-of-pearl above the treetops. The air was cool and exquisitely clear.

It was as well that our day began with such beauty and peace, for the wharves of Boulaq, where we went after breakfast, were not at all peaceful. I began to understand what our fellow travelers had warned me about. There were over a hundred boats at their moorings; the confusion and noise were indescribable.

The boats are much alike, varying only in size. The cabins occupy the after part of the deck, and their roof forms an upper deck which, when furnished and canopied, provides a charming open-air drawing room for the passengers. The crew occupy the lower deck. Here is the kitchen, a shed containing a charcoal stove, and a collection of pots and pans. The dahabeeyahs are shallow, flat-bottomed boats with two masts; and when the huge sails are spread to catch the brisk northerly breeze, they present a most attractive picture.

Our problem, then, was to decide which boat to hire. At first even I was bewildered by the variety. It did not take long, however, to realize that some of the boats were impossible. There are degrees of uncleanliness; I could tolerate, indeed, I expected, a state of sanitation inferior to that of England, but . . . ! Unfortunately, the bigger boats were usually the better kept. I did not mind the expense, but it seemed a trifle ridiculous for the two of us—and my maid—to rattle about in a boat that contained ten staterooms and two saloons.

At Evelyn's insistence we had hired a dragoman that morning at the hotel. I saw no reason why we should; I had learned some Arabic phrases during the voyage to Alexandria, and had every confidence in my ability to deal with an Egyptian boat captain. However, I yielded to Evelyn. Our dragoman was named Michael Bedawee; he was a Copt, or Egyptian Christian, a short, plump, coffee-colored man with a fierce black beard and a white turban

—although I must confess that this description would fit half the male population of Egypt. What distinguished Michael was the friendliness of his smile and the candor of his soft brown eyes. We took to him at once, and he seemed to like us.

With Michael's help we selected a boat. The *Philae* was of middle size, and of unusual tidiness; Evelyn and I both liked the looks of the reis, or captain. His name was Hassan, and he was an Egyptian of Luxor. I approved of the firm set of his mouth and the steady gaze of his black eyes—and the glint of humor in them when I assayed my few words of Arabic. I suppose my accent was atrocious, but Reis Hassan complimented me on my knowledge of his language, and the bargain was soon concluded.

With the pride of ownership Evelyn and I explored the quarters that would be our home for the next four months. The boat had four cabins, two on either side of a narrow passageway. There was also a bathroom, with water laid on. At the end of the passage a door opened into the saloon, which was semicircular, following the shape of the stern. It was well lighted by eight windows and had a long curved divan along the wall. Brussels' carpets covered the floor; the paneling was white with gold trim, giving a light, airy feeling. Window curtains of scarlet, a handsome dining table, and several mirrors in gold frames completed the furnishings.

With the ardor of ladies equipping a new house, we discussed what else we should need. There were cupboards and shelves in plenty, and we had books to fill the shelves; I had brought a large box of father's books on Egyptian antiquities, and I hoped to purchase more. But we should also need a piano. I am totally without musical ability, but I dearly love to hear music, and Evelyn played and sang beautifully.

I asked Reis Hassan when he would be ready to depart; and here I received my first check. The boat had just returned from a trip. The crew needed time to rest and visit their families; certain mysterious overhaulings needed to be done on the vessel

27

itself. We finally settled on a date a week hence, but there was something in Hassan's bland black eyes that made me wonder. . . .

Nothing went as I had planned it. Finding a suitable piano took an unreasonable amount of time. I wanted new curtains for the saloon; their shade clashed horribly with my crimson evening frock. As Evelyn pointed out, we were in no hurry; yet I had a feeling that she was even more anxious than I to be on our way. Every evening when we entered the dining room I felt her shrink. Sooner or later it was more than probable that she should encounter an acquaintance, and I could understand why she shrank from that.

Our days were not wasted; there is a great deal to see and do in Cairo. The bazaars were a source of constant amusement; the procession of people passing through the narrow passages would have been entertainment enough, without the fascination of the wares on display. Each trade occupies a section of its own: saddlers, slipper makers, copper and bronze workers, carpet sellers, and vendors of tobacco and sweetmeats. There are no real shops, only tiny cupboards, open at the front, with a stone platform or mastaba, on which the merchants sit cross-legged, awaiting customers. I could not resist the rugs, and bought several for our drawing room on the *Philae*—soft, glowing beauties from Persia and Syria. I tried to buy some trinkets for Evelyn; she would only accept a pair of little velvet slippers.

We visited the bazaars and the mosques and the Citadel; and then planned excursions somewhat farther afield. Of course I was anxious to see the remains of the ancient civilization, but I little realized what was in store for me that day, when we paid our first visit to Gizeh.

Everyone goes to see the pyramids. Since the Nile bridge was built, they are within an easy hour-and-a-half drive from the hotel. We left early in the morning so that we should have time to explore fully.

I had seen engravings of the Great Pyramid and read extensively about it; I thought I was prepared for the sight. But I was not. It was so much grander than I had imagined! The massive bulk bursts suddenly on one's sight as one mounts the steep slope leading up to the rocky platform. It fills the sky. And the color! No black-and-white engraving can possibly prepare one for the color of Egyptian limestone, mellow gold in the sunlight against a heavenly-blue vault.

The vast plateau on which the three pyramids stand is honeycombed with tombs—pits, fallen mounds of masonry, crumbling smaller pyramids. From the midst of a sandy hollow projects the head of the Sphinx, its body buried in the ever-encroaching sand, but wearing more majesty on its imperfect features than any other sculpture made by man.

We made our way to the greatest of the three pyramids, the tomb of Khufu. It loomed up like a mountain as we approached. The seeming irregularities of its sides were now seen to be huge blocks, each one higher than a man's head; and Evelyn wondered audibly how one was supposed to mount these giant stairs.

"And in long skirts," she mourned.

"Never mind," I said. "We shall manage."

And we did, with the help of six Arabs—three apiece. One on either side and one pushing from behind, we were lifted easily from block to block, and soon stood on the summit. Evelyn was a trifle pale, but I scarcely heeded her distress or gave her courage its due; I was too absorbed in the magnificent view. The platform atop the pyramid is about thirty feet square, with blocks of the stripped-off upper tiers remaining to make comfortable seats. I seated myself and stared till my eyes swam—with strain, I thought then; but perhaps there was another reason.

On the east, the undulating yellow Mokattam hills formed a frame for a picture whose nearer charms included the vivid green ' strip of cultivated land next to the river, and, in the distance, shining like the towers of fairyland, the domes and minarets of

Cairo. To the west and south the desert stretched away in a haze of gold. Along the horizon were other man-made shapes—the tiny pyramid points of Abusir and Sakkarah and Dahshoor.

I gazed till I could gaze no more; and was aroused from a reverie that had lasted far too long by Evelyn plucking at my sleeve.

"May we not descend?" she begged. "I believe I am getting sunburned."

Her nose was certainly turning pink, despite the protection of her broad-brimmed hat. Remorsefully I consented, and we were lowered down by our cheerful guides. Evelyn declined to enter the pyramid with me, having heard stories of its foul atmosphere. She knew better than to try to dissuade me. I left her with some ladies who had also refused the treat, and, hitching up my skirts, followed the gentlemen of the party into the depths.

It was a horrid place—stifling air, debris crunching underfoot, the dark barely disturbed by the flickering candles held by our guides. I reveled in every moment of it, from the long traverse of the passage to the Queen's Chamber, which is so low that one must walk bent over at the waist, to the hazardous ascent of the Grand Gallery, that magnificent high-ceilinged slope up which one must crawl in semidarkness, relying on the sinewy arms of the Egyptians to prevent a tumble back down the stone-lined slope. There were bats as well. But in the end I stood in the King's Chamber, lined with somber black basalt, and containing only the massive black coffin into which Khufu was laid to rest some four thousand years ago; and with the perspiration rolling down my frame, and every breath an effort, I felt the most overpowering sense of satisfaction I had felt since childhood—when William, my brother, dared me to climb the apple tree in the garden, and I, perched on the highest bough, watched him tumble out of a lower one. He broke his arm.

When I finally joined her outside, Evelyn's face was a sight to behold. I raked my fingers through my disheveled hair and remarked, "It was perfectly splendid, Evelyn. If you would like to go, I would be happy to see it again. . . ."

"No," Evelyn said. "Not under any circumstances."

We had been in Cairo for a week by then, and I really had hopes of getting underway within another fortnight. I had been to Boulaq several times, assisting Reis Hassan—bullying him, as Evelyn quaintly put it. In recent days I had not been able to find him on the boat, although once I saw a flutter of striped petticoat that looked like his disappear over the stern as I approached.

After Gizeh, Hassan was left in peace. I had a new interest— but to call it an interest is to understate my sentiments. I admired, I desired—I lusted after pyramids! We went back to Gizeh. I visited the Second and Third pyramids there. We went to Sakkarah to see the Step Pyramid. There are other pyramids at Sakkarah. Being built of rubble within a facing of stone, unlike the solid-stone pyramids of Gizeh, the smaller Sakkarah pyramids are only heaps of debris now that the outer facing stones have been taken away for building purposes; but I did not care. They were, or had been, pyramids, and pyramids were now my passion. I was determined to get into one of these smaller mounds, whose burial chamber is beautifully inscribed with hieroglyphic picture writing, and I would have done it, too, but for Evelyn. Her outcries, when she saw the funnel-shaped well into which I proposed to lower myself, were terrible to hear. I pointed out that with two men holding the rope I should do quite nicely; but she was adamant. I had to yield when she threatened to follow me down, for I saw that she was appalled at the idea.

Travers was no more sympathetic to my pyramid inquiries. She mourned aloud over the state of my clothes, some of which had to be given away as beyond repair, and she objected to the mementos of bats which I inadvertently carried away from the interiors of the pyramids. One morning, when I proposed a trip to Dahshoor, where there are several splendid pyramids, Evelyn flatly refused. She suggested that instead we visit the museum of Boulaq. I agreed. It was not far from the wharves; I could go and assist Hassan after the museum.

I was looking forward to meeting M. Maspero, the French director of antiquities. My father had been in correspondence with him, and I hoped my name would be familiar. It was; and we were fortunate to find Maspero at the museum. He was usually away, his assistant informed us, digging for the treasures which had made him known throughout the scholarly world.

This assistant, Herr Emil Brugsch, I knew by reputation, for it was he who had been the first European to gaze upon the famous cache of royal mummies that had been discovered a few years earlier. While we waited for M. Maspero, Brugsch told us of the robber family of Thebes who had discovered the hiding place of the mummies ten years before. The discoverer, a shifty character named Abd er-Rasool Ahmed, had been searching for a missing goat amid the rocky cliffs near his village of Gurnah. The goat had fallen into a crevice, or shaft, forty feet deep; upon descending, Ahmed made an incredible discovery—the mummies of the great pharaohs of Egypt, hidden in ancient times to keep their sacred bodies safe from the thieves who had looted their original tombs!

His eyes never leaving my face, Herr Brugsch explained, with affected modesty, that he was responsible for the detective work that had eventually discovered the mummies. Collectors had sent him photographs of objects bearing royal names, and he had realized that these must have come from a tomb. Since the known royal tombs were in Thebes, he had alerted the police to watch out for a peasant from that city who had more money than he could have come by honestly. Thus suspicion was focused on the Abd er-Rasool family; and, the thieves having fallen out in the meantime over the disposition of the loot, one of them betrayed the secret to Brugsch.

I did not care for this gentleman. His brother is a respectable and well-known scholar, and Mr. Emil has been employed by Maspero and his predecessor, M. Mariette, for many years; but his bold stare and hard face affected me unpleasantly, as did his calloused description of the interrogation of the unfortunate Abd er-Rasool brothers. Not a muscle in his tanned face moved as he described beatings with palm rods, and heated pots being placed on the heads of the suspects. Yet I could not help but be fascinated by an eyewitness account of the incredible discovery. Brugsch admitted that his sensations, as he was lowered into the pit, were not wholly comfortable. He was armed, of course, but his weapons would not have availed against treachery, and all the inhabitants of the area hated the representatives of the government. And then his feelings, as he stood in the stifling gloom of the little cave, amid a jumble of royal dead . . . ! He knew the bodies must be moved at once, in order to prevent their being stolen, and he accomplished this difficult task in only eight days. He was describing the northward voyage of the barge—the banks of the river lined with mourning women, rending their garments and pouring dust on their heads as the bodies of the ancient kings floated by—when Maspero joined us.

The director of antiquities was a stout, genial man with twinkling eyes and a short black beard. A true Frenchman, he bowed over my hand and greeted Evelyn with admiration. He spoke of my father in the highest terms. Seeing how busy he was, we soon excused ourselves, and he begged pardon for not showing us over the museum himself. Perhaps he would join us later, he said, glancing at Evelyn.

"You have made another conquest," I said softly to Evelyn, as we walked away. "M. Maspero could hardly keep his eyes away from you."

"Nor Herr Brugsch his eyes from you," Evelyn replied with a smile. "He was anxious to escort you; did you see his scowl when M. Maspero told him he had work for him to do?"

"Don't try to give your admirers to me," I retorted. "I am not in need of such mendacious flattery; and if I were, Herr Brugsch would not be my choice."

I was glad the director was not with us when we began our tour. Courtesy must have prevented me from telling him what I thought of his museum. Not that the place wasn't fascinating; it contained many marvelous things. But the dust! And the clutter! My housewifely and scholarly instincts were equally offended.

"Perhaps you are not being fair," Evelyn said mildly, when I expressed my feelings. "There are so many objects; new ones are discovered daily; and the museum is still too small, despite the recent enlargement."

"All the more reason for neatness and order. In the early days, when European adventurers took away what they discovered in Egypt, there was no need for a national museum. Then M. Mariette, Maspero's predecessor, insisted that Egypt should keep some of its national treasures. The cooperation between Great Britain and France, to regulate and assist this unfortunate country, has resulted in the French being given control over the antiquities department. I suppose they must have something; after all, we control finance, education, foreign affairs, and other matters. But we could do with a little English neatness here, instead of French nonchalance."

We had penetrated into a back room filled with objects that seemed to be leftovers from the more impressive exhibits in the front halls of the museum—vases, bead necklaces, little carved ushebti figures, flung helter-skelter onto shelves and into cases. There were several other people in the room. I paid them little heed; in mounting indignation, I went on, "They might at least dust! Look at this!"

And, picking up a blue-green statuette from a shelf, I rubbed it with my handkerchief and showed Evelyn the dirty smudge that resulted.

A howl—a veritable animal howl—shook the quiet of the room. Before I could collect myself to search for its source, a whirlwind descended upon me. A sinewy, sun-bronzed hand snatched the statuette from me. A voice boomed in my ear.

"Madam! Do me the favor of leaving those priceless relics alone. It is bad enough to see that incompetent ass, Maspero, jumble them about; will you complete his idiocy by destroying the fragments he has left?"

Evelyn had retreated. I stood alone. Gathering my dignity, I turned to face my attacker.

He was a tall man with shoulders like a bull's and a black beard cut square like those on the statues of ancient Assyrian kings. From a face tanned almost to the shade of an Egyptian, vivid blue eyes blazed at me. His voice, as I had good cause to know, was a deep, reverberating bass. The accents were those of a gentleman. The sentiments were not.

"Sir," I said, looking him up and down. "I do not know you—"

"But I know you, madam! I have met your kind too often—the rampageous British female at her clumsiest and most arrogant. Ye gods! The breed covers the earth like mosquitoes, and is as maddening. The depths of the pyramids, the heights of the Himalayas—no spot on earth is safe from you!"

He had to pause for breath at this point, which gave me the opportunity I had been waiting for.

"And you, sir, are the lordly British male at his loudest and most bad-mannered. If the English gentlewoman is covering the earth, it is in the hope of counteracting some of the mischief her lord and master has perpetrated. Swaggering, loud, certain of his own superiority . . ."

My adversary was maddened, as I had hoped he would be. Little flecks of foam appeared on the blackness of his beard. His subsequent comments were incomprehensible, but several fragile objects vibrated dangerously on their shelves.

I stepped back a pace, taking a firm grip on my parasol. I am not easily cowed, nor am I a small woman; but this man towered over me, and the reddening face he had thrust into mine was suggestive of violence. He had very large, very white teeth, and I felt sure I had gotten a glimpse of most of them.

A hand fell on his shoulder. Looking up, I saw Evelyn with a young man who was a slighter, beardless copy of my adversary—dark-haired, blue-eyed, tall, but not so bulky.

"Radcliffe," he said urgently. "You are alarming this lady. I beg you—"

"I am not at all alarmed," I said calmly. "Except for your friend's health. He seems about to have a fit. Is he commonly subject to weakness of the brain?"

The younger man now had both hands on his companion's shoulders. He did not seem concerned; indeed, he was smiling broadly. He was an attractive young fellow; from the way Evelyn looked at him I suspected she shared my opinion.

"My brother, madam, not my friend," he said cheerfully. "You must forgive him—now, Radcliffe, calm yourself. The museum always has this effect on him," he explained, looking at me. "You must not blame yourself for upsetting him."

"I certainly should not blame myself if my harmless behavior brought on such a violent, inexcusable breach of common courtesy—"

"Amelia!" Evelyn caught my arm as a roar of rage burst from the bearded person. "Let us all be calm, and not provoke one another."

"I am not provoking anyone," I said coolly.

Evelyn exchanged a glance with the young man. As if some message had passed between them, they both moved, the young fellow tugging at his agitated brother, Evelyn using a gentler but equally firm grip to pull me away. The other visitors were watching us with ill-bred curiosity. One lady pulled her companion out

36

of the room. Another couple followed, leaving a single spectator, an Arab in flowing robes, headcloth, and bright-green goggles, who continued to watch the antics of the incomprehensible foreigners with amused contempt.

Rapid footsteps in the hall heralded the arrival of M. Maspero, who had apparently been alarmed by the uproar. When he saw us his pace slowed, and a smile spread over his face.

"*Ah, c'est le bon Emerson.* I should have known. You have met one another? You are acquainted?"

"We are not acquainted," said the person called Emerson, in a slightly modified shout. "And if you make any attempt to introduce us, Maspero, I shall fell you to the ground!"

M. Maspero chuckled. "Then I will not risk it. Come, ladies, and let me show you some of our finer objects. These are unimportant—a miscellany only."

"But they are most interesting," Evelyn said in her gentle voice. "I admire the soft colors of the jewelry."

"Ah, but these trinkets are not valuable—no gold, only beads and amulets, made of faience, common as sand. We find such bracelets and necklaces by the hundreds."

"Faience?" Evelyn repeated. "Then the lovely coral, the delicate blue-green which resembles turquoise, are not the real stones?"

The black-bearded male person had turned his back on us and was pretending to sneer at a collection of ushebtis; I knew he was eavesdropping, however. His brother was not so rude. The young fellow stood looking shyly at Evelyn, and when she asked about the jewelry he started to answer. The ebullient Maspero anticipated him.

"*Mais non, mademoiselle,* they are imitations of coral, turqoise, lapis lazuli, made from a colored paste common in ancient Egypt."

"They are lovely, all the same," I said. "And the very age of them staggers the imagination. To think that these beads adorned the slim brown wrist of an Egyptian maiden four thousand years before our Saviour was born!"

Blackbeard whirled around. "Three thousand years," he corrected. "Maspero's chronology, like all his work, is inexcusably inaccurate!"

Maspero smiled, but I think his next act was prompted to some extent by the annoyance he was too courteous to express directly. Lifting a necklace of tiny blue and coral beads, he handed it to Evelyn with a courtly bow.

"Keep it as a memento of your visit, if you treasure such things. No, no"—he waved away Evelyn's protests—"it is of no consequence; I only regret I have nothing finer for such a charming lady. For you, too, Mademoiselle Peabody"—and another string of beads was pressed into my hand.

"Oh, but—" I began, with an uneasy glance at the black-bearded person, who was shaking like an engine about to burst.

"Do me the honor," Maspero insisted. "Unless you fear the foolish tales of curses and avenging Egyptian ghosts—"

"Certainly not," I said firmly.

"But what of the curses of M. Emerson?" Maspero asked, his eyes twinkling. "*Regardez*—he is about to say unkind things to me again."

"Never fear," Emerson snarled. "I am leaving. I can only stand so many minutes in this horror house of yours. In God's name, man, why don't you classify your pots?"

He rushed off, pulling his slighter companion with him. The young fellow turned his head; his gaze went straight to Evelyn and remained fixed on her face until he had been removed from the room.

"He has almost the Gallic temperament," said Maspero admiringly. "One observes the magnificence of his rages with respect."

"I cannot agree with you," I said. "Who is the fellow?"

"One of your fellow countryman, dear lady, who has interested himself in the antiquities of this country. He has done admirable work excavating, but I fear he does not admire the rest of us. You heard his abuse of my poor museum. He abuses my excavation methods with the same ardor. But, indeed, there is no archaeologist in Egypt who has been spared his criticism."

"I don't care to speak of him," I said, with a sniff.

"We think your museum is fascinating, M. Maspero," Evelyn added tactfully. "I could spend days here."

We spent several hours more inspecting the exhibits. I would not have said so for the world, but I felt a certain sympathy for the odious Emerson's criticisms. The exhibits were not arranged as methodically as they might have been, and there was dust everywhere.

Evelyn said she was too tired to go down to the boat that day, so we took a carriage back to the hotel. She was pensive and silent during the drive; as we neared Cairo, I said slyly,

"Mr. Emerson's young brother does not have the family temper, I believe. Did you happen to hear his name?"

"Walter," said Evelyn, and blushed betrayingly.

"Ah." I pretended not to notice the blush. "I found him very pleasant. Perhaps we will meet them again at the hotel."

"Oh, no, they do not stay at Shepheard's. Walt—Mr. Walter Emerson explained to me that their money all goes for excavation. His brother is not supported by any institution or museum; he has only a small yearly income and, as Walter says, if he had the wealth of the Indies he would consider it insufficient for his purposes."

"You seem to have covered quite a lot of ground in a very short time," I said, watching Evelyn out of the corner of my eye. "It is a pity we can't continue the acquaintance with the younger Mr. Emerson, and avoid his insane brother."

"I daresay we shall not meet again," Evelyn said softly.

I had my own opinion on that score.

In the afternoon, after a rest, we went to shop for medical supplies. The guidebooks advise travelers to carry a considerable quantity of medicines and drugs, since there are no doctors south of Cairo. I had copied the list of suggested remedies from my guide, and was determined to do the thing properly. If I had not been a woman, I might have studied medicine; I have a natural aptitude for the subject, possessing steady hands and far less squeamishness about blood and wounds than many males of my acquaintance. I planned to buy a few small surgical knives also; I fancied I could amputate a limb—or at least a toe or finger— rather neatly if called upon to do so.

Our dragoman, Michael, accompanied us. I thought he seemed quieter than usual, but I was occupied with my list: blue pills, calomel, rhubarb, Dover's powder, James's powder, carbolic acid, laudanum, quinine, sulfuric acid, ipecacuanha. . . . It was Evelyn who asked Michael what the trouble was. He hesitated, looking at us in turn.

"It is my child, who is ill," he said finally. "She is only a girl-child, of course."

The faltering of his voice and his troubled countenance be- trayed a paternal emotion that contradicted the words, so I modified what had begun as an indignant comment into an offer of assistance. Michael protested, but it was clear that he would welcome our help. He led us to his home.

It was a narrow old house with the intricately carved wooden balconies that are typical of Old Cairo. It seemed to me appall- ingly dirty, but compared with the squalor and filth we had seen elsewhere, it could have been worse. The sickroom where the child lay was dreadful. The wooden shutters were closely barred, lest evil spirits enter to harm the child further, and the stench was frightful. I could scarcely see the small sufferer, for the only illumination came from a clay lamp filled with smoking fat, with a wick of twisted cloth. My first move, therefore, was to go to the windows and throw them open.

A wavering shriek of protest arose from the women huddled on the floor. There were six of them, clad in dusty black and doing nothing that I could see except add to the contamination of the air and keep the child awake by their endless wailing. I evicted them. The child's mother I allowed to remain. She was a rather pretty little thing, with great black eyes, and was herself, I suspected, not more than fifteen years of age.

Careless of her dainty gingham skirts, Evelyn was already seated on the floor by the pallet where the child lay. Gently she brushed the tangled black curls from its face and dislodged a cluster of flies swarming around its eyes. The mother made a gesture of protest, but subsided after a frightened glance at me. Evelyn and I had already had cause to be horrified at the way these people allow insects to infest the eyes of the children; I had seen pitiful infants so beset by flies that they looked as if they were wearing black goggles. If they attempted to brush the stinging, filthy creatures away, the mothers slapped their hands. One sees tiny children who have already lost the sight of one or both eyes through this dreadful custom; and, of course, infant mortality is extremely high. One authority claims that three children out of five die young.

I looked at Michael's agonized face, and at the flushed face of the small sufferer, and I decided this was one child that would not succumb if I could help it. How fortunate that we had just come from purchasing medical supplies!

The cause of the child's illness was not hard to discover. She had fallen and cut herself, as children will; infection had entered the wound, which naturally had not been washed or cleaned. One small arm was puffed and swollen. When I cut into the swelling, after disinfecting the knife as best I could, the infected matter spurted out in an evil-smelling flood. I cleaned and dressed the wound, then lectured the distracted parents on the necessity of keeping it clean. Evelyn was a tower of strength. It was not until we got back to the hotel that she was quietly and thoroughly sick. I dismissed Michael for the remainder of the day, telling him to go home and keep his horde of female relatives out of the child's room.

By evening Evelyn was feeling better, and I insisted that we dress and dine downstairs, instead of having a bowl of soup in our room, as she wished to do. Although she never complained, I knew she was often depressed on her own account. We had as yet heard no word of the Earl's fate, but Evelyn expected news of his death daily, and it fretted her tender heart to think of him dying alone. For my part, I felt the old reprobate was meeting the end he richly deserved.

In her soft-rose evening dress, with its wide lace cuffs and ruffled underskirt, Evelyn looked quite charming; the wistful droop of her mouth only added to her appealing appearance. I put on my crimson satin, feeling we needed something bright and cheerful, although I still felt self-conscious in the dress. We made a fine show. Several of our gentlemen acquaintances followed us into the lounge after dinner, and attempted to win a smile from Evelyn. Suddenly I saw a rosy flush spread over her face. I suspected the cause even before I followed her gaze to the doorway. There stood young Walter Emerson, looking very handsome in evening dress. He had eyes only for Evelyn, and crossed the room so quickly that he nearly stumbled over a low table.

He had brought his brother with him. I had to stifle a laugh at the sight of the irascible Emerson, he wore a look of such gloom. His evening clothes looked as if they had been pulled out of a traveling bag and put on without the benefit of pressing; his collar seemed to be too tight. He had lost all his swagger and shambled along behind Walter like a great black bear, darting suspicious glances at the elegantly garbed travelers around him.

After greeting me hastily, Walter turned to Evelyn and they were soon deep in conversation. The other gentlemen, being ignored, faded away; and I was left face to face with Emerson. He stood looking down at me with an expression of sullen dejection.

"I am to make my apologies," he growled.

"I accept them," I said, and indicated the place next to me on the sofa. "Do sit down, Mr. Emerson. I am surprised to see you here. I understood that social life was not to your taste."

"It was Walter's idea," said Emerson bluntly. He sat down, edging as far away from me as the limited confines of the sofa would allow. "I hate such things."

"What things?" I inquired, enjoying myself hugely. It was delightful to see the arrogant Emerson cowed by society.

"The hotel. The people. The—the—in short, all this."

He waved a contemptuous hand at the handsome chamber and its finely dressed occupants.

"Where would you rather be?" I asked.

"Anywhere in Egypt but here. Specifically, at the site of my excavations."

"In the dust of the desert, away from all the comforts of civilization? With only ignorant Arabs for company—"

"Ignorant perhaps; but lacking the hypocrisies of civilization. Good God, how it maddens me to hear the smug comments of English travelers concerning the 'natives,' as they call them! There are good and bad among the Egyptians, as there are in any race; but by and large they are an admirable people, friendly, cheerful, loyal, intelligent—when taught. . . . For centuries these people were oppressed by a vicious, cruel despotism. They are riddled by disease, poverty, and ignorance, but through no fault of their own."

He was recovering his confidence. His fists clenched on his knees, he glared at me. I rather liked him for his defense of an oppressed people, but I could not resist baiting him.

43

"Then you should approve of what we British are doing in Egypt. By assuming responsibility for the finances of the country—"

"Bah," said Emerson vigorously. "Do you think we are acting out of benevolence? Ask the inhabitants of Alexandria how they enjoyed being shelled by British gunboats, two years ago. We are not so uncivilized as the Turk, but we have the same purpose— our own self-interest. And we are letting those imbecile French mismanage the antiquities department! Not that our own so-called scholars are any better."

"Are they all wrong?" I inquired. "All but you?"

My irony went unnoticed. Emerson considered the question seriously.

"There is one young fellow—Petrie is his name—who seems to have some idea of method in archaeology. He is excavating in the Delta this winter. But he has no influence; and meanwhile every year, every passing day sees destruction that cannot be remedied. We are destroying the past! Digging like children for treasure, wrenching objects out of the ground without keeping proper records of how and where they were found. . . ."

I glanced at Evelyn. I could not hear what she and Walter were discussing, Emerson's voice was too loud, but she seemed to find the conversation enjoyable. I turned my attention back to Emerson, who was still ranting.

". . . scraps of pottery! Something should be done with pottery, you know. One should study the various types—discover what kinds of pottery accompany certain kinds of ornaments, weapons, furnishing. . . ."

"For what purpose?"

"Why, there are a dozen purposes. Pottery, like other objects, changes and develops with time. We could work out a basic chronological sequence which would enable us to date not only the pottery, but other objects found with it. And it is not only

44

pottery that can be useful. Every object, every small scrap of the past can teach us something. Most of these objects are now tossed into rubbish heaps, or carried off by ignorant tourists, lost forever to science. Maspero saves only the impressive objects, and half of those are lost or smashed or stolen, in that reputed museum of his."

"I understand," I said. "For example, studies might be made of anatomical remains. The race to which the ancient Egyptians belonged might be ascertained, and the racial mixtures. Are they the same stock today as they were in ancient times? But scholars do not collect bones and mummies, do they, except to display the latter as curiosities."

Emerson's jaw dropped. "Good God," he said. "A woman with an inquiring mind? Is it possible?"

I overlooked the insult, having become interested in what he was saying. I was about to pursue the subject further when there was a dramatic interruption.

Evelyn was sitting next to the sofa, with Walter leaning on the back of her chair. She suddenly started to her feet. Turning, I saw that her face had gone white as linen. She was staring with a fixed look of horror toward the entrance to the room.

I glanced about. The room was crowded with people, but I saw nothing that might explain her agitation. Before I could make a more searching perusal, Evelyn had collapsed onto the floor. When Walter, clumsy with agitation, managed to reach her and raise her in his arms, she was in a dead faint, from which she was restored with some difficulty.

She would not answer our questions; she was only capable of reiterating her desire to return to our rooms.

"Let me carry you," Walter begged. "You are no burden; you cannot walk—"

He put out his arms. She shrank back, as if he had offered to strike her.

45

"No, no," she gasped. "Amelia will help me. I can walk, indeed I can. Pray do not touch me."

Poor Walter was as white as Evelyn. But there was nothing to be done but accede to her wishes. She walked, falteringly, but without any assistance except mine, to the stairs. As we started up, I had only time to assure Walter that I would let him know next morning how Evelyn was, if he cared to come by.

My maid was waiting when we reached our rooms. Evelyn rejected her attentions, which were given grudgingly enough; she seemed to shrink from any company but mine, but still refused to tell me what was wrong. At her request, I dismissed Travers, telling her to go to bed.

"I believe I will send Travers home," I said, seeking to strike a casual note, since Evelyn would not talk of the matter uppermost in both our minds. "She hates everything—the country, the Egyptians, the boat—"

"And me," said Evelyn, with a faint smile.

"She doesn't think highly of me, either," I said, pleased to see Evelyn regaining her spirits. "We can manage without her quite nicely. I shall make arrangements tomorrow. Evelyn, won't you tell me now—"

"Later," Evelyn said. "I will explain later, Amelia, when I have. . . . Won't you return to the saloon? You were having such a nice talk with Mr. Emerson. I am sure he is still there. You might reassure him and his. . . . You might reassure them, and make my apologies. I am well; I only need rest. I will go straight to bed. I really am quite well."

This speech, delivered in a rapid monotone, was quite unlike the girl I had come to know. I looked at her searchingly; she refused to meet my eyes. I started to speak, fully prepared to break down a reticence which now alarmed me; then came a loud knock at the door of the sitting room.

Evelyn started convulsively. A renewed pallor spread over her

46

face. I stared at her, too bewildered to speak. Who could this visitor be, who knocked so peremptorily? And at such an hour! It was not too late for evening social activities, but it was certainly too late for anyone to be coming to our rooms. I could not believe that Walter's anxiety would drive him to such a step. Moreover, it was clear from Evelyn's demeanor that she suspected who the visitor might be, and that her suspicion caused her deep dread.

Her eyes met mine. Her shoulders straightened, and she set her lips in a firm line before she opened them to speak. "Open the door, Amelia, if you will be so good. I am being a miserable coward. I must face this."

I suppose her speech conveyed a clue to my mind. I remember I felt no surprise when I opened the door and saw the man who stood there. I had never seen him before, but his swarthy complexion, his sleek black hair, his bold good looks confirmed the suspicion Evelyn's manner had aroused.

"Ah," I said. "Signor Alberto, I presume."

3

ALBERTO placed one hand on his heart and bowed. His look, as well as his manner, verged on insolence; and as his eyes moved from my face toward the inner doorway where Evelyn stood, pale and still as a statue, it was all I could do not to slap him.

"You invite me in?" he asked, looking at me. "I think you prefer I would not speak of matters close to our hearts except in the privacy."

I stepped back; silently I motioned him in, gently I closed the door behind him. I wanted to slam it. Alberto rushed toward Evelyn.

"Ah, my lost darling, my heart's beloved! How can you desert me? How can you leave me with agony for your fate?"

Evelyn raised her hand. Alberto stopped, a few feet away from her. I really believe the rascal would have taken her into his arms if she had not moved. Now he cocked his head on one side and said, in tones of deep reproach, "You push me! You crush me! Ah, I understand. You have found a rich protectress. She give you gifts and you abandon the poor lover who give only love."

My parasol was standing in the corner. I went and got it. Evelyn was silent throughout; I think she was too thunderstruck at the man's insolence to speak. I approached Alberto and jabbed him in the waistcoat with my parasol. He jumped back.

"That will do," I said briskly. "You abandoned this lady; she did not abandon you, although she would have been wise to do so. How dare you come here after writing that abominable message to her, after taking all her possessions—"

"Message?" Alberto rolled his eyes. "I leave no message. Going out, to seek employment, so I buy food for my beloved, I was strike by a horse while I cross the street. Weeks I lie in the terrible hospital, in delirious, crying out for my Evelyn. When I recover, I stagger to the room which was my paradise. But she is gone! My angel has flow away. I leave no message! If there is message my enemy must leave it. I have many enemy. Many who hate me, who try to steal my happiness, who envy me my angel."

He looked meaningfully at me.

I have rarely seen such an unconvincing dramatic performance. Yet I was not sure it might not convince Evelyn; love has a most unfortunate effect on the brain, and I feared some lingering fondness for the rascal might still move her.

I need not have feared. Evelyn's color had returned; indeed, her cheeks were flushed becomingly with an emotion that I recognized to be anger.

"How dare you?" she said in a low voice. "Have you not done me enough harm? Oh, you are right to reproach me; I deserve your contempt. Not for having left you, but for ever coming away with you in the first place. But how dare you come here and insinuate such things about this lady? You are not worthy to occupy the same room with her. Begone, and never trouble my sight again!"

Alberto staggered back a few paces. He was counterfeiting shock and anguish, but the ferrule of the umbrella, which I had against his stomach, might have assisted his retreat.

"You cannot speak with true meaning. You are sick. No—you do not understand. I come to marry you. I offer you my hand and name. There is no other way for you. No other man marry you now, not when he know—"

He was an agile fellow; he jumped nimbly back as I tried to bring the parasol down on his head, and when I raised it for a second attempt, Evelyn caught at my arm.

"Pray don't break a good parasol," she said, with a curling lip. "He is not worth it."

"But he is trying to blackmail you," I said, panting with rage. "He is threatening you with exposure unless you agree—"

"He may publish my infamy to the world," Evelyn said coldly. "Believe me, Amelia, he has no more power over me. If any lingering trace of fondness had remained, this would have ended it."

Smoothing down his hair, which had been disarranged by his rapid movement, Alberto stared at us in affected horror.

"Blackmail? Threat? *Dio mio*, how you do not understand me! I would not—"

"You had better not," I interrupted. "The first sign of trouble from you, you rascal, and I'll have you put in prison. Egyptian prisons are vastly uncomfortable, I am told, and I have a good deal more influence with the present government than you do."

Alberto drew himself up.

"Now you threaten me," he said with satisfaction. "No need for threat. If the lady do not want me, I go. I come only for honor. I see now. I understand. There is another! It is true, no? Who is he, this villain who steal my darling's heart?"

Evelyn, who had born up magnificently, now showed signs of breaking—which was no wonder.

"I can't stand any more of this," she whispered. "Amelia, can we not make him go away? Can we call for help?"

"Certainly," I said.

I passed Alberto—who drew back nervously—and threw open the door. There is usually a floor attendant on duty, and I meant to summon him. But there was no need. Sitting on the floor, across the hall from our door, was our dragoman, Michael. I did not stop to ask why he was there. He leaped to his feet when he saw me, and I beckoned him in.

"Take this man by the collar and throw him out," I said, gesturing at Alberto.

Michael looked surprised, but he did not hesitate. As he reached out for Alberto, the latter stepped back.

"No need, I go, I go," he exclaimed. "I leave Egypt. My heart is broke, my life is—"

"Never mind that," I said. "One question before you go. How did you find us here, and how did you get the money to follow us?"

"But I go to the British consul at Rome, what else? I work way on boat—I am seasick, I am cold, but I work to follow my heart's—"

"Enough of that. Go, now, or Michael will—"

"I go." Alberto drew himself up. He rolled his eyes one last time at Evelyn; then Michael took a step forward, and Alberto bolted out the door with more speed than dignity.

"I follow, to be sure he is gone," said Michael.

"Thank you," Evelyn said gratefully. "Your little girl, Michael—how is she? Did you want us to come to her again?"

"No," Michael said. "No, lady. I come to tell you she is better. She wakes up, she asks for food. I come to thank you; to tell you when you want anything from Michael, you ask, even if it is his life. Now I will follow the evil man."

With a gesture that oddly combined humility and dignity, he departed; and as the door closed, Evelyn broke into a storm of weeping.

The storm was soon over. While I rushed around searching for smelling salts and handkerchiefs, Evelyn recovered herself and insisted that I sit down. She relieved me of my parasol, which I was still holding.

"You are more upset than you will admit," she said. "Let me order you a glass of wine."

"No, there is no need. But perhaps you—"

"No." Evelyn sat down and looked at me steadily. "My predominant emotion, strangely, is one of relief. I feel as if I had exorcised some evil spirit."

"It was Alberto you saw in the lounge, when you fainted."

"Yes. You will not believe me, Amelia; but when I saw him standing there, watching me with that insolent sneering smile, I thought him a demon of the mind, conjured up to remind me of my past. I was so happy just then, with—with—"

"With Walter. Why do you shrink from speaking his name? Do you love him?"

"I cannot use that word; not after. . . . But, yes; I could love him, if I had the right to love any decent man."

"Oh, come, you are being absurdly melodramatic! We are almost in the twentieth century; abandon your old-fashioned morality."

"Do you think Walter would ask me to marry him if he knew of my past?"

"Well . . ." I shrugged uncomfortably. "He seems a nice young man, but he is a man, after all. But why should he ever know?"

There was no need for Evelyn to answer. He would know because she would tell him. Candor was an integral part of her nature. She smiled sadly at me.

"Let us change the subject, Amelia. All I meant to say was that I was foolishly relieved to find Alberto mere flesh and blood. We have finished with him now; but how amazing that he should actually follow me here!"

"Yes. I wonder . . ."

"What?"

"If perhaps your grandfather has not recovered after all."

Evelyn gasped. "Heavens, Amelia, how cynical! And how clever of you. Oh, how I hope it may be so!"

"Do not hope too much. I daresay there are other, equally cynical reasons that may explain Alberto's appearance here. I shall take steps, tomorrow, to see what I can find out. I must also go to Boulaq and hurry Reis Hassan. The sooner we leave Cairo, the better for both of us."

"Yes," Evelyn said, smiling wistfully. "It is becoming crowded with people whom I do not wish to see. But Walter will not be here much longer. He and Mr. Emerson are leaving in two days."

"Where do they go?"

"I cannot remember the name. It is several hundred miles to the south; the remains of the city of the heretic pharaoh."

"Amarna," I said. "Yes. Well, child, let us go to bed. It has been a tiring day."

But the day was not yet over.

Evelyn dropped off to sleep almost at once. She was worn out, poor girl, by her emotional experiences. I could hear her quiet breathing as I lay sleepless under my canopy of white netting. Her bed and canopy were across the room from mine, which stood near the window. There was a small balcony outside. I had left the shutters open, as I always did; the netting protected us from insects, and the night air was particularly sweet and cool. Moon-light streamed in through the window, illumining the objects in its path but leaving the corners of the large room deep in shadow. A ray of silver light shone distractingly on my bed.

53

I am not often unable to sleep, but the events of the day had given considerable food for thought. Oddly enough, I found myself principally preoccupied with the exasperating Mr. Emerson and his peculiar ideas. Peculiar—but stimulating. I thought about them for some time; and then forcibly turned my thoughts to more important matters.

Walter and Evelyn. . . . Now there was a worrying subject. If she had been what she pretended to be, an impoverished gentlewoman serving as my companion, a marriage between the two might have been eminently suitable. But I suspected that the elder Mr. Emerson controlled his young brother; that there was not sufficient income to support a wife for Walter and an archaeological expedition for Emerson, and that, if a choice had to be made, Emerson would have the deciding vote. And poor Evelyn was right; she would have to tell Walter the truth, and I doubted that any man would take it in the proper way. He might marry her and then spend the rest of his life nobly forgiving her. Nothing can be more infuriating than being forgiven over and over again.

I turned restlessly in my bed. The springs squeaked and something outside the window—a night bird, or an insect—squeaked as if in answer. I turned over on my side, with my back to the brilliant moonlight, and lay still, determined to woo sleep. Instead, my thoughts turned to Alberto, and I began to speculate about his motive for following Evelyn. I could not credit the creature with the slightest degree of altruism or love; he must have another reason for pursuing her. I thought of several possible answers. No doubt he had other prospects in mind when he deserted her. Perhaps one such scheme had brought him to Egypt, the destination of so many travelers from Italy, and, finding Evelyn under the protection of a wealthy woman—for so I must seem to him—he had decided to see what could be gotten from me.

With such thoughts churning around in my mind I was no nearer sleep than I had been. They distracted me from the usual night noises, however; I was unaware of extraneous sounds until one sudden noise, close at hand, struck my ear. It was a squeaking sound from one of the boards of the floor. I knew it well; the faulty plank was between my bed and the window, and my foot had pressed it several times that day.

I turned onto my back. I was not alarmed; I assumed that either I had been mistaken about the origin of the sound or that Evelyn had waked up and crept to the window for a view of the moonlit garden.

Standing over the bed, so close that its body brushed the folds of white netting, was an incredible apparition.

It appeared to be swathed in a white mist, like an emanation of fog. This blurred the features, but the general outline of the figure was plain enough. It might have walked out of the main hall of the Boulaq museum, where Maspero kept his prized, life-sized statues of ancient Egyptian ladies and gentlemen. Like the painted statues, this apparition had the hues of life, though they were faded by the cold moonlight. The bronzed body, bare to the waist; the broad collar of orange and blue beads; the folded linen headdress, striped in red and white.

I was thunderstruck. But not by fear—no, never suppose for a moment that I was afraid! I was simply paralyzed by surprise. The figure stood utterly motionless. I could not even detect the rise and fall of its breast. It lifted an arm, then, in a gesture of unmistakable menace.

I sat up and, with a shout, reached out for the thing. I do not believe in apparitions. I wanted to get my hands on it, to feel the warmth and solidity of human flesh. Unfortunately, I had forgotten the confounded mosquito netting.

(My Critic reminds me that "confounded" is not a word a lady should use. I reply that some strong expression is called for, and that I have avoided others far stronger.)

It was the netting, of course, that had given the apparition its ghostly aura, and it fit so well with the presumed supernatural appearance of the thing that I had forgotten its existence. I plunged head foremost into a muffling cloud of fabric; the bed sheet and the skirts of my nightgown wound about my limbs. By the time I had fought my way out of these encumbrances I was gasping for breath—and the room was empty. I had succeeded only in waking Evelyn, who was calling out agitatedly and trying to escape her own netting.

We met at the window; Evelyn caught me by the shoulders and tried to shake me. I must have looked like a wild woman with my hair breaking loose from its night braids and streaming over my shoulders. My determined rush toward the window had persuaded Evelyn, as she later confessed, that I was bent upon self-destruction.

After I had assured myself that there was no trace of the visitant on the balcony or in the garden below, I explained to Evelyn what had happened. She had lighted a candle. By its flame I saw her expression, and knew what she was about to say.

"It was no dream," I insisted. "It would not be surprising that I should dream of ancient Egyptian ghosts; but I believe I know the difference between reality and sleep."

"Did you pinch yourself?" Evelyn inquired seriously.

"I had not time to pinch myself," I said, pacing angrily up and down. "You see the torn netting—"

"I believe you fought a gallant fight with the bed sheets and the netting," Evelyn said. "Real objects and those seen in dreams blend into one another—"

I let out a loud exclamation. Evelyn looked alarmed, fearing she had offended me; but it was not her disbelief that had prompted my cry. Bending over, I picked up from the floor the hard object that my bare instep had painfully pressed upon. In silence I held it out for Evelyn's inspection.

It was a small ornament, about an inch long, made of blue-green faience, in the shape of the hawk god, Horus—the kind of ornament that often hangs on necklaces worn by the ancient Egyptian dead.

II

I was more determined than ever to leave Cairo. Of course I did not believe in ghosts. No; some malignant human agent had been at work in the moonlit room, and that worried me a good deal more than ghosts. I thought immediately of Alberto as a possible culprit, but there really seemed no reason why he should undertake such a bizarre trick. His was not the type of the murderer; he was vicious, but weak. And what would it profit him to murder either Evelyn or myself?

A criminal of another kind might hope to profit, however, and I came to the conclusion that my visitor had been a would-be thief, a little more imaginative than his fellows, who hoped by his imitation of an ancient Egyptian to confound a wakeful victim long enough to effect his escape. It was a rather ingenious idea, really; I almost wished I could meet the inventive burglar.

I decided not to summon the police. The Egyptian police are perfectly useless, and I had not seen the man's face closely enough to identify him, even supposing that the authorities could track one man through the teeming streets of Cairo. The man would not return; he had found me wakeful and threatening, and he would look for easier prey.

Having come to this conclusion, I was somewhat easier in my mind, so I explained it all to Evelyn, hoping to calm her nerves. She agreed with my deductions, but I think she still half believed I had been dreaming.

I did take the precaution of investigating Alberto's activities.

I was unable to discover where he had been staying. There are hundreds of small inns in Cairo, and presumably he had used one of these, for he certainly had not been observed in any of the European hotels. I did learn, however, that a man of his description had taken a ticket on the morning train for Alexandria, and I decided that we could dismiss Alberto from our thoughts.

Walter was not so easy to dismiss. He called next morning, as early as was decently possible. Evelyn refused to see him. I understood, and commended, her motives; the less she saw of him, the easier the eventual parting would be. Not knowing her true feelings, Walter naturally misunderstood. I assured him that physically she was recovered and then informed him she could not receive visitors. What else could he assume but that she did not want to see *him?* He even went so far as to ask whether it was some act of his that had brought on her fainting fit the night before. I assured him that this was not so, but the poor lad was unconvinced. Looking like a wan Byronic hero, he asked me to say good-bye to Evelyn for him. He and his brother were leaving next day for their dig.

I felt so sorry for the young fellow I almost blurted out part of the truth; but I knew I had no right to violate Evelyn's confidence. So I went upstairs, to console the other half of the pair of heartbroken lovers, and a tedious business it was too, when a little common sense on both parts would have settled the matter to the satisfaction of all.

With Michael's assistance I contrived to hurry the boat crew. Michael's newborn devotion was complete; he did everything he could to assist us, although at times I think he shared the opinion of the men—that I was an interfering, illogical female. One of my acquaintances at Shepheard's had informed me I had made an error in selecting a Christian as my dragoman, for the Copts are not accepted as readily as coreligionists by Moslem crews and captains. However, Reis Hassan and Michael seemed to get on well enough, and the preparations proceeded apace. The piano was moved into the saloon, and the curtains were hung; they looked very handsome. The crew began to straggle in from their home villages. I sent Travers off to England, and saw her go with no regrets.

We were very busy during those days, shopping for more supplies and visiting Michael, where we played with the little girl and practiced our Arabic on the ladies of the household; having the piano tuned, paying final visits to Gizeh (I went in the Great Pyramid again, but Evelyn would not), going to the museum several more times, and making calls on the British authorities. I found another of my father's old acquaintances in the finance ministry; he scolded me for not having called earlier so that he could have the opportunity of entertaining me. He was very kind; so much so, that I began to feel uncomfortable at the way his eyes examined me. Finally he burst out,

"My dear Miss Amelia, you really have changed; are you aware of how much you have changed? The air of Egypt must agree with you; you seem much younger than you did when I last saw you in Sussex."

I was wearing a dress Evelyn had selected for me, a mustard-yellow foulard trimmed in green, with draped skirts.

"Fine feathers, my dear sir," I said briskly. "They are becoming even to elderly hens. Now, I wonder if you could help me—"

I had come, of course, to find out about Evelyn's grandfather. I could see that my friend was surprised at my interest, but he was too much of a gentleman to ask the cause. He informed me that word of the earl's death had reached him within the past fortnight. He knew no details, only the bare fact; it was not a subject of consuming interest to him. I was inhibited because I could not ask the questions I needed to ask without betraying Evelyn's secret. I did not want her identity to become known in Egypt, since we proposed to spend the rest of the winter there. So I had to go away with my curiosity partially unsatisfied.

However, I was able to meet Major—now Sir Evelyn—Baring, the consul general and British agent, who came into the office as I was leaving it. He reminded me of my brothers. Solid British respectability lay upon him like a coating of dust. His neat moustache, his gold-rimmed pince-nez, the rounded configuration of his impeccably garbed form, all spoke of his reliability, capability, and dullness. However, he had done an admirable job of trying to restore financial stability to a country heavily in debt, and even when I met him he was known to be the chief power in Egypt. He was faultlessly courteous to me, assuring me of his willingness to be of assistance in any possible way. He had known my father, he said, by reputation. I was beginning to get an image of my dear papa sitting quietly in the center of a web whose strands extended all over the globe.

We planned to leave on the Friday. It was on the Thursday evening that our visitor arrived, and conversation with him made clear several points that had hitherto been cloudy—and raised new problems not so easily solved.

We were in the lounge; I had insisted we go down. Evelyn had been pensive and sad all day, brooding about her grandfather and, I suspected, about the thought of Walter speeding southward away from her. The Emersons did not hire even a small dahabeeyah; Walter had explained that they rented space on a steamer which carried their supplies, and that they slept on deck with the crew, rolled in their blankets. I thought of my delicate Evelyn living in such conditions and could not wholly regret the loss of Walter.

We were both tired, having been occupied all day with such last-minute details as always occur when one prepares for a journey; and I believe I was dozing just a little when an exclamation from Evelyn aroused me. For a moment I thought we were about to have a repetition of the evening of Alberto's appearance. Evelyn had risen to her feet and was staring toward the door. Her expression was not so much one of alarm, however, as of disbelief; and when I turned, to see the cause of her amazement, I beheld a young gentleman coming quickly toward us, a broad smile on his face and his hand extended in greeting.

He seemed for a moment as if he would embrace her. Propriety prevailed; but he took her limp hand in both his big brown ones and wrung it enthusiastically.

"Evelyn! My dear girl! You cannot imagine the relief, the pleasure. . . . How could you frighten me so?"

"And you cannot imagine my surprise," Evelyn exclaimed. "What on earth are you doing here?"

"Following you, of course; what other reason could I have? I could not rest while I was in doubt as to your safety. But we forget ourselves, Evelyn." He turned to me with the same broad smile. "I need not ask; this must be Miss Peabody. The kindly, the noble, the greathearted Miss Peabody, to whom I owe my dear cousin's recovery. Oh, yes, I know all! I visited the British consul in Rome; that is how I traced you here. And knowing what that gentleman did not, of the circumstances that had brought Evelyn to Rome—no, Cousin, we will not speak of them, not now or ever again; but knowing of them I am able to give Miss Peabody's conduct the credit it deserves. My dear Miss Peabody! Excuse me, but I cannot restrain my enthusiasm; I am an enthusiastic fellow!"

Seizing my hand, he wrung it as thoroughly as he had wrung Evelyn's, beaming like a younger edition of the immortal Pickwick all the while.

"Really, sir," I said. "I am quite overwhelmed—"

"I know, I know." Dropping my hand, the young gentleman burst into the jolliest peal of laughter imaginable. "I do overwhelm people. I can't help it. Please sit down, ladies, so that I may do so; then we will have a pleasant talk."

"Perhaps you might even consider introducing yourself," I

suggested, tenderly massaging my fingers.

"Forgive me, Amelia," Evelyn exclaimed. "Let me present my cousin, Mr. Lucas Hayes."

"*I* will let you; whether *he* will be silent long enough to be presented, I don't know." I looked keenly at the young man, who was smiling broadly, undisturbed by my sharpness. "But I fancy it is no longer Mr. Hayes. Should I not say 'your lordship?' "

A shadow clouded Evelyn's face. The new earl leaned over and patted her hand.

"*You* will say Lucas, I hope, Miss Peabody. I feel I know you so well! And it may be painful for Evelyn to be reminded of her loss. I see the news has reached you."

"We only learned of it a few days ago," Evelyn said. "I had tried to prepare myself, but. . . . Please tell me about it, Lucas. I want to hear everything."

"You are sure you wish to?"

"Oh, yes. I must hear every detail, even if it is painful to me; and although I know I should not, I cannot help hoping that he forgave me, at the end . . . that he had time for one kind word, one message. . . ."

She leaned forward, her hands clasped, her blue eyes misty with tears. She looked very pretty and appealing; the young earl's face reflected his admiration.

"Evelyn, I am sure he felt kindness, even though. . . . But I will tell you all. Only let me marshal my thoughts."

While he marshaled them I had leisure to study him with a curiosity I made no attempt to conceal. He was a tall, broad-shouldered young chap, dressed with an elegance that verged on foppishness. His patent leather boots shone like glass; his waistcoat was embroidered with rosebuds. A huge diamond glittered in the midst of an immense expanse of snowy shirt front, and his trousers were so close-fitting that when he sat down I expected something to rip. The candid cheerfulness of his face was very

62

English, but his swarthy complexion and large dark eyes betrayed his father's nationality. I looked then at his hands. They were well shaped, if rather large and brown, and were as well tended as a woman's. I always think hands are so expressive of character. I had noticed that Emerson's were heavy with callouses and disfigured with the scars and scratches of manual labor.

There is no use trying to conceal from the reader that I found myself illogically prejudiced against my new acquaintance. I say illogically, because his manner thus far had been irreproachable, if ebullient. His subsequent speeches proved him to be a man of honor and of heart. Still, I did not like him.

Lucas began his explanation.

"You know, I imagine, that after your—your departure, our revered progenitor fell into such a rage that he suffered a stroke. We did not expect that he would recover from it, but the old gentleman had amazing powers of recuperation; I have noted that a vicious temper does seem to give its possessors unusual strength. . . . Now, Evelyn, you mustn't look at me so reproachfully. I had some affection for our grandfather, but I cannot overlook his treatment of you. You must allow me an occasional word of criticism.

"When I heard what had transpired, I went at once to Ellesmere Castle. I was not the only one to respond; you, who know our family, can imagine the scene of pandemonium I found on my arrival. Aunts and uncles and cousins of every degree had descended, like the scavengers they are—eating and drinking as hard as they could, and trying every despicable stratagem to get into the sickroom, where the sufferer lay like a man in a beleaguered fort. I couldn't decide which of them was the worst. Our second cousin Wilfred tried to bribe the nurse; Aunt Marian sat in a chair outside the door and had to be pushed back whenever it was opened; young Peter Forbes, at his mother's instigation, climbed the ivy outside the window of the sickroom and was only repelled by the footman and your humble servant."

The waiter coming by at that moment, Lucas ordered coffee. He caught my eye and burst into another of those hearty peals of laughter.

"My dear Miss Peabody, you have a countenance as expressive as an open book. I can read your thoughts; shall I tell you what you are thinking? You are thinking that I am the pot that calls the kettles black—that I am as thorough a scavenger as the rest. And, of course, you are absolutely correct! I respected our grandfather for his good qualities. He had a few; if I had more time, I might be able to recall one of them. . . . No, dear Miss Peabody, frankness is my worst failing. I cannot pretend to emotions I do not feel, even to improve my position in the world, and I will not be such a hypocrite as to pretend I loved our grandfather. Evelyn is a little saint; she would find some excuse for a man who knocked her down and trampled on her. . . ."

He broke off as I made a warning gesture. Evelyn's face was flushed; her eyes were fixed on her hands, folded tightly in her lap.

"Evelyn is a saint," Lucas repeated more emphatically. "Only a saint could have loved grandfather. But I could not help feeling sorry for the old gentleman just then. It is pitiable to lie dying, and have no one there who loves you.

"I was in a stronger position than my fellow scavengers, for I was the heir, and the doctors and lawyers who surrounded my grandfather knew this. While he was incapable of speech or movement, the authority was mine, and I exercised it to rid the house of the family. If curses have any effect, I am due to perish miserably. But I did not care for that; and I cannot help but think that the silence and peace I produced in the castle helped Grandfather's recovery. For, to the astonishment of the doctors, he began to mend. Within a few weeks he was tottering around his room swearing at the nurses and throwing crockery at his valet, as was his endearing habit. However, the doctors had warned him that any exertion or emotion might bring on another stroke; and this one would certainly be fatal.

"One of his first acts, Evelyn, on your departure, was to call his solicitor and make a new will. You know that; you know that he left you five pounds with which to buy a mourning ring. He had made me his heir—not through affection, but because he detested the other relatives even more than he did me. When he recovered sufficiently, I at once spoke to him of the impropriety of his treatment of you. I had no objection to inheriting, but there was plenty for both of us, and I could not enjoy my share if I thought you were in need.

"Needless to say, my interference was received without favor. Indeed, I had to abandon the attempt for fear of bringing on another seizure. Dear Grandfather hinted to me that I ought to leave, but I had the concurrence of his medical advisers when I remained in spite of the hints. He was still rather feeble, and it was necessary to spare him as much as possible. I was the only one with the proper authority to fend off annoying visitors, and I exercised it to the full.

"I honestly did believe that he was beginning to soften toward you, until. . . . It happened one afternoon when I was away from the house. It was virtually the first time I had left, and I had business. . . . Ah, well, let me be candid. I needed amusement. It had been a dreary month. I blame myself; for in my absence Grandfather dragged his poor old bones from his bed and set the servants to packing your belongings. Nothing of any value, alas; only your clothing and ornaments, and the dozens of little trinkets and mementos he had given you. Not a single one was missed; I was told that Grandfather stormed in and out of your rooms gathering up objects and throwing them into boxes. A demonic energy had seized him; by the time I returned home, the boxes had been packed, corded, and dispatched by the local carter. The castle was swept clean of any object that could remind him of you;

and he had collapsed, like the old bundle of bones he was. The house was in an uproar, with doctors arriving and conferring, the servants in hysterics, and snow falling heavily, as in a scene from a dreary novel. It was frightful!

"From that evening, Grandfather never recovered. By morning he was much worse, and although he tried once or twice to speak, he never uttered a consecutive sentence. But, dearest Evelyn, I am convinced he wanted to speak of you. I am sure he forgave you and wanted you back. I hope you will believe that."

Evelyn's head was bowed. Crystal drops splashed down onto her hands.

"A very affecting narrative," I said drily. "Evelyn, you will spoil that dress. Satin water-stains badly."

Evelyn took a deep breath and dabbed at her eyes. Lucas had the effrontery to wink at me. I ignored him.

"Well," I said, "that solves one problem, does it not, Evelyn? The motives of our visitor become more comprehensible. The individual to whom I refer had not heard of the final fatality, but was informed of the preceding recovery. Hope springs eternal."

"You need not be so tactful," Evelyn said dully. "Lucas must know to whom we refer. His manner has been generosity itself, but I will not insult him by glossing over my dreadful—"

"You will insult me if you ever refer to the matter again," Lucas interrupted. "The past is finished; unless I should be fortunate enough to encounter a certain individual someday in a quiet spot. . . . Evelyn, let me finish my narrative. You have heard the distressing part, let me proceed to happier matters."

"Happier?" Evelyn smiled sadly.

"Happier, I hope. I hope you cannot be insensible to my actions, my feelings. . . . As soon as the obsequies of our ancestor had been celebrated, I set out in pursuit of you. And here I am, only waiting for your consent to share our fortune—I cannot call it mine—and, if you will, our title, our lives, and our name!"

66

He leaned back in his chair, beaming on both of us like a youthful Father Christmas.

I really did have a hard time maintaining my dislike of Mr. Lucas; my prejudices struggled and were almost subdued. The offer was magnificent, noble; and it was made with a delicacy I would not have believed possible.

Then the meaning of Lucas's last phrase penetrated my brain, and I exclaimed, "Sir, are you proposing marriage?"

"I don't think my words are open to any other interpretation," said Lucas, grinning broadly.

Evelyn sat openmouthed and staring. Twice she tried to speak; twice her voice failed her. Then she cleared her throat, and on the third attempt succeeded.

"Lucas, this is too much. I cannot believe—you cannot mean—"

"Why not?" Leaning forward, he captured her hands in his. "We were meant for each other, Evelyn. Common sense, worldly values and, I hope, mutual affection design us for one another. Oh, I know you don't love me. I know your heart is bruised and fearful. Let me offer it a refuge in my heart! Let me teach you to love me as I adore you."

His intense dark eyes shone with an ardent light; his handsome features were set in an expression of tenderness. I really did not see how a girl could resist him. But, as I had learned, Evelyn was made of sterner stuff than she appeared. And, as I was about to learn, the new sentiment that had entered her heart was stronger than I had supposed.

"Lucas," she said gently. "I cannot tell you how much your offer moves me. All my life I will honor and revere you as one of the noblest gentlemen of my acquaintance. But I cannot marry you."

"If you fear censure—" Lucas began.

"I do fear it—for your sake rather than my own. But that is not

67

why I refuse your generous offer. I will never marry. There is an image enshrined in my heart—"

Lucas dropped her hands. His expression was one of disbelief. "Not that wretched—"

"No." Evelyn flushed. "Certainly not."

"I am relieved to hear it!" Lucas looked thoughtful. Then his face cleared. "Dearest Evelyn, I am not disheartened. I was prepared for a refusal, although the reason you cite does rather take me by surprise. However, it does not alter the facts of the case. Such a sudden affection—forgive me, Cousin, but it is the truth —cannot be a deep affection. With time, I will overcome it. In lieu of parent, I turn to Miss Peabody, and ask her permission to pay court to you in the proper fashion!"

He did turn to me, his hand on his heart and a broad smile on his lips. I couldn't help smiling back, although it was a rather sour smile.

"I can hardly prevent you from enjoying the society of your cousin," I said. "But you will have to work fast, Mr. Lucas; we leave tomorrow morning for a trip down the Nile. So you have only a few hours in which to press your suit."

"Tomorrow morning," Lucas exclaimed. "I have no undue modesty about my powers of persuasion, but really—!"

"I am sorry," Evelyn said, in her gentle voice. "Lucas, I cannot encourage you. I will never change my mind. But I regret that we will not enjoy your company for a longer time."

"Really, Evelyn, we must discuss this," Lucas said. "I am as stubborn as you are, and much louder; I do not intend to abandon my hopes. But my dear girl, you don't suppose that I am making marriage a prerequisite to the enjoyment of the rights that are morally yours, even though they have not been established legally. Half of our grandfather's fortune belongs to you. I will settle it upon you immediately when we return home. That is where you belong, at home. You can have your own establishment, anywhere you like—if the Dower House at Ellesmere does not suit you, we will find another—"

He stopped speaking. Evelyn was shaking her head.

"My grandfather had the right to dispose of his property as he chose. I cannot take what is not mine, Lucas, and if you try to give it to me, I will give it back. Further, I have agreed to spend the winter with Amelia. One companion has already deserted her; I will not do so, she is depending on me."

"Then in the spring . . . ?"

"I do not promise that."

"No, but. . . . I see your argument with regard to Miss Peabody; it would indeed be a poor return for her kindness to abandon her now, at the last minute. Altogether, it is a good idea. Winter in Egypt, recover your health and spirits; in the meantime we can work out a good lie with which to confound our friends at home when they wonder where you have been all this time."

"No, Lucas, really—"

"A good lie is absolutely essential, my love. Never mind what they suspect; together we will outface them."

"Lucas, you bewilder me," Evelyn exclaimed. "You pay no heed to anything I have said—"

"I do, I do. But I do not take it as final. No, my dear cousin, Egypt is a splendid place in which to spend the winter; I have always wanted to come here. If I cannot convince you of my sincerity by spring, I will abandon my hopes. Come, Miss Peabody, you are our Minerva, our font of wisdom; what do you say?"

"Oh, I am to be allowed to say something? Well, my dear Lord Ellesmere, then I must confess you have some justice on your side; and you, Evelyn, cannot refuse your cousin's desire to assist you. If you will not accept all the money he wants to give you, you can in clear conscience accept a respectable annuity. If you wish to go home—"

"Oh, Amelia, how can you say so?"

"Very well," I said, sniffing to conceal my pleasure. "Then we will carry out our trip down the Nile. When it is over, you will consider your cousin's offer. Does that seem fair to both of you?"

Lucas snatched my hand and shook it enthusiastically. Evelyn nodded. She was not favorable to the idea, but was too fair-minded to object.

"However," I continued, "Mr. Lucas will have to conduct his courtship from a distance. I can hardly offer him a room on our dahabeeyah. It would not be proper."

"I had not thought you the sort of lady who worried about propriety," Lucas said, with a meaningful look. "However, I shall hire my own dahabeeyah and be on your trail as soon as possible. You shan't escape me so easily, ladies. I shall sail where you sail and moor where you moor!"

"That sounds very romantic," I said coolly. "I hope you will not be disappointed; it is not so easy to arrange these things in Egypt."

"So I have been informed." Lucas rose, squaring his shoulders. "Therefore I must get at the business immediately."

"You can do nothing tonight," I said.

"Ah, you underestimate me, dear lady! Tomorrow, when I accompany you to your boat, I will hire one for myself. Nor is it too late, tonight, to acquire a dragoman. The lobby still teems with the wretched fellows, and I am told they are essential to travelers. Perhaps you could recommend a good one."

"No," I said.

"Michael might know of someone," Evelyn said, with a smiling glance at me.

"He has gone home," I said.

"He is sure to be somewhere about," Evelyn said gently. "He never leaves until we have retired. Indeed, I think the fellow sleeps here, he's so devoted to you since you saved the life of his child. He would do anything for you."

"You are the one he is devoted to," I said. "I cannot imagine where you get these notions, Evelyn."

Michael had taken quite a fancy to Evelyn and was, as she had thought, still in the hotel. We found him and, taking our leave of his lordship, left the two of them in conversation.

I was really vexed with Evelyn for helping her cousin to further his plans; if I had not known her so well, I would have imagined she wanted to encourage him. But that was Evelyn's weakness. She was too kind, and too truthful. Both, I have found, are inconvenient character traits.

4

I HAD thought to avoid Mr. Lucas by making an outrageously early departure next morning. I underestimated him. The rosy streaks of dawn were scarcely brushing the sky when we descended into the lobby of the hotel, to find Lucas waiting, with an armful of flowers for Evelyn and a knowing smile for me. He insisted on accompanying us to Boulaq, and as the little boat carried us across to the waiting dahabeeyah he stood on the shore waving both arms like a semaphore and showing all his teeth in a smile.

With much bustle and a babble of cheerful voices the men took their places. The mooring ropes were loosed; the oarsmen pushed off from the bank; the great sail swelled as it took the wind; and we were off, with a six-gun salute from our crew, answered by other boats along the bank.

We sat on the high upper deck, with an awning to protect us from the sun. Rugs, lounge chairs, and tables had transformed this area into a comfortable drawing room, and the waiter, young Habib, at once appeared with mint tea and cakes. Evelyn lost her thoughtful look and sat up, pointing and exclaiming at the sights. The worst pessimist in the world must have responded to the happiness of such an excursion on such a day. The sun was well up, beaming down from a cloudless sky. The gentle breeze fanned our cheeks. The palaces and gardens on the riverbank glided by as smoothly as in a dream, and with every passing minute new beauties of scenery and architecture were displayed to our eager eyes. In the distance the shapes of the pyramids were etched against the sky; the air was so clear that they seemed like miniature monuments, only yards away.

We sat on the deck the whole of that day; the experience was so new and so enchanting it was impossible to tear ourselves away. At dinner time delectable smells wafted up from the kitchen near the prow. Evelyn ate with a better appetite than I had seen her display for days; and when we retired to the saloon as the evening fell, she performed Chopin beautifully on the pianoforte. I sat by the window watching the exquisite sunset and listening to the tender strains; it is a moment that will always remain in my memory.

We had many such moments as the days went on; but I must curtail my enthusiasm, for I could write another of those repetitious travel books about the trip—the eerie singing of the crewmen as we lay moored at night; the exchanges of salutes with the Cook's steamers plying the river; the visits to the monuments of Dahshoor (pyramids) and Abusir (more pyramids).

Most travelers hurry up the river as fast as possible, planning to stop at various historic sites on the return voyage. The voyage upstream is the difficult one, against the current, which, as the reader knows, flows from south to north; one is dependent upon the prevailing northerly wind, and, when this fails, as it often does, upon the brawny arms of the men. After we watched them tow the heavy boat through an area of sandbanks in a dead calm, we could not bear to inflict this labor on them any more often than was absolutely necessary. To see the poor fellows harnessed to a rope, like ancient slaves, was positively painful.

I had private reasons for wishing to push on as quickly as possible. The energetic Mr. Lucas would find difficulty in hiring a dahabeeyah as promptly as he hoped, but I did not underestimate his stubbornness, and I fancied a few weeks of peace and quiet before he caught us up.

However, my study of history had told me that the common method of travel is the wrong way. The monuments near Cairo are among the oldest; in order to see Egyptian history unroll before us in the proper sequence, we must stop on our way south instead of waiting till the return voyage. I wanted to see Twelfth Dynasty tombs and Eighteenth Dynasty temples before viewing the remains of the later Greek and Roman periods. I had therefore made out an itinerary before we left Cairo and presented it to Reis Hassan.

You would have thought I had suggested a revolution, the way that man carried on. I was informed, through Michael, that we must take advantage of the wind, and sail where, and as, it permitted.

I was beginning to understand a little Arabic by then, and I comprehended a few of the comments Michael did not translate. According to the reis I was a woman, and therefore no better than a fool. I knew nothing about boats, or wind, or sailing, or the Nile; who was I, to tell an experienced captain how to run his boat?

I was the person who had hired the boat. I pointed this out to Reis Hassan. I hoped I need not say who won the argument. Like all men, of all colors and all nations, he was unable to accept an unpalatable fact, however; and I had to argue with him every time I proposed to stop.

Except for running aground on sandbanks, which is a common-enough occurrence, we made admirable time. The wind was good. I therefore encountered some stiff resistance from the reis when I told him we would stop at Beni Hassan, which is some 167 miles south of Cairo. Brandishing my copy of M. Maspero's history, I explained to him that the tombs at Beni Hassan are of the time of Usertsen of the Twelfth Dynasty; chronologically they follow the pyramid of Gizeh, where we had been, and precede the antiquities of Luxor, where we proposed to go. I doubt that he understood my argument. However, we stopped at Beni Hassan.

The village was typical. I would have reported a man who kept his dog in such a kennel. Small mud hovels, roofed with corn-stalks, looked as if they had been flung down at random on the ground. These huts are clustered around an inner courtyard, where the cooking is carried on; there is a fire, a stone for grinding corn, a few storage jars, and that is all. The women spin, or grind, or nurse their infants. The men sit. Children, chickens, and dogs tumble about in an indiscriminate mass, equally dirty, equally unclad; and yet the children are pretty little things when they are not disfigured by flies and disease.

When we appeared, the village seethed as if someone had stirred it with a stick. We were besieged by outstretched hands —some empty, begging for the inevitable backsheesh; some holding objects for sale—antiquities, stolen from the tombs, or manufactured by enterprising merchants to delude the unwary. It is said that some Europeans and Americans engage in this immoral trade.

Evelyn recoiled with a cry as an indescribably horrid object was thrust under her very nose. At first it appeared to be a bundle of dry brown sticks wrapped in filthy cloth; then my critical gaze recognized it for what it was—a mummy's hand, snapped off at the wrist, the dried bones protruding; black from the bitumen in which it had been soaked in ancient times. Two tawdry little rings adorned the bony fingers, and scraps of rotten wrappings were pushed back to display the delicacy in all its gruesome reality.

The seller was not at all put off by our mutual exclamations of disgust; it required Michael's added comments to convince him that we would not own such a repulsive object. Many travelers buy such mementos, even entire mummies, which are exported from the country like bundles of wood instead of human remains.

Evelyn's sensitive face was pensive as we went on. "How strange and pitiful," she said musingly. "To reflect that that horrid object was perhaps once clasped ardently by a husband or lover! It was very small, was it not, Amelia—a woman's hand?"

"Don't think about it," I said firmly.

"I wish I could stop thinking about it. My reflections should dwell on the frailty of the flesh, on human vanity, and the other precepts of Christian faith. . . . Instead I shudder at the horror of what is, after all, only a bit of cast-off flesh—the discarded garment of the soul. Amelia, if it had touched me I should have died!"

We went up to the tombs. You may rest assured, dear reader, that I had not wasted my time during the voyage. I had with me the Reverend Samuel Birch's little books on the study of Egyptian hieroglyphs; and my hours of pouring over these sources were repaid in full when I was able to point out to Evelyn the group of hieroglyphic signs which spells the name of the chief of this district during the Twelfth Dynasty. There is no thrill equal to seeing the actual signs, painted on crumbling rock walls instead of printed on a page; finding in them meaning and sense. . . .

But I fear I am being carried away by my scholarly enthusiasm. The tombs had considerable interest even for casual tourists; the painted scenes on the wall are gay and pretty, showing the activities in which the dead man loved to indulge during his lifetime, as well as the industries pursued on his estates. His serfs blow glass and work gold into jewelry; they tend the flocks, fashion pottery, and work in the fields.

Some years later these same splendid tombs were savagely mutilated by native Egyptians extracting fragments of the paintings for sale to antiquities dealers. But even when we saw them I was aware of some of the abuses Emerson had talked about. Fragments of paint and plaster were constantly flaking off the walls, which were dulled by the smoke from the candles carried by the guides. Visiting travelers were no more careful than the uninformed Egyptians; as we stood in one tomb I watched an American gentleman calmly walk away with a fallen bit of stone that bore a pretty picture of a young calf. I shouted at him, but Evelyn prevented me when I would have pursued him to retrieve the fragment. As she pointed out, someone else would have taken it anyway.

The name of Emerson has now returned to the narrative; but the reader must not suppose that it was absent from our thoughts during the halcyon days of sailing. Evelyn did not refer to Walter; but when I introduced his name the eager light in her eye, the unguarded way in which she turned toward me told me that, though absent from her tongue, the name was not far from her thoughts.

As for myself, I thought often of Emerson, though not, of course, in the same way Evelyn regarded his young brother. No; the thought of Emerson was a stinging mosquito, which produced an itching spot that constantly demanded to be rubbed. (The Critic comments upon the inelegance of this comparison. I insist upon leaving it in.) Emerson's criticisms kept recurring to me; I saw evidence of neglect and vandalism to the monuments wherever we went, and I itched (you see the appropriateness of my analogy), I positively itched to be in charge of the entire antiquities department. I would have settled things properly!

We got to know some of our crew quite well. The cook was an elderly, toothless black gentleman from Assuan, who produced the most delicious meals upon two small charcoal burners. The waiters, Habib and Abdul, were handsome boys who might have stepped straight out of an ancient Egyptian painting, with their broad shoulders and long, slim bodies. We got to be very fond of them, especially Habib, who laughed in the most infectious manner whenever I spoke to him in Arabic. The crewmen I could only vaguely distinguish by their complexions, which ranged from black to café-au-lait; they looked identical otherwise, in their flowing striped robes and white turbans.

I acquired a new name during the voyage. The Egyptians have nicknames for everyone, and some of them are quite amusing and disrespectful. Maspero told us of a friend of his, an American gentleman named Wilbour, who is the proud possessor of a magnificent white beard. The Arabs call him "Father of the Beard." My name was equally descriptive; they called me the Sitt Hakim, the lady doctor. I felt I deserved the title; scarcely a day went by when I was not patching up some scrape or cut, although, to my regret, I was not called upon to amputate anything. When we stopped in the native villages I was always being approached by dark-eyed mothers, some no more than children themselves, carrying their pitiful babies. I had used virtually all my stock of eye medicines by the time we left Beni Hassan—and knew, unfortunately, that my efforts were like a single drop of water in a desert. The key to the regeneration of Egypt lies in the women. So long as they are forced into marriage and motherhood long before they are ready for such responsibilities—sold to the highest bidder like animals, untrained in even the rudiments of sanitation and housekeeping, untaught, unassisted, and degraded—so long will the country fail to realize its potential. I determined that I would speak to Major Baring about this as soon as we returned to Cairo. I didn't suppose that the man had any notion of matters outside of his account books; men never do.

With such reflections and studies the days passed delightfully. Evelyn's companionship added immeasurably to my enjoyment.

She was the perfect friend: sensitive to beauty, responsive to my moods and to the frequent distressing sights of poverty and disease; interested in learning all she could of the history that unrolled before us; cheerful; uncomplaining. I found myself dreading the spring. It would have been so pleasant to look forward to years of Evelyn's company; we could have lived like sisters, enjoying the domestic comforts of England, and traveling whenever we got bored with domesticity. But that was clearly not to be expected. Whether Evelyn yielded to her cousin's suit or not, she would certainly marry one day; and I rather believed that Lucas would prevail. He had every argument on his side. So I decided to enjoy the moment and forget about the future.

After Beni Hassan, the next site of interest to historians is near a village called Haggi Qandil. The region has a more famous name; it is sometimes called Tell-el-Amarna, and it was the city of the heretic king Khuenaten—if indeed he was a king, and not a queen in disguise, as some archaelogists have claimed. I had seen copies of the strange portraits of this monarch, and had to admit that his form bore more resemblance to the feminine than to the masculine.

Even more intriguing was the speculation on the religious beliefs of this peculiar personage. He had abandoned the worship of the old gods of Egypt and given his devotion to the sun, Aten. Did he worship only this god? Was he the first monotheist of whom history gives us a record? And what connection could there be between this supposed monotheism and the monotheism of the Hebrews? Moses was raised at the court of Egypt. Perhaps the elevated faith of Yahweh derived, ultimately, from the iconoclastic religion of an ancient Egyptian pharaoh!

Evelyn was rather shocked when I proposed this idea, and we had a pleasant little argument. I gave her a lecture on Khuenaten; she was always anxious to learn.

"He abandoned the royal city of Thebes," I explained, "and

79

built a new capital dedicated to his god, on land that had never been contaminated by other worship. Herr Lepsius discovered some of the boundary inscriptions placed on the rocks around the city by Khuenaten. There are also tombs in the cliffs, rather interesting ones; the drawings are quite different in style from the usual tomb decorations. If the wind suits, I think a visit there might be profitable. What do you say?"

I was leafing through my copy of Brugsch's *Geographical Dictionary* (Heinrich Brugsch, the archaeologist, not his disreputable brother) as I spoke; but I watched Evelyn out of the corner of my eye, and saw the betraying color rise in her cheeks. She put down her pencil—she was quite a good little artist, and had made a number of nice sketches along the way—and gazed out across the river toward the cliffs.

"What is the name of the place, Amelia?"

I riffled busily through the pages of Brugsch.

"The ancient name of the place was—"

"The modern name is El Amarnah, is it not?"

"There are three villages on the spot, el-Till and el-Haggi Qandil and El-Amariah. A corruption of these names—"

"Yes, yes, I recall—I recall Walter speaking of it. That is where he and Mr. Emerson are working. You would have no reason to remember that, of course."

I decided that Evelyn was being sarcastic. She seldom allowed herself this luxury, so I overlooked it on this occasion.

"Is that so?" I said casually. "Well, I suppose there is no reason why we should necessarily encounter the Emersons. The site is large and the tombs are scattered. We will take it as settled, then. I will speak to Reis Hassan."

Owing to a difficulty with the wind, we did not reach the village of Haggi Qandil for two days. Indeed, we had some trouble reaching it at all; if I had not been determined, Reis Hassan would not have stopped. He mentioned unfavorable winds, disease in the village, the remoteness of the archaeological remains from the river, and a number of other irrelevant arguments. You would have thought the good captain would have learned by now the futility of arguing with me; but perhaps he enjoyed it. Honesty compels me to admit that Hassan may have had some reason on his side. We ran aground on a sandbank outside the village and had to be carried ashore by the villagers. We left Reis Hassan staring gloomily at his crew, who were trying to free the boat and making very little progress.

Michael, our dragoman, led the way into the village. It was a typical Egyptian village—perhaps a trifle more wretched than others. The narrow streets were heaped with refuse of all kinds, steaming under the hot sun. Dust and windblown sand coated every surface. Mangy dogs lay about the streets, their ribs showing. They bared their teeth at us as we passed, but were too miserable even to rise. Half-naked children stared from eyes ringed with flies, and whined for backsheesh.

Michael plunged into the crowd, shouting orders, and eventually we were presented with a choice of donkeys. We chose the least-miserable-looking of the lot, and then I proceeded to a ritual which had caused considerable amusement along the way, and which puzzled even our loyal Michael. Following my orders, interpreted by Michael, the reluctant owners took the filthy cloths from the animals' back, swabbed them down with buckets of water, and smeared on the ointment I supplied. The donkeys were then covered with fresh saddle cloths, supplied by me, which were laundered after every use. I think it was the only time in the lives of these little donkeys that the cloths were ever removed; sores and insects proliferated under them.

The scowls on the faces of the donkeys' owners turned to broad smiles as I tipped them liberally for their unusual effort; I took the opportunity to add a short lecture on the economic advantage of tending one's livestock, but I was never sure how much of this discourse Michael translated. With the now laughing attendants running alongside, we trotted off across the desert toward the tombs.

The cliffs, which run closely along the river in other areas, fall back here, leaving a semicircular plain some seven miles long by four miles wide at its greatest extent. The cultivated land is only a narrow strip less than half a mile wide; beyond, all is baking yellow-brown desert, until one reaches the rocky foothills of the cliffs into which the tombs were cut.

We were bouncing along in fine style, squinting against the glare of the sun, when I beheld a figure coming toward us. The air of Egypt is so clear one can make out details at distances impossible in England; I saw at once that the person approaching was not a native. He wore trousers instead of flapping skirts. My internal organs (if I may be permitted to refer to these objects) gave an odd lurch. But soon I realized that the man was not Emerson. Evelyn recognized him at the same time. We were side by side; I heard her soft exclamation and saw her hands clench on the reins.

Walter did not recognize us immediately. He saw only two European travelers, and ran toward us with increased speed. Not until he was almost upon us did he realize who we were; and he stopped so abruptly that a spurt of sand shot up from under his heels. We continued to trot decorously toward him as he stood swaying and staring like a man in a dream.

"Thank God you are here!" he exclaimed, before we could greet him. "That is . . . you are really here? You are not a vision, or a mirage?"

His eyes were fixed on Evelyn's face; but his agitation was so great I deduced some other cause of trouble than frustrated love.

"We are really here," I assured him. "What is wrong, Mr. Walter?"

"Emerson. My brother." The lad passed his hand across his

damp forehead. "He is ill. Desperately, dangerously ill. . . . You have no doctor with you, of course. But your dahabeeyah—you could take him to Cairo . . . ?"

His brother's danger and Evelyn's unexpected appearance had turned the poor boy's brains to mush. I realized that I must take charge.

"Run back to the boat and get my medical kit, Michael," I said. "Hurry, please. Now, Mr. Walter, if you will lead the way . . ."

"A doctor . . ." mumbled Walter, still looking at Evelyn as if he didn't believe in her.

"You know there is no doctor nearer than Cairo," I said. "Unless I see Mr. Emerson, I cannot tell whether he is fit to be moved. It would take days to get him to Cairo. Lead on, Mr. Walter."

I jabbed him with my parasol. He started, turned, and began to run back in the direction from which he had come. The donkeys, aroused by my voice, broke into a trot. Skirts flying, parasols waving, we dashed forward, followed by a cloud of sand.

Emerson had situated himself in one of the tombs that had been dug into the rock wall of the hills bounding the plain. The entrances looked like black rectangles against the sunbaked rock. We had to climb the last few yards, along a sort of path that led up the cliff. Walter devoted himself to Evelyn; the donkey attendants would have helped me, but I swatted them off with my parasol. I needed no assistance. I was panting a trifle when I finally reached the entrance to the tomb, but it was—yes, I confess it —it was with agitation rather than exertion.

The lintel and jambs of the entrance were covered with carved reliefs. I had no time for them then; I entered. Once inside, I cast a quick, comprehensive glance about, and understood why Emerson had chosen to take up his abode in the resting place of the ancient dead, rather than pitch a tent. The room was long and narrow—a passageway, as I later discovered, rather than a chamber. The far end was lost in shadow, but diffused sunlight illumined the area next to the entrance. Wooden packing cases served as tables. Some were covered with tins of food, others with books and papers. A lamp showed how the room was lighted by night. A few folding camp chairs were the only other pieces of furniture, save for two camp beds. On one lay the motionless form of a man.

He lay so still that horror gripped me; I thought for a moment that we had come too late. Then an arm was flung out and a hoarse voice muttered something. I crossed the room and sat down on the floor by the cot.

I would not have known him. The beard, which had been confined to lower cheeks and jaw, spread upward in a black stubble that almost met his hairline. His eyes were sunken and his cheekbones stood out like spars. I had no need to touch him to realize that he was burning with fever. Heat fairly radiated from his face. His shirt had been opened, baring his throat and chest, and exposing a considerable quantity of black hair; he was covered to the waist with a sheet which his delirious tossing had entwined around his limbs.

Evelyn sank to her knees beside me.

"What shall I do, Amelia?" she asked quietly.

"Dampen some cloths in water. Walter, you must see that we do not run out of water; send the men for more. I don't suppose he can eat; has he taken water to drink?"

"He won't take it," Walter said.

"He will take it for me," I said grimly, and began to roll up my sleeves.

By the time Michael arrived with my bag, we had managed to make Emerson more comfortable. Constant application of water to his face and breast had lowered his temperature somewhat, and I had forced a few drops past his cracked lips. He knocked my bonnet off and sent me sprawling before I succeeded; but resistance merely increased my determination. I then gave him a stiff dose of quinine, lying flat across his chest and pinching his nose shut, while Walter held his arms and Evelyn sat on his legs. Not surprisingly, he fell into an uneasy sleep after these exertions, and I was able to turn my attention to arrangements for the future. Michael was sent back to the dahabeeyah for bedding and supplies. Evelyn went with him, to help him select the personal things we would need. I ordered her to remain on board, but she refused, with the quiet determination she showed at certain times. So I directed Walter to pick out a nice tomb for us.

He was staring at me in the most peculiar fashion. He did not speak, but he kept opening and closing his mouth. If he had not been such a handsome fellow, he would have reminded me of a frog.

"There is a nice tomb close by, I trust," I repeated, resisting the desire to poke at him with my parasol. "Go along, Walter, we mustn't waste time; I want the place all swept out and tidy by the time our luggage arrives. Where are your workmen? Some of them can take care of that matter."

"Nice tomb," Walter repeated stupidly. "Yes. Yes, Miss Peabody, there are several other tombs nearby. I don't know whether you would call them nice. . . ."

"Walter, you are incoherent," I said. "This is no time to lose your head. I understand your concern, but there is no need for it now. I am here. I have no intention of leaving until Mr. Emerson is on his feet again. I have always wanted to spend some time with an archaeological expedition; it should be a delightful experience. There is no point in moving your brother, for the crisis will come in the next few hours, long before we could reach the nearest town. I believe there is no cause for alarm. He has a strong constitution; and at the risk of sounding repetitious, may I say again that I am on the job."

Walter was sitting on the floor next to me. He watched as I

wrung out another cloth and slapped it on Emerson's chest. Then, quite without warning, he leaned forward, took me by the shoulders, and kissed me soundly on the cheek.

"I believe you, Miss Peabody; there is no cause for alarm with you here. I believe you would square off at Satan if he came around and inconvenienced you!"

Before I could reply he had jumped to his feet and bolted out.

I turned back to my patient and wrung out another cloth. There was no one there but myself and Emerson, and he was sleeping; so I permitted myself to smile. Some Eternal Designer had robbed Peter to pay Paul; one Emerson had an extra share of charm and the other had none. Poor Evelyn; no wonder she had succumbed! Luckily Emerson presented no such danger to any woman.

I had to admit, though, that he looked rather pathetic in his present state. A fallen colossus is more pitiable than a felled weakling. As I went on wiping his hot face, some of the lines of pain smoothed out, and he gave a little sigh, like that of a child sinking into restful sleep.

The crisis of the fever came that night, and we had our hands full. Neither Evelyn nor I saw our beds until dawn. Walter had made some of his workers clean out a tomb for us, and Michael fitted it up quite comfortably; but I would not leave my patient, and Evelyn would not leave me. Or perhaps it was Walter she was reluctant to leave. I had no time or energy to inquire, for Emerson became delirious toward sunset, and it took all my strength and Walter's to keep him from harming himself, or us. I acquired a handsome bruise across one cheek when Walter's grip on his brother's arm failed for a moment. I have never seen a man carry on so; you would have thought him an Egyptian soul traversing the perils of the Afterworld, and us crocodile-headed monsters trying to keep him from Heaven. Well, we kept wrestling him back onto the bed, and I forced more medicine down him; and in the early hours of the morning he fell into a coma that must end, as I knew, in death or recovery.

In a way, those succeeding hours were worse than the violent struggles of the earlier time. Walter knelt by the bed, unaware of anything except his brother's gasping breath. The fever rose, in spite of our efforts. My hands were sore from wringing out cloths, and my very bones ached—especially those of my left hand, for at some point before he dropped into his coma Emerson had seized it and would not let go. It was terrifying to feel the hard grip of that hand and see the immobility of the rest of his body; I had the superstitious feeling that he was clinging as if to a lifeline, and that if I forced his fingers apart he would drop into the bottomless abyss of death.

As the night wore on I grew giddy and light-headed with lack of sleep. The scene was uncanny: the smoky lamplight casting its shadows over the taut faces of the watchers and the sunken countenance of the sick man; the utter stillness of the night, broken at long intervals by the wavering howl of a jackal, the loneliest, most desolate sound on earth.

Then, in the darkest hour before dawn, the change came. It was as palpable as a breath of cold air against the face. For a moment my eyes failed, and I felt nothing. I heard a sound, like a strangled sob, from Walter. When I opened my eyes I saw him lying across the foot of the bed, his face hidden and his hand resting on his brother's arm. Emerson's face was utterly peaceful. Then his breast rose in a single long inspiration—and continued to move. The hand that held mine had gone limp. It was cool. He would live.

I could not stand; my limbs were too cramped with crouching. Walter had to half carry me to my bed. He would sit with Emerson the rest of the night, in case there was a relapse, but I had no fear of that. I fell into slumber as one falls into a well, while Evelyn was bathing my hands and face.

When I woke later that morning I could not imagine for a moment where I was. Stone walls instead of the white paneling of my cabin; a hard surface below instead of my soft couch. I started to turn, and let out a cry of pain; my left hand, on which I had tried to raise myself, was swollen and sore.

Then memory came back; I levered myself up from the pallet on which I had slept and fumbled for my dressing gown. Across the room Evelyn still slept the sleep of exhaustion. A beam of light streaming through a gap in the hastily curtained doorway touched her fair hair and made it glow like gold.

When I stepped out onto the ledge in front of my improvised bedchamber, the heat struck like a blow. In spite of my anxiety I could not help pausing for a look. Below me a panorama of desert rolled away to the blue curve of the river, with the western cliffs beyond like ramparts of dull gold. The huts of the village were cleansed by distance; half hidden by the graceful shapes of palm trees, amid the green of the cultivated fields, they looked picturesque instead of nasty. Midway between the village and the cliffs a huddle of black shapes, busy as ants, moved amid a great dusty cloud of sand. I surmised that this was the site of the current excavation.

I walked along the ledge to the next tomb, whence I could hear sounds of altercation. My anxiety had been unnecessary. Emerson was himself again.

I wish it clearly understood that my feelings that bright morning were those of pure Christian charity. For Emerson I felt the compassion and interest one always feels toward a person one has nursed.

These sentiments did not last two minutes.

When I entered I saw Emerson half out of bed, restrained only by Walter's arm. He was partially clad; his nether limbs were covered by the most incredible garments, pink in color. He was shouting at Walter, who waved a small dish under his nose like a weapon.

Emerson stopped shouting when he saw me. His expression was hardly welcoming, but I was so glad to see his eyes aware and sensible, instead of glaring wildly with fever, that I gave him a cheerful forgiving smile before I inspected the contents of the dish Walter was holding.

I forgot myself then; I admit it. I had picked up several forceful expressions from Father, and I used them in his presence, since he never heard a word I said; but I endeavored to avoid them in other company. The sight of the sickly gray-green contents of the dish were too much for my self-control.

"Good Gad," I burst out. "What is that?"

"Tinned peas," said Walter. He looked apologetic, as well he might. "You see, Miss Peabody, they are an excellent cheap source of food. We also have tinned beef and beans and cabbage, but I thought this might be more—"

"Throw it out," I said, holding my nose. "Tell your cook to boil a chicken. One can obtain chickens, I hope? If this is what you eat, no wonder your brother had fever. It is a wonder he doesn't also have dysentery and inflamed bowels."

Walter brought his hand to his brow in a military salute and marched out.

I turned to Emerson. He had flung himself back onto the bed and pulled the sheet up to his chin.

"Go on, Miss Peabody," he said, drawling offensively. "Comment on my other organic failures if you will. I understand I am to thank you for saving my life. Walter is inclined to dramatize things; however, I thank you for ministering to me in your inimitable fashion. Consider yourself thanked. Now go away."

I had intended to go, until he told me to. I sat down on the bed and reached for his hand. He jerked it away.

"I wish to take your pulse," I said impatiently. "Stop acting like a timid maiden lady."

He let me hold his wrist for a few moments. Then he pulled his hand free.

"I wish Miss Nightingale had stayed at home where she belongs," he growled. "Every wretched Englishwoman now wants to become a lady of the lamp. Now, madam, if your instincts are satisfied, take yourself away or—or I shall rise from my bed!"

"If that is what you intend, I shall certainly remain. You cannot get up today. And don't think to frighten me by threats. I watched you all night, remember; your anatomy is not prepossessing, I agree, but I am tolerably familiar with it."

"But my pavement," Emerson shouted. "What is happening to my pavement? You fiend of a woman, I must go and see what they are doing to my pavement!"

"My pavement" had been a recurrent theme in his delirium, and I had wondered what he was talking about. The only allusion that occurred to me was the description in the Gospel of Saint John: "When Pilate therefore heard that saying, he brought Jesus forth, and sat down in the judgment seat in a place that is called the Pavement. . . ." However, although I considered Emerson quite capable of blasphemy, I doubted that he would compare his illness with that divine Martyrdom.

"What pavement?" I asked.

"My painted pavement." Emerson looked at me consideringly. "I have found part of Khuenaten's royal palace. Pavements, walls, and ceilings were painted. Some have miraculously survived."

"Good—that is, how amazing! Do you mean that the royal heretic's palace once stood where that waste of sand now stretches?"

"You know of Khuenaten?"

"Yes, indeed. He is a fascinating personality. Or do you think he was a woman?"

90

"Balderdash! That is typical of the fools who manage archaeological research today. Mariette's notion, that he was taken captive by the Nubians and cas——that is, operated upon—"

"I have read of that theory," I said, as he stuttered to a halt. "Why is it not possible? I believe the operation does produce feminine characteristics in a male."

Emerson gave me a peculiar look.

"That is one way of putting it," he said drily. "It seems more likely to me that Khuenaten's physical peculiarities are an artistic convention. You will note that his courtiers and friends are shown with similar peculiarities."

"Indeed?"

"Yes. Look there." Emerson started to sit up and clutched the sheet to him as it slid. He was a *very* hairy man. "This tomb belonged to a high noble of Khuenaten's court. Its walls are decorated with reliefs in the unique Amarna style."

My curiosity aroused, I reached for the lamp. This motion produced a scream of rage from Emerson.

"Not the lamp! I only use it when I must. The fools who light the tombs with magnesium wire and lamps are vandals; the greasy smoke lays a film on the reliefs. The mirror—take the mirror. If you hold it at the proper angle it will give you sufficient light."

I had observed the mirror and wondered at this unexpected sign of vanity. I ought to have known. It took me some time to get the hang of the business, with Emerson making sarcastic remarks; but finally a lucky twist of the wrist shone a beam of reflected light through the doorway in which I stood, and I stared with wonder and delight.

The reliefs were shallow and worn, but they had a vivacity that at once appealed to me. There seemed to be a parade or procession; all the small running figures followed the mighty form of pharaoh, ten times the size of lesser men. He drove a light chariot, handling his team of prancing horses easily; in the chariot with

91

him was a slightly smaller crowned person. Their heads were turned toward one another; it seemed as if their lips were about to touch.

"He must have loved her very much, to give her such a prominent place at his side," I mused aloud. "I am inclined to agree with you, Emerson; no man who was less than a man would violate tradition by showing his devotion to his beautiful wife. Even her name, Nefertiti—'the beautiful woman has come' . . ."

"You read the hieroglyphs?" Emerson exclaimed.

"A little."

I indicated, without touching it, the oval cartouche in which the queen's name was written, and then moved my finger toward the empty ovals which had once contained the names of Khuenaten.

"I have read of this—how the triumphant priests of Amon destroyed even the royal heretic's name after he died. It is strangely disturbing to see the savagery of their attack. How they must have hated him, to obliterate even his name!"

"By doing so they hoped to annihilate his soul," Emerson said. "Without identity, the spirit of the dead could not survive."

The incongruity of the conversation, with a gentleman in pink undergarments, did not strike me until Evelyn appeared in the doorway, and as abruptly disappeared. From without, her timid voice inquired whether she might come in.

"Oh, curse it," Emerson exclaimed, and pulled the sheet over his head. From under it a muffled voice bade Evelyn enter.

Evelyn entered. She was properly dressed in a pale-green cotton frock, and looked as neat and dainty as if she had had all the amenities of the dahabeeyah at her disposal instead of a basin of tepid water. She was a little flushed. Knowing her as I did, I concluded that she was amused, although I could not imagine why. Emerson pulled the sheet down to the bridge of his nose.

Over its folds a pair of blue eyes regarded Evelyn malevolently. She did not look at him.

"Do come in, Evelyn, and look at these carvings," I exclaimed, flashing my mirror about expertly. "Here is the king riding in his chariot and his queen beside him—"

"I am sure they are fascinating, Amelia, but do you not think it might be better to wait for a more propitious time? Mr. Emerson needs rest, and you are not really dressed for a social call. . . ." There was a suspicious quiver in her voice. She suppressed it and went on, "Walter seems to be having some trouble with the chicken you ordered."

"I suppose I must take charge, as usual." With a last lingering glance at a group of running soldiers, I replaced the mirror.

"So long as you are taking charge, you might have a look at my pavement," Emerson said grudgingly. "You stand here chattering like a parrot, and every moment the paint is chipping away—"

"You were the one who uncovered it," I reminded him. "What are you planning to do to protect it?"

"I've had a wooden shelter built, but that is only a small part of the problem. The question is, what preservative can we apply that won't damage the paint? It is crumbled to powder; an ordinary brush simply smears the surface. And the varnishes that have been used in such cases are atrocious; they darken and crack. . . ."

"But you, of course, have found a solution," I said.

"A solution is precisely what it is. A mixture of weak tapioca and water, brushed on the painting—"

"You said brushing marred the paint."

Emerson looked as dignified as a man can look under such adverse circumstances.

"I brush it on with the edge of my finger."

I stared at him with reluctant admiration.

"You are determined, I'll say that for you."

"It is slow work; I have to do it myself, I can't trust any of the workmen. I have only covered part of it." He groaned feelingly. "I tell you, woman, I must get up and see to my pavement."

"I'll see to your pavement," I said. "Stay in bed or you will have a relapse and be ill for weeks. Even you must see that that would be foolish."

I did not wait for an answer; it would only have been rude. I started along the ledge. Evelyn caught my sleeve.

"Amelia, where are you going?"

"To see Mr. Emerson's pavement, of course. Have you ever known me to break my word?"

"No, but. . . . Do you not think you might assume a more appropriate costume?"

In some surprise I glanced down. I had forgotten I was wearing my dressing gown and slippers.

"Perhaps you are right, Evelyn."

As the reader has no doubt realized, female fashion has never interested me. However, while in London, I had learned of the Rational Dress League, and had had a dress made in that style. It was of slate-colored India cloth, with a plain, almost mannish bodice and a few simple frills at the cuffs as its only ornament. But the daring feature of this costume was the *divided skirt*. The two legs were so full that they resembled an ordinary kilted skirt and did not give me nearly the freedom of action I desired, but they were a good deal more practical than the so-called walking dresses then in vogue. I had kept this garment at the very bottom of my trunk; in Cairo I had not had quite the courage to wear it. Now I took it out, shook out the creases, and put it on.

As I scrambled down the rocky, hot path, I appreciated the divided skirt; but I still yearned for trousers. At the foot of the slope I found Walter arguing with the cook, a morose-looking individual with only one functional eye. I never did make out what the argument was about, but I settled it, and saw the chicken, which the cook had been waving under Walter's nose, plucked and in the pot before I proceeded. Walter offered to accompany me, but I sent him back to his brother. Emerson needed a watchdog; I did not.

I found the place where the workers were employed and introduced myself to the foreman, Abdullah. He was a stately figure of a man, almost six feet tall; his flowing snowy robes, long gray beard and voluminous headcloth gave him the look of a biblical patriarch. He was not a native of one of the local villages, but came from Upper Egypt and had worked with Emerson before.

Abdullah directed me to the pavement, which was some distance away. It was easy to find, however, because of the low wooden roof that had been erected over it.

There was a great stretch of it—twenty feet across by perhaps fifteen feet long—miraculously, magnificently preserved. The colors were as fresh as if they had just been applied—exquisite blues, glowing reds, and cool greens, with touches of white and deep blue-black to emphasize details. Birds flew with outstretched wings in luxuriant gardens where flowers bloomed. Young animals, calves and kids, frolicked amid the undergrowth, kicking up their heels. I could almost hear them bellowing and bleating with the sheer joy of living.

I was still squatting on the ground, looking, when Evelyn and Walter found me.

"Amelia, it is the hottest part of the day; the workers have stopped for food and rest, and all sensible people are indoors. Come back and have lunch."

"I won't eat a bite of that miserable-looking chicken," I said. "Evelyn, look; only look. I have never seen anything like it. And to think that the gold-trimmed sandals of the beautiful Nefertiti may have walked across this surface!"

"It is exquisite," Evelyn agreed. "How I would love to sketch it!"

"What a splendid idea!" Walter exclaimed. "And how pleased my brother would be to have a copy, in case of accident. I am the official expedition artist, among other things, and I am very bad at it."

Evelyn promptly disclaimed any skill, but Walter continued to press her. I grew tired of their mutual raptures after a time and staggered to my feet.

We had an atrocious lunch—stringy, tough chicken and some unidentifiable vegetables cooked into a tasteless mass. My devoted Michael was at hand; I took him aside for a whispered conference. I decided to put off discussing future arrangements with Evelyn and Walter until that evening. It was rather hot, and after my disturbed night I was ready to take a siesta.

Michael was a jewel. When Evelyn and I came out of our tomb in the late afternoon, the place was transformed. Tables and chairs, even a small rug, had been spread out along the ledge, making a charming little piazza or balcony—a balcony with a view such as few property owners enjoy. The cool breeze of evening fanned our cheeks, and across the river the most splendid sunset I had ever seen, even in Egypt, turned the sky to a glowing tapestry of light. From below, a succulent odor wafted up to my appreciative nostrils. Michael had brought food as well as furniture, and was supervising the criminal of a cook.

I sank down luxuriously in one of the chairs. Michael came trotting up the cliff with tall glasses of lemonade. Walter soon joined us. I was about to ask when I might check on my patient, when a sound of rattling pebbles turned all our heads around.

Emerson stood in the door of his tomb. He was fully dressed and looked comparatively respectable, except for his face; it was as gray as the shadows in the darkening western cliffs; and one of his hands was tightly clenched on the stone jamb.

Men are never of any use in an emergency. I was the only one who moved; and I reached Emerson just in time to catch him by the shoulders and prevent his head from striking against the rock as he fell. It was hard, prickly rock; I could feel a thousand sharp points through my skirts as I sat down, rather more suddenly than I had planned, for Emerson was a considerable weight. I was forced to hold him tightly against me with both arms, or he would have tumbled off the ledge.

"There is absolutely no limit to this man's arrogant stupidity," I exclaimed, as Walter came rushing to us. "Fetch Michael and help your brother back to bed, Walter. And for pity's sake," I added angrily, as Emerson's unconscious head rolled against my breast and bristly black hairs scratched me through the fabric of my bodice, "for pity's sake, get rid of this beard!"

5

EMERSON was luckier than he deserved. His injudicious act did not bring on a relapse, but it was obvious that he would be too weak to assume command for some days. Clearly something had to be done; equally clearly, I was the one to do it.

I brought Emerson out of his faint, forced another dose of quinine down him, and left Abdullah sitting on his legs to keep him down. His curses floated out across the valley as I left him.

Without, the sky had darkened. A glittering web of stars covered the indigo-blue vault; the afterglow transformed the cliffs into glowing ghost shapes, the shadows of rock. Side by side Evelyn and Walter sat looking out across the valley.

I had intended to discuss my plans with them; but one look told me they wouldn't care. I did not need to see their faces, their very outlines were eloquent.

I had decided there was no purpose in removing Emerson to a more civilized milieu. By the time we reached Cairo he should be on the road to recovery—unless the removal from his beloved antiquities induced a stroke from sheer rage, which was more than likely. I had told Michael we would remain where we were for approximately a week, by which time Emerson should be out of danger. Michael assured me that the boat crew would be delighted to rest for a week, so long as they were paid. He was distressed that I refused to stay on the boat, traveling back and forth to the excavations daily. I saw no need for this, it would simply be a waste of time.

For the next two days everything went smoothly. At least I thought it did. Later I discovered that there had been ominous signs, if anyone of intelligence had been watching for them. Unfortunately I was not. I was totally preoccupied with my—that is, with Emerson's pavement.

His notion of tapioca and water was good, but I improved on it, adding a teaspoonful of starch and two of bismuth to each quart of water. He had been correct about the impossibility of using an ordinary brush to apply the mixture. I had used my right hand, my left hand—and was almost ready to remove shoes and stockings in order to use my toes—when Evelyn intervened.

She had been copying the painting, and was doing splendidly. I was amazed at her skill; she caught not only the shapes and colors, but the vital, indefinable spirit underlying the mind of the ancient artist. Even Emerson was moved to admiring grunts when she showed him her first day's work. She spent the second morning at the task, and then went up for a rest, leaving me at work. Having covered the edges of the painting, I had set some of the workers to building walkways across the pavement; the supports rested on blank spaces where pillars had once stood, so there was no defacement of the painting, but I had to watch the men closely. They thought the process utterly ridiculous, and would have dragged planks across the fragile surface if I had not supervised them every moment.

They had finished the job and I was lying flat across the walk working on a new section when Evelyn's voice reached me. Glancing up, I was surprised to see that the sun was declining. My last useful finger was beginning to bleed, so I decided to stop; bloodstains would have been impossible to remove from the painting. I crawled back along the boards. When I reached the edge, Evelyn grasped me by the shoulders and tried to shake me.

"Amelia, this must stop! Look at your hands! Look at your complexion! And your dress, and your hair, and—"

"It does seem to be rather hard on one's wardrobe," I admitted, gazing down at my crumpled, dusty, tapioca-spotted gown. "What is wrong with my complexion, and my hair, and—"

Making exasperated noises, Evelyn escorted me back to the tomb, and put a mirror in my hands.

I looked like a Red Indian witch. Although the wooden shelter had protected me from the direct rays of the sun, even reflected sunlight has power in this climate. My hair hung in dusty elf-locks around my red face.

I let Evelyn freshen me and lead me out to our little balcony. Walter was waiting for us, and Michael promptly appeared with cool drinks. This evening was an occasion, for Emerson was to join us for the first time. He had made a remarkable recovery; once he grasped the situation he applied himself to recuperation with the grim intensity I might have expected. I had agreed that he might dress and join us for dinner, provided he wrapped up well against the cool of evening.

He had acrimoniously refused any assistance in dressing. Now he made a ceremonious appearance, waving Walter aside; and I stared.

I knew the beard was gone, but I had not seen him since the operation. I had overheard part of the procedure that morning.

It was impossible *not* to overhear it; Emerson's shouts of rage were audible a mile away, and Walter had to raise *his* voice in order to be heard.

"Excessive hair drains the strength," I had heard him explain, in a voice choked with laughter. "Hold his arms, Michael; I am afraid I may inadvertently cut his throat. Radcliffe, you know that fever victims have their hair cut off—"

"That is an old wives' tale," Emerson retorted furiously. "And even if it were not, hair on the head and hair on the face are not the same."

"I really cannot proceed while you struggle so," Walter complained. "Very well. . . . Miss Peabody will be pleased."

There was a brief silence.

"Peabody will be pleased that I retain my beard?" Emerson inquired.

"Miss Peabody claims that men grow beards in order to hide weak features. Receding chins, spots on the face. . . ."

"Oh, does she? She implies my chin is weak?"

"She has never seen it," Walter pointed out.

"Hmph."

That was all he said; but since silence followed the grunt, I knew Walter had won his point.

Seeing, as I now did, the beardless countenance of Emerson, I understood why he had cultivated whiskers. The lower part of his face looked a little odd, being so much paler than the rest, but the features were not displeasing—although the mouth was set in such a tight line I could not make out its shape. The chin was certainly not weak; indeed, it was almost too square and protuberant. But it had a dimple. No man with a dimple in his chin can look completely forbidding. A dimple, for Emerson, was out of character. No wonder he wished to hide it!

Emerson's defiant eyes met mine, and the comment I had been about to make died on my lips.

"Tea or lemonade?" I inquired.

When I handed him his cup, a half-stifled expletive burst from his lips. Walter followed his gaze.

"My dear Miss Peabody, your poor hands!"

"There must be some better way of going about it," I muttered, trying to wrap my skirt around the members in question. "I haven't given the matter much thought as yet."

"Naturally not," Emerson said gruffly. "Women don't think. A little forethought would prevent most of the suffering they constantly complain about."

Walter frowned. It was the first time I had seen the young fellow look at his brother with anything but affectionate admiration.

"You should be ashamed to speak so, Radcliffe," he said quietly. "Miss Peabody's hand was swollen and painful for hours after you passed the crisis of your sickness, you held it so tightly; and I had to carry her to her bed because her limbs were cramped from kneeling beside you all night long."

Emerson looked a little uncomfortable, but I think I was even more embarrassed. Sentimentality always embarrasses me.

"No thanks, please," I said. "I would have done as much for a sick cat."

"At least you must stop working on the pavement," Walter said. "Tomorrow I will take over the task."

"You can't do the pavement and supervise the workers at the same time," I argued, conscious of an inexplicable annoyance.

Emerson, slouching in his chair, cleared his throat.

"Abdullah is an excellent foreman. There is no need for Walter to be on the spot at all times. Or is there, Walter?"

How he had sensed the truth I do not know, but Walter's uneasy silence was answer enough.

"Come," Emerson insisted, in a voice of quiet firmness. "I knew this evening that something was worrying you. What is it?

Fruitless speculation will be worse for me than the truth, Walter; be candid."

"I am willing to be candid, but it isn't easy to be explicit," Walter said, smiling faintly. "You know how one becomes sensitive to the feelings of the men. There are so many meaningful signs—the singing of the work crews, the way in which they move about, the joking and laughter—or the lack thereof. I don't know how long it has been going on. I only sensed it today."

"Then it has not been going on long. You are too experienced to be unaware, preoccupied though you are." Emerson glanced meaningfully at Evelyn, who sat listening with her hands folded in her lap. "Are the men hostile? Are they hiding something they don't want us to know about?"

Walter shook his head; the dark hair tumbled over his high brow, giving him the look of a worried schoolboy.

"Neither of those, I think. Your illness disturbed them; you know how superstitious they are, how ready to find evil demons behind every accident. But I can't really account for the feeling. There is a general laxity, a slowing down, a—a stillness. As if they knew something we don't know—and are afraid of it."

Emerson's brows drew together. He struck his hand on his knee.

"I must see for myself."

"If you venture out into that sun tomorrow, you will be back in bed by noon," I said firmly. "Perhaps I can have a look around myself. But I hate to neglect my pavement, even for a day."

"Peabody, you are not to touch the pavement tomorrow," Emerson said. "Infection is in the air here; you will lose a finger or two if you continue to rub them raw."

I am not accustomed to be spoken to in that tone. Oddly enough, I was not angered by the order, or by the name. Emerson was looking at me with a kind of appeal. His mouth had relaxed. It was, as I had suspected, a well-shaped organ.

"Perhaps you are right," I said.

Evelyn choked on her tea and hastily set the cup down.

"Yes," I continued. "No doubt you are right. Then I will supervise the workers tomorrow and see what I can ascertain. What are you digging up at present, Walter?"

The conversation became technical. Evelyn showed us the progress of her drawing; this time Emerson unbent far enough to mutter, "Not at all bad," and suggest that Evelyn might copy some of the tomb reliefs when she had finished the pavement.

"A trained artist would be a godsend on expeditions like this," he exclaimed, his eyes flashing with enthusiasm. "We cannot save all the relics; we are like the boy with his finger in the dike. But if we had copies of them before they are destroyed . . ."

"I would like to learn something of the hieroglyphic signs," Evelyn said. "I could copy them more accurately if I knew what they meant. For example, there seem to be a dozen different kinds of birds, and I gather each has a different meaning. When the inscriptions are worn it is not always possible to see what the original form was; but if one knew a little of the language . . ."

Emerson beetled his eyebrows at her, but it was clear that he was impressed; before long he was drawing birds on his napkin and Evelyn was attempting to copy them. I looked at Walter. His ingenuous face was luminous with pleasure as he watched his admired brother and the girl he loved. Yes, he loved her; there could be no question of that. She loved him too. And at the first declaration from him, she would ruthlessly destroy their happiness because of a convention that seemed more absurd the more I considered it. Knowing what was in store, my heart ached at the sight of Walter's face.

We sat late on our little balcony that night, watching the afterglow fade and the stars blaze out; even Emerson was companionably silent under the sweet influence of the scene. Perhaps we all had a premonition of what was to come; perhaps we knew that this was our last peaceful evening.

I was brushing my hair next morning when I heard the hubbub below. Within a few minutes Walter came running up the path and shouted for me. I went out, fearing some disaster; but his expression was one of excitement rather than alarm.

"The men have made a discovery," he began. "Not in the ruins of the city—up in the cliffs. A tomb!"

"Is that all? Good Gad, the place is overfurnished with tombs as it is."

Walter was genuinely excited, but I noticed that his eyes strayed past me to where Evelyn stood before the mirror, listening as she tied a ribbon around her hair.

"But this one has an occupant! All the other tombs were empty when we found them—robbed and rifled in antiquity. No doubt this new tomb has also been robbed of the gold and jewels it once contained, but there is a mummy, a veritable mummy. What is even more important, Miss Peabody, is that the villagers came to me with the news instead of robbing the tomb. That shows, does it not, that the fancies I expressed last evening were only fancies. The men must trust us, or they would not come to us."

"They trust Mr. Emerson because he pays them full value for every valuable object they find," I said, hastily bundling my hair into its net. "They have no reason to resort to antiquities dealers under those conditions."

"What does it matter?" Walter was fairly dancing with impatience. "I am off, I cannot wait to see, but I thought you might like to accompany me. I fear the trail will be rough. . . ."

"I fear so, too," I said grimly. "I must apply myself to the question of appropriate costume. My rationals are an improvement on skirts, but they do not go far enough. Do you think, Evelyn, that we could fashion some trousers out of a skirt or two?"

The trail *was* rough, but I managed it. A few of the villagers accompanied us. As we walked, Walter explained that the tombs we were inhabiting were known as the Southern Tombs. Another group of ancient sepulchers lay to the north, and were, logically enough, referred to as the Northern Tombs. The newly discovered tomb was one of this group.

After several long miles I finally saw a now-familiar square opening in the cliffs above us, and then another beyond the first. We had reached the Northern Tombs, and a scramble up a steep slope of detritus soon brought us to the entrance to the new tomb.

Walter was a different man. The gentle boy had been supplanted by the trained scholar. Briskly he gave orders for torches and ropes. Then he turned to me.

"I have explored these places before. I don't recommend that you come with me, unless you are fond of bats in your hair and a great deal of dust."

"Lead on," I said, tying a rope in a neat half-hitch around my waist.

I had Walter thoroughly under control by then. He would not have argued with me if I had proposed jumping off a pyramid.

I had been in a number of ancient tombs, but all had been cleared for visitors. I was somewhat surprised to find that this one was almost as clear, and far less difficult than Walter had feared. There was a good deal of loose rubble underfoot, and at one point we had to cross a deep pit, which had been dug to discourage tomb robbers. The villagers had bridged it with a flimsy-looking plank. Other than that, the going was not at all bad.

Walter too was struck by the relative tidiness. He threw a comment over his shoulder.

"The place is too well cleared, Miss Peabody. I suspect it has been robbed over and over again; we will find nothing of interest here."

The corridor ended, after a short distance, in a small chamber cut out of the rock. In the center of the room stood a rough wooden coffin. Lifting his torch, Walter looked into it.

"There is nothing to be afraid of," he said, misinterpreting my expression. "The wrappings are still in place; will you look?"

"Naturally," I said.

I had seen mummies before, of course, in museums. At first glance this had nothing to distinguish it from any other mummy. The brown, crumbling bandages had been wrapped in intricate patterns, rather like weaving. The featureless head, the shape of the arms folded across the breast, the stiff, extended limbs—yes, it was like the other mummies I had seen, but I had never seen them in their natural habitat, so to speak. In the musty, airless chamber, lighted only by dimly flaring torches, the motionless form had a grisly majesty. I wondered who he—or she—had been: a prince, a priestess, the young mother of a family, or an aged grandfather? What thoughts had lived in the withered brain— what emotions had brought tears to the shriveled eyes or smiles to the fleshless lips? And the soul—did it live on, in the golden grain fields of Amenti, as the priests had promised the righteous worshiper, as we look forward to everlasting life with the Redeemer these people never knew?

Walter did not appear to be absorbed in pious meditation. He was scowling as he stared down at the occupant of the coffin. Then he turned, holding the torch high as he inspected the walls of the chamber. They were covered with inscriptions and with the same sort of reliefs to which I had become accustomed in the Southern Tombs. All centered on the majestic figure of pharaoh, sometimes alone, but usually with his queen and his six little daughters. Above, the god Aten, shown as the round disk of the sun, embraced the king with long rays that ended in tiny human hands.

"Well?" I asked. "Will you excavate here, or will you remove the poor fellow from his coffin and unwrap him in more comfortable surroundings?"

For a moment Walter looked unnervingly like his shaven

brother as he tugged thoughtfully at his lower lip.

"If we leave him here, some enterprising burglar will rend him apart in the hope of finding ornaments such as were sometimes wrapped in the bandages. But I don't hope for much, Miss Peabody. Some tombs were used for later burials, by poor people who could not build tombs of their own. This looks to me like just such a late mummy, much later than the period in which we are interested, and too poor to own any valuable ornaments."

He handed his torch to one of the villagers and spoke to the man in Arabic—repeating the comment, I assumed. The man burst into animated speech, shaking his head till the folds of his turban fluttered.

"Mohammed says our mummy is not a commoner," Walter explained, smiling at me. "He is a prince—a princely magician, no less."

"How does he know that?"

"He doesn't. Even if Mohammed could read the hieroglyphs, which he cannot, there is no inscription on the coffin to give the mummy's name. He is only trying to increase the backsheesh I owe him for this find."

So Mohammed was the discoverer of this tomb. I studied the man with interest. He looked like all the other villagers—thin, wiry, epicene, his sunbaked skin making him look considerably older than his probable age. The life span in these villages is not high. Mohammed was probably no more than thirty, but poverty and ill health had given him the face of an old man.

Seeing my eye upon him he looked at me and grinned ingratiatingly.

"Yes," Walter said thoughtfully. "We must take our anonymous friend along. Radcliffe can unwrap him; it will give him something to do."

Emerson was delighted with the find; he fell on the mummy with mumbled exclamations, so after making sure his temperature and pulse were normal, I left him to his ghoulish work. When he joined us on the ledge that evening, however, he was vociferously disappointed.

"Greco-Egyptian," he grumbled, stretching his long legs out. "I suspected as much when I saw the pattern of the wrappings. Yes, yes; the signs are unmistakable. I am familiar with them from my own research; no one has done any work on this problem, although a chronological sequence could be worked out if one—"

"My dear fellow, we are all of us familiar with your views on the deplorable state of archaeology in Egypt," Walter broke in, with a laugh. "But you are wrong about the mummy. Mohammed swears it is that of a princely magician, a priest of Amon, who placed a curse on this heretical city."

"Mohammed is a scurvy trickster who wants more money," growled Emerson. "How does he know about heretics and priests of Amon?"

"There is another project for you," Walter said. "Investigating the traditions and folk memories of these people."

"Well, his folk memory is wrong in this case. The poor chap whose wrappings I removed this afternoon was no priest. It frankly puzzles me to find him here at all. The city was abandoned after Khuenaten's death, and I did not think there was a settlement here in Ptolemaic times. These present villages did not occupy the site until the present century."

"I doubt that the tomb was used by the official who had it built," Walter said. "The reliefs in the corridor were not finished."

"What have you done with our friend?" I asked. "I hope you are not planning to make him the third occupant of your sleeping dormitory; I don't think he can be healthy."

Emerson burst into an unexpected shout of laughter.

"Being dead is the ultimate of unhealthiness, I suppose. Never

109

fear; the mummy is resting in a cave at the bottom of the path. I only wish I could account for his original position as easily."

"I might have a look at the tomb in the morning," I said. "That would leave the afternoon for working on the pavement—"

"And what do you expect to find?" Emerson's voice rose. "Good God, madam, you seem to think you are a trained archaeologist! Do you think you can walk in here and—"

Walter and Evelyn broke in simultaneously in an attempt to change the subject. They succeeded for the moment; but Emerson was sulky and snappish for the rest of the evening. When I tried to feel his forehead to see if he had developed a temperature, he stalked off to his tomb, fairly radiating grumpiness.

"Don't mind him, Miss Peabody," Walter said, when he was out of earshot. "He is still not himself, and enforced inactivity infuriates a man of his energy."

"He is not himself," I agreed. "In normal health he is even louder and more quarrelsome."

"We are all a little on edge," Evelyn said in a low voice. "I don't know why I should be; but I feel nervous."

"If that is the case we had better go to bed," I said, rising. "Some sleep will settle your mind, Evelyn."

Little did I know that the night was to bring, not a cure for troubled minds, but the beginning of greater trouble.

It is a recognized fact that sleepers train themselves to respond only to unfamiliar noises. A zoo keeper slumbers placidly through the normal nightly roars of his charges; but the squeak of a mouse in his tidy kitchen can bring him awake in an instant. I had accustomed my sleeping mind to the sounds of Amarna. They were few indeed; it was one of the most silent spots on earth, I think. Only the far-off ululation of an occasional love-sick jackal disturbed the silence. So, on this particular night, it was not surprising that the sound at the door of our tomb, slight though it was, should bring me upright, with my heart pounding.

Light penetrated cracks in the curtain, but I could see nothing without. The sound continued. It was the oddest noise—a faint, dry scratching, like the rubbing of a bony object on rock.

Once my pulse had calmed, I thought of explanations. Someone on the ledge outside the tomb—Michael, keeping watch, or Walter, sleepless outside his lady's chamber? Somehow my nerves were not convinced by either idea. In any case, the sound was keeping me awake. I fumbled for my parasol.

The frequent mention of this apparatus may provoke mirth in the reader. I assure her (or him, as the case may be) that I was not intending to be picturesque. It was a very sturdy parasol, with a stiff iron staff, and I had chosen it deliberately for its strength.

Holding it, then, in readiness for a possible act of violence, I called softly, "Who is there?"

There was no response. The scratching sound stopped. It was followed, after a moment or two, by another sound, which rapidly died away, as if someone, or something, had beat a hasty but quiet retreat.

I leaped from bed and ran to the doorway. I confess that I hesitated before drawing back the curtain. A parasol, even one of steel, would not be much use against a feral animal. The scratching sound might well have been produced by claws; and although I had been told that there were no longer any lions in Egypt, they had abounded in ancient times, and an isolated specimen might have survived in this desolate region. As I stood listening with all my might I heard another sound, like a rock or pebble rolling. It was quite a distance away. Thus reassured, I drew back the curtain and, after a cautious glance without, stepped onto the ledge.

The moon was high and bright, but its position left the ledge in shadow. Against this dark background an object stood out palely. It was at the far end of the ledge, where it curved to pass around a shoulder of rock; and I was conscious of an odd constriction of my diaphragm as I glimpsed it.

111

The shape was amorphous. It was of the height and breadth of a man, but it more resembled a white stone pillar than a human form, split at the bottom to present an imitation of a man's lower limbs. Stiff, stubby appendages like arms protruded at shoulder height, but they were not arms; human arms were never so rigid.

As I stared, blinking to cure what I thought must be a failure of my vision, the shape disappeared. It must have moved around the corner of the path. A faint moaning sigh wafted back to me. It might have been the sigh of the wind; but I felt no movement of air.

I retreated to my bed, but I did not sleep well the rest of the night. The first pale streaks of dawn found me wide awake, and I was glad to arise and dress. I had managed to convince myself that what I saw was a large animal of some kind, raised on its back legs as a cat or panther will rise; so the full horror of the night did not strike me until I stepped out onto the ledge, which was now illumined by the rising sun. As I did so, something crackled under my foot.

Sunrise in Egypt is a glorious spectacle. The sun, behind the cliffs at my back, shone fully upon the western mountains; but I had no eye for the beauties of nature then. The sound and feel of the substance my foot had crushed was horribly familiar. With reluctance I bent to pick it up, though my fingers shrank from the touch of it.

I held a small fragment of brown, flaking cloth, so dry that it crackled like paper when my fingers contracted. I had seen such cloth before. It was the rotting bandage which had once wrapped an ancient mummy.

6

I STOOD on the ledge for some time, trying to think sensibly. Emerson had spent some hours with the mummy. Fragments of the fragile cloth, caught on the fabric of his garments, might have been brushed off when he sat down at dinner the night before. But as soon as the idea entered my mind, common sense dismissed it. There was a regular trail of the stuff leading down the ledge as far as I could see. If Emerson's clothes had been so untidy I would have noticed. Further, Emerson's chair was some six feet away from the door of our chamber. He had never approached our door last night; and the largest heap of framents was there, as if it had been deposited by a creature who stood for a long time on our threshold.

I don't know what instinct moved me to action—fear for Evelyn's nerves, perhaps, or concern for the superstitions of the

113

workers. At any rate, I dashed inside, snatched up a cloth, and swept the horrible fragments off the ledge. Evelyn was still sleeping; and from below, the fragrance of coffee reached my nostrils. Michael was on duty early.

I was not the only early riser. As I stood by the campfire sipping my tea, Emerson came down the path. He gave me a surly nod and paused for a moment, as if daring me to order him back to bed. I said nothing; and after a while he went on and disappeared into the cave where his precious mummy had been deposited.

He had not been within for more than a few seconds when the sweet morning air was rent by a hideous cry. I dropped my cup, splashing my foot with hot tea; before I could do more, Emerson burst out of the cave. His inflamed eyes went straight to me. He raised both clenched fists high in the air.

"My mummy! You have stolen my mummy! By Gad, Peabody, this time you have gone too far! I've watched you; don't think I have been unwitting of your machinations! My pavement, my expedition, my brother's loyalty, even my poor, helpless carcass have fallen victim to your meddling; but this—this is too much! You disapprove of my work, you want to keep me feeble and helpless in bed, so you steal my mummy! Where is it? Produce it at once, Peabody, or—"

His shouts aroused the rest of the camp. I saw Evelyn peering curiously from the ledge above, clutching the collar of her dressing gown under her chin. Walter bounded down the path, trying to stuff his flying shirttails into his waistband and simultaneously finish doing up the buttons.

"Radcliffe, Radcliffe, what are you doing? Can't you behave for five minutes?"

"He is accusing me of stealing his mummy," I said. My own tones were rather loud. "I will overlook his other ridiculous accusations, which can only be the product of a disturbed brain—"

"Disturbed! Certainly I am disturbed! Of all the ills on earth,

114

an interfering female is the worst!"

By this time we were surrounded by a circle of staring faces; the workers, coming in from the village, had been attracted by the uproar. They could not understand Emerson's remarks, but the tone of anger was quite comprehensible; their dark eyes were wide with alarm and curiosity as they watched Emerson's extraordinary performance. Foremost in the crowd stood Mohammed, the man who had led us to the tomb the day before. There was the most peculiar expression on his face—a kind of sly smirk. It interested me so much that I failed to respond to Emerson's latest outburst, and turned away, leaving him waving his fists at empty air. Mohammed saw me. Instantly his mouth turned down and his eyes widened in a look of pious alarm that would have suited an angel.

Seeing the futility of communication with Emerson when he was in this state, Walter turned to the cave where the mummy was kept. He was soon out again; his expressive face told me the truth before he spoke.

"The mummy is gone," he said, shaking his head in disbelief. "Only scraps of the wrappings remain. Why would anyone steal such a poor specimen?"

"These people would steal their grandmothers and sell them if there were a market for decrepit old ladies," Emerson growled.

I had observed that his fits of rage, though violent, were soon over. Afterward he seemed greatly refreshed by the outburst and would, in fact, deny that he had ever lost his temper. He now spoke to me as if he had never made his outrageous accusations.

"What about breakfast, Peabody?"

I was meditating a suitably crushing retort when Walter spoke again.

"It is really incomprehensible. The men could have made off with the mummy when they first found it. And what has become of the bandages you removed?"

"That, at least, is easily explained," Emerson answered. "I

could not unwrap the bandages. The perfumed resins in which the body was soaked had glued the wrappings into a solid mass. I had to make an incision and open the thorax. As you know, Walter, the body cavities often contain amulets and scraps of—Peabody! Miss Peabody, what is the matter?"

His voice faded into a dim insect buzzing, and the sunlight darkened. A ghastly vision had flashed upon my mind. If the moon had been higher—if I had seen the nocturnal visitor more distinctly—would I have beheld the violated body, gaping wide?

I am happy to say that this was the first and last time I succumbed to superstition. When I opened my eyes I realized that Emerson was supporting me, his alarmed face close to mine. I straightened, and saw a dark flush mantle his cheeks as I pushed his arms away.

"A momentary weakness," I said. "I think—I think perhaps I will sit down."

Walter quickly offered his arm, and I did not disdain it.

"You are wearing yourself out, Miss Peabody," he said warmly. "We cannot allow such sacrifices. Today you must rest; I insist upon it."

"Hmmm," said Emerson. His eyes expressed neither concern nor appreciation, but rather speculation as they examined my face.

As the day wore on I could not help recalling Evelyn's remark of the previous evening. I had discounted her mention of nervousness then; now I could not deny that the atmosphere was uneasy. I myself was unable to settle down to anything. After working on the pavement for a time I went to the site where Walter and Abdullah were directing the workers.

There were more than fifty people at work. The men were removing the sand that had covered the foundations of temples and houses, shoveling it into baskets which were then carried away by children, boys and girls both. It was necessary to dump

116

the sand some distance away, lest it cover future excavations. The work was tedious, except when the men reached the floor level, where abandoned objects might be found; yet all the workers, children and adults alike, usually worked cheerfully and willingly. They are very musical people, the Egyptians, although their wailing, yodeling singing sounds odd to European ears; but today no brisk chorus speeded the work. The children who carried the baskets were slow and unsmiling.

I joined Abdullah, the foreman, where he stood on a little rise of sand watching the diggers.

"They do not sing today," I said. "Why not, Abdullah?"

Not a muscle moved in the dignified brown face; but I sensed an inner struggle.

"They are ignorant people," he said, after a time. "They fear many things."

"What things?"

"Afreets, demons—all strange things. They fear ghosts of the dead. The mummy—they ask where it has gone."

That was all he could, or would, say. I went back to my pavement in some perturbation of spirit. I could hardly sneer at the ignorance of the natives when I had experienced equally wild thoughts.

The reader may well ask why I had not spoken of my adventure. I asked myself the same question; but I knew the answer, and it did not reflect creditably on my character. I was afraid of being laughed at. I could almost hear Emerson's great guffaws echoing out across the valley when I told him of seeing his lost mummy out for a midnight stroll. And yet I felt I ought to speak. I knew I had not seen an animated mummy. My brain knew it, if my nervous system did not. I spent the rest of the day brushing tapioca and water over my lovely pavement and carrying on a vigorous internal debate—common sense against vanity.

When we gathered on the ledge for our customary evening

meeting, I could see that the others were also distraught. Walter looked very tired; he dropped into a chair with a sigh and let his head fall back.

"What a wretched day! We seem to have accomplished nothing."

"I shall come down tomorrow," said Emerson. He looked at me. "With Peabody's permission or without it."

Walter sat upright.

"Radcliffe, why do you address Miss Peabody so disrespectfully? After all she has done for us . . ."

It was unusual for Walter to speak so sharply—another indication, if I had needed one, of the strained atmosphere.

"Oh, I don't mind," I said calmly. "Sticks and stones may break my bones, you know. As for your returning to work tomorrow . . ."

I looked Emerson up and down. The clinical appraisal annoyed him, as I had known it would; he squirmed like a guilty schoolboy, and exclaimed, "What is your diagnosis, Sitt Hakim?"

Truthfully, I was not pleased with his appearance. He had lost considerable flesh. The bones in his face were too prominent, and his eyes were still sunken in their sockets.

"I disapprove," I said. "You are not strong enough yet to be out in the sun. Have you taken your medicine today?"

Emerson's reply was not suitable for the pages of a respectable book. Walter sprang to his feet with a hot reproof. Only the appearance of Michael, with the first course of our dinner, prevented an argument. We went early to bed. I could see that Emerson fully intended to return to the excavations next day, so he needed his sleep, and after my disturbed night I too was weary.

Yet I did not sleep well. I had disturbing dreams. I awoke from one such dream in the late hours of the night, and as my sleep-fogged eyes focused, I saw a slim white form standing by the doorway. My heart gave such a leap I thought it would choke me.

118

When I recognized Evelyn, I almost fainted with relief.

She turned, hearing my gasp.

"Amelia," she whispered.

"What is it? Why are you awake at this hour? Good Gad, child, you almost frightened me to death!"

She looked ghostly as she glided toward me, her bare feet making no sound, her white nightdress floating out behind her. I lighted a lamp; Evelyn's face was as pale as her gown. She sank down on the edge of my bed, and I saw that she was shivering.

"I heard a sound," she said. "Such an eerie sound, Amelia, like a long, desolate sigh. I don't know how long it had been going on. It woke me; I am surprised it didn't waken you too."

"I heard it, and it became part of my dream," I answered. "I dreamed of death, and someone weeping over a grave. . . . Then what happened?"

"I didn't want to wake you; you had worked so hard today. But the sound went on and on, until I thought I should die; it was so dreary, so unutterably sad. I had to know what was making it. So I went and drew the curtain aside and looked out."

She paused, and went even paler.

"Go on," I urged. "You need not fear my skepticism, Evelyn. I have reasons, which you will hear in due course, for believing the wildest possible tale."

"You cannot mean that you too—"

"Tell me what you saw."

"A tall, pale form, featureless and stark. It stood in shadow, but. . . . Amelia, it had no face! There was no sign of nose or mouth or eyes, only a flat, white oval; no hair, only a smooth-fitting covering. The limbs were stiff—"

"Enough of this equivocation," I cried impatiently. "What you saw resembled . . . was like . . . seemed to be . . . in short—a Mummy!"

Evelyn stared at me.

"You saw it too! You must have done, or you could not accept this so readily. When? How?"

"One might add, 'why?' " I said wryly. "Yes, I saw such a form last night. This morning I found scraps of rotted wrappings on the ledge outside our chamber."

"And you said nothing of this to Walter—or to me?"

"It sounded too ridiculous," I admitted, "particularly after I learned that the mummy we discovered had mysteriously disappeared in the night."

"Ridiculous, Amelia? I wish I could think so. What are we to do?"

"I will have the courage to speak now that I have you to support me. But I shudder to think what Emerson will say. I can hear him now: 'A walking mummy, Peabody? Quite so! No wonder the poor fellow wants exercise, after lying stiff for two thousand years!' "

"Nevertheless, we must speak."

"Yes. In the morning. That will be time enough for my humiliation."

But the morning brought a new sensation, and new troubles.

I was up betimes. Emerson, another early riser, was already pacing about near the cook tent. A pith helmet, set at a defiant angle, proclaimed his intentions for the day. I glanced at it, and at his haggard face, and sniffed meaningfully; but I made no comment. Breakfast was prepared; we returned to our table on the ledge, where Evelyn and Walter joined us; and the meal was almost finished when Emerson exploded.

"Where are the men? Good God, they should have been here an hour ago!"

Walter withdrew his watch from his pocket and glanced at it.

"Half an hour. It appears they are late this morning."

"Do you see any signs of activity in the direction of the village?" Emerson demanded, shading his eyes and peering out across the sand. "I tell you, Walter, something is amiss. Find Abdullah."

The foreman, who slept in a tent nearby, was nowhere to be found. Finally we made out a small white figure crossing the sand. It was Abdullah; he had apparently been to the village in search of his tardy work force. We were all at the bottom of the path waiting when he came up to us. He spread out his hands in an eloquent gesture and looked at Emerson.

"They will not come."

"What do you mean, they won't come?" Emerson demanded.

"They will not work today."

"Is there some holiday, perhaps?" Evelyn asked. "Some Moslem holy day?"

"No," Emerson answered. "Abdullah would not make such an error, even if I did. I would think the men are holding out for higher pay, but. . . . Sit down, Abdullah, and tell me. Come, come, my friend, let's not stand on ceremony. Sit down, I say, and talk."

Thus abjured, Abdullah squatted on the bare ground, in that very same posture in which his ancestors are so often depicted. His English was not very good, so I shall take the liberty of abridging his remarks.

A conscientious man, he had set out for the village when the workmen failed to appear on time. The squalid little huddle of huts presented a disquieting appearance. It was as deserted and silent as if plague had struck. No children played in the dusty streets; even the mangy curs had taken themselves off.

Alarmed, Abdullah had gone to the house of the mayor—who was, I learned for the first time, the father of Mohammed. He had to pound on the barred door before he was finally admitted, and it took him some time to extract the facts from the mayor. At first

121

he said only that the men would not come. Upon being pressed, he said they would not come the next day either—or any other day. His son was with him; and it was from Mohammed that Abdullah finally received a statement. As Abdullah repeated this, his face retained its well-bred impassivity, but his eyes watched Emerson uneasily.

The workers had been disturbed by the mummy Mohammed had found. The man repeated his absurd claim—that the mummy was that of a princely priest-magician, a servant of the great god Amon whom Pharaoh Khuenaten had toppled from his spiritual throne. The deposed god's wrath found a vessel in his priest; through him, Amon had cursed the heretic city and anyone who set foot on its soil to resurrect it, forever. The villagers knew that none of them had made off with the mummy. Its disappearance could be accounted for in only one way: restored to the light of day, and animated by its discovery that new heretics were at work to uncover the accursed city, it had taken to its feet and left the camp. But it had not left the city—no, indeed. It walked by night, and on the previous midnight it had visited the village. Its moans had awakened the sleepers, and a dozen men had seen its ghastly form pacing the streets. The villagers were too wise not to heed the warning, which Mohammed helpfully interpreted: no more work for the infidels. They must leave Khuenaten's unholy city to the desolation of the sands, and take themselves off. Unless they did so, the curse would be visited on them and all those who assisted them in the slightest way.

Emerson listened to this bizarre hodgepodge without the slightest change of expression.

"Do you believe this, Abdullah?" he asked.

"No." But the foreman's voice lacked conviction.

"Nor do I. We are educated men, Abdullah, not like these poor peasants. Amon-Ra is a dead god; if he could once curse a city, he lost that power centuries ago. The mosques of your faith stand on the ruins of the temples, and the muezzin calls the faithful to prayer. I do not believe in curses; but if I did, I would know that our god—call him Jehovah or Allah, he is One—has the power to protect his worshipers against demons of the night. I think you believe that too."

I had never admired Emerson more. He had taken precisely the right tone with his servant, and as Abdullah looked up at the tall form of his employer, there was a glint of amused respect in his dark eyes.

"Emerson speaks well. But he does not say what has become of the mummy."

"Stolen." Emerson squatted on his lean haunches, so that he and Abdullah were eye to eye. "Stolen by a man who wishes to cause dissension in the camp, and who has invented this story to support his aim. I do not name this man; but you remember that Mohammed was angry because I brought you in to be foreman instead of giving him the position. His doting father has not disciplined him properly; even the men of the village resent him."

"And fear him," Abdullah said. He rose to his feet in a single effortless movement, his white robes falling in graceful folds. "We are of one mind, Emerson. But what shall we do?"

"I will go down to the village and talk to the mayor," Emerson said, rising. "Now go and eat, Abdullah. You have done well, and I am grateful."

The tall foreman walked away, not without an uneasy look at Emerson. Evelyn glanced at me. I nodded. I had not wished to speak in front of Abdullah, but the time had come to tell my story. Before I could start, Walter burst out,

"What an incredible tale! You would think I should be accustomed to the superstitious folly of these people, but I am constantly amazed at their credulity. They are like children. A mummy, walking the village streets—could there be anything more absurd?"

I cleared my throat self-consciously. This was not a good prelude to the tale I was about to tell.

"It is absurd, Walter, but it is not imagination. The villagers are not the only ones to see the Mummy. Evelyn and I both saw such a shape here in the camp."

"I knew you were hiding something," Emerson said, with grim satisfaction. "Very well, Peabody, we are listening."

I told all. I did not tell the story well, being only too conscious of Emerson's sneer. When I had finished, Walter was speechless. My support came, unexpectedly, from Emerson himself.

"This proves nothing, except that our villain—and we have a good notion as to his identity, have we not?—has gone to the trouble of dressing up in rags and wandering around in order to frighten people. I confess I am surprised; I had not thought Mohammed would be so energetic, or so imaginative."

As he spoke the last word, a memory popped into my mind. In the hotel in Cairo another imaginative miscreant had penetrated my room, dressed as an ancient Egyptian. I started to speak and then changed my mind; there surely could be no connection between the two events.

"I am off to the village," Emerson said. "I have dealt with these people before; I think I can persuade the mayor. Walter?"

The distance to the village was several miles. I am sure I need not say that I made part of the expedition. Evelyn remained behind, feeling herself unequal to the exertion; with Abdullah and Michael in camp, she was amply protected. Emerson, who had opposed my coming with his customary temper tantrum, was annoyed that I kept up with him easily. Of course I could not have done so if he had been at his normal strength, and I was increasingly concerned for him as he plodded through the sand.

The brooding silence of the village was most disturbing. I thought at first we would not be admitted to the slightly more pretentious hovel that housed the mayor of the village, but Emerson's repeated blows on the rickety door finally produced a response. The door opened a mere crack; the sharply pointed nose and wrinkle-wrapped eyes of the old sheikh peered out. Emerson gave the door a shove. He caught the old gentleman as he staggered back and politely set him on his feet. We were in the house.

I wished immediately that I was out. The stench of the place was indescribable. Chickens, goats, and people crowded the dark little room; their eyes shone like stars in the shadows. We were not invited to sit down, and indeed there was no surface in the place on which I would have cared to sit. Obviously the chickens roosted on the long divan that was the room's most conspicuous piece of furniture.

Emerson, arms folded and chin jutting, carried on the discussion in Arabic. I could not understand what was being said, but it was easy to follow the course of the conversation. The mayor, a wrinkled little old man whose pointed nose almost met his bony chin, mumbled his responses. He was not insolent or defiant; this attitude would have been easier to combat than his obvious terror.

Gradually the other human inhabitants of the place slipped away; only the goats and the chickens remained. One friendly goat was particularly intrigued with the sleeve of my dress. I pushed him away absentmindedly, trying to keep track of what was transpiring between the speakers, and slowly the truth dawned on me. The mayor could hardly bear to be in the same room with us. He kept retreating until his back was up against the wall.

Then someone slipped through the narrow aperture that gave entry into the back room—the only other chamber this mayoral palace contained. I recognized Mohammed. With his appearance the conversation took a new turn. His father turned to him with pathetic pleasure, and Mohammed took over his role in the argument. He *was* insolent; his very tone was an offense. Emerson's fists clenched and his lips set tightly as he listened. Then Mohammed glanced at me and broke into English.

"The Mummy hate stranger," he said, grinning. "Stranger go. But not women. Mummy like English women—"

Emerson was on him in a single bound. The poor old father squealed in alarm; but it was Walter who plucked his infuriated brother from Mohammed's throat. The man collapsed, moaning, when Emerson's fingers were detached, but even in the bad light I saw the look he gave his assailant; and a chill ran through me.

"Come away," Walter said in a low voice, holding his brother's rigid arm. "Come away, there is nothing more we can do here."

We did not linger in the village, but traversed its single narrow street as quickly as we could. When we reached the clean emptiness of the desert, Emerson stopped. His face was shining with perspiration; under his tan he was a sickly gray in color.

"I think I owe you both an apology," he said thickly. "That was stupid of me; I have ruined any chance we might have had of convincing the mayor."

"I heard what the fellow said," Walter replied. "I don't blame you, Radcliffe; it was all I could do to control myself. I feel sure Mohammed is out to drive us away; your action was ill advised, but I don't think it mattered."

"I am amazed at his effrontery," I exclaimed. "Doesn't he realize what he risks from the authorities in opposing you?"

Emerson's face darkened.

"Egypt is more unsettled than those complacent fools in Cairo realize. The mad dervish in the Sudan has stirred up the peasants; most Egyptians secretly yearn for his success and gloat at every British defeat. I wouldn't give a shilling for the lives of foreigners here if the Mahdi should approach the First Cataract."

"But surely there is not the slightest danger of that! Gordon is still making a valiant defense at Khartoum, and Wolseley's expedition is about to relieve him. How can untrained native rebels succeed against British troops?"

Emerson's answer was all the more convincing because I secretly believed it myself; but I would not give him the satisfaction of looking as if I agreed.

"Those untrained rebels have already massacred half a dozen British armies, including that of Colonel Hicks. I have the gravest fears for Gordon's safety; it will be a miracle if the relief expedition arrives in time. The whole business in the Sudan has been a masterpiece of blunders from start to finish. In the meantime, we seem to be facing a minor rebellion here, and I won't tolerate it."

Stumbling a little, he started walking.

"Where are you going?" I asked. "The camp is this way."

"There are two other villages on the plain. If the men of Haggi Qandil will not work, we will try el Till and al Amarnah."

"I fear it will be useless." Walter caught up with his brother and tried to take his arm. Emerson shook it off. "Radcliffe, stop and listen; you aren't fit to walk all over the desert today, and you can be sure that Mohammed's story has reached the other villages as well. They battle among themselves, but they are of the same stock. Your efforts will not avail there any more than they did at Haggi Qandil."

Emerson's feet were dragging, but his chin was set stubbornly. I decided to end the matter before he fell flat on his face.

"Let him go, Walter," I said. "You know he is too stubborn to listen to reason. What we need now is a council of war; we must consult Abdullah, and also Michael, who is an astute man. I can think of several things we might do, but we may as well wait until after your brother has fainted, then he won't be in our way, arguing and shouting. I think we can drag him back to camp from here. If not, Abdullah and Michael can come for him."

Emerson was still on his feet when we reached the camp. Walter took him into their tomb for restorative action; then we met for the suggested council of war.

This was the first time Michael had heard of what was happening. He spent his nights on the dahabeeyah, considering the three-mile walk trivial; as a Christian and a stranger he was not welcome in the village. Squatting on the rug at my side he listened without comment; but his fingers strayed to the gold crucifix around his neck, and he kept touching it throughout the remainder of the discussion. I asked him for his suggestions.

"Leave this place," he said promptly. "I am protected from demons"—and his fingers closed over the crucifix—"but in this place are also evil men. The boat waits; we all go, the gentlemen too."

"Surely you don't believe in demons, Michael," Evelyn said in her gentle voice.

"But, lady, it is in the Holy Book. God lets demons and afreets exist; how can we say the Holy Book is a lie? I do not fear demons, no, I am a true believer. But this is not a good place."

Abdullah nodded vigorously. His faith was not Michael's, but beneath both Christianity and Islam lie the dark superstitions of the pagan religion.

"Michael has made one of the proposals I intended to make," I said, nodding at Michael, who beamed with gratified pride. "You must face the fact, gentlemen, that you can do no more here at this time. I suggest you withdraw and recruit workers from some other part of Egypt. They will not be subject to the influence Mohammed can bear; and when the local villagers see that the work is proceeding without incident, they will realize that the idea of a curse is nonsense."

Walter was clearly impressed with the argument, and with the additional point I had not made—his brother's health. He looked at Emerson, who said nothing; but his chin jutted out so far that I had to repress an urgent desire to strike it.

"There are other sites in Egypt that need work," Evelyn added. "Many of them, from what you tell me. Why not try another

128

place until the resentment has died down here?"

"An interesting suggestion," Emerson said. His voice was very quiet; it grated like a grinding stone. "What do you say, Abdullah?"

"Very good, very good. We go. Work at Sakkarah, Luxor. I know tombs in the Valley of the Kings," he added, with a sly glance at Emerson. "Royal tombs, many not found yet. I find you good king's tomb and we go to Thebes, where is my home, where I have friends who work gladly."

"Hmm," said Emerson. "There certainly are undiscovered tombs in the Valley of the Kings. It is a tempting suggestion, Abdullah. You seem to forget, however, that one cannot excavate in Egypt without permission from the Antiquities Department. I had a difficult enough time wringing this concession out of Maspero; he certainly will not allow me to dig in any spot where he hopes to find interesting objects. There is also a minor matter of money to be considered. Walter—what is your opinion?"

Walter had been looking at Evelyn. He started when his brother addressed him, and faint color stained his tanned cheeks.

"Why, Radcliffe, you know I will do whatever you wish. But I urge one thing most strongly. Whether you and I go or stay, the ladies must leave. Not that our situation holds any danger; but it is unpleasant, and the ladies have already given too much time to us. They must depart; today, if possible."

A tear glimmered in my eye as I gazed at the gallant young fellow. He was a true Briton, ordering the girl he loved out of danger and remaining loyal to his billy goat of a brother. Evelyn clasped her hands and gazed at me beseechingly. She felt the same loyalty to me, and would not oppose my decision. There was no need for her appeal. I had no intention of being removed, like a bundle of laundry, to a safe spot behind the lines of battle.

"The suggestion is well meant, but I cannot accept it," I said briskly. "Either we all go, or all of us remain."

129

Emerson now turned his full attention to me. He drew a deep breath; the buttons of his shirt strained across his broad chest. They were all loose, and I reminded myself to fetch my sewing kit as soon as the argument was over.

"Ah, Miss Peabody," he said, in a low growl. "My dear Miss Peabody. May I take the liberty of inquiring how the devil—" His voice rose to a roar; a gesture from Walter stopped him, and he continued in a moderated voice that shook with the strain of control. "How on earth did you come to be mixed up in my affairs? I am a patient man; I seldom complain. But my life was calm and peaceful until you came into it. Now you behave as if you were the leader of the expedition! I quite agree with Walter; the women must go. Now don't argue with me, Peabody! Do you realize that I could have you bundled up and carried off to your boat? Michael and Abdullah would be delighted to do the job."

I glanced down at Michael, who was listening in openmouthed interest.

"No, Michael would not obey you. He would prefer to see me out of here, I'm sure, but he would not disregard my wishes. Now, Emerson, don't waste time arguing. I can see that you intend to remain here, and I must admit that I am reluctant to abandon the work—to see the British lion skulk away with its tail between its legs. . . ."

"Oh, God," said Emerson. He rolled his eyes until the whites showed. I felt that the remark was not intended as a prayer, but decided not to make an issue of it. I continued.

"Having decided to remain, we must consider the next step. You cannot obtain workmen here. Unless my crew . . ." I glanced at Michael, who shook his head, and went on, "No, I thought they would not. And I fear any workers you might import might be subject to the same harassment. I suggest, then, that today we all work at finishing up the pavement. Evelyn must complete her sketch; I will apply the rest of the tapioca. Tonight we will proceed to the obvious course of action. We must catch the

Mummy, and unmask him!"

Walter sat upright and clapped his hands.

"Miss Amelia, you are a wonder. Of course! With four of us on guard—"

"Six of us," I said. "I think that is sufficient; there is no need to bring the boat crew into this. I suggest that one of us watch the village. Mohammed must slip out in his disguise if he wants to haunt us, and since he is determined to get rid of us, he will probably pay us a visit tonight. The rest of us will lie in wait for him. Have you firearms?"

Evelyn let out a little cry of alarm.

Emerson's face underwent a series of silent convulsions. He said in a muffled voice, "I do not have firearms. They are dangerous and unnecessary."

"Then we will have to use clubs," I said.

Emerson's lips writhed. "I can't stand this," he muttered, and sprang to his feet. As he walked away, I saw that his shoulders were shaking uncontrollably, and I realized he must be weaker than I had thought.

"Have a good rest," I called out after his retreating form. "We should all sleep this afternoon, in order to be alert tonight."

Emerson's only response was a sort of muted roar. He disappeared into his tomb, and I turned to Walter, who was staring after his brother.

"He is weak with exhaustion, Walter. You had better—"

"No," said Walter. "I don't think so."

"What is wrong with him, then?"

Walter shook his head dazedly. "It is impossible. . . . But if I did not know better, I would swear he was laughing."

III

The rest of the day proceeded according to plan—*my* plan. Evelyn finished her sketch of the pavement. It was a lovely thing; she

131

had caught perfectly the muted pastel shades of the original. I then sent her back to rest while I finished applying the protective coating. It was early evening before I was done, and when I returned to camp I found dinner underway. Thanks to my efforts, there was a new spirit about the place. We were a small, reduced force, but we were united. Even Michael and Abdullah seemed cheerful and alert. Over dinner we made the rest of our plans.

Walter and Abdullah were to watch the village, with special attention to the mayor's house. Like all primitive groups, the village retired as soon as the sun went down. We did not expect any activity much before midnight, but the watchers were to take their places as soon as it was completely dark. Should Mohammed emerge, they were to follow him. He probably did not keep his mummy disguise in the house; Emerson felt sure that his father was not one of the plotters. The old man's fear had seemed genuine. Mohammed, then, would go to the spot—of which there were many in the crumbling cliffs—where he had concealed his costume, and assume it there. The watchers were not to interfere with him until they saw him actually in his disguise. They would then apprehend him; one would hold him captive while the other ran to give us the news. In a body we would haul the miscreant back to the village and expose his trickery.

On the remote chance that Mohammed was able to elude our gallant watchers, the rest of us prepared a second line of defense. Evelyn, with Michael to guard her, would retire to her chamber, though not to her bed, of course. From the doorway Michael would keep watch. Meanwhile, Emerson and I would take up our positions in his tomb chamber, which was some distance down the ledge from the one we ladies occupied. Any visitor would have to pass this door in order to reach Evelyn, who would thus be doubly protected. I must confess I felt a trifle uneasy on Evelyn's behalf. Mohammed's vile remark fit only too neatly with the mute evidence of the crumbled wrappings outside the door of the chamber where Evelyn slept.

As soon as it was dark, Walter and Abdullah slipped away. I settled Evelyn, with Michael standing by; he was holding a long cudgel, and although he began to show signs of uneasiness as the mysterious dusk gathered, I felt sure he would use the club if anything threatened Evelyn. I did not expect such a necessity would arise. If the Mummy eluded the watchers at the village, Emerson and I would take care of him.

After assuming a suitable costume, I crept along the ledge to Emerson's tomb. He was seated at the packing case that served as a desk, writing by the light of a lamp. When I slid stealthily into the chamber, he dropped his pen and stared.

"Is this a masquerade party, Peabody? The Mummy will win first prize in any case; your old gypsy lady will not compete."

"Obviously dark clothing is necessary if I wish to be unseen," I replied, in some annoyance. "The black head scarf keeps my hair from flying about, and the dirt is necessary to darken the comparative pallor of my face and hands. I was about to suggest the same precautions for you. And put out the lamp, if you please."

"I will put out the lamp at the usual time," Emerson said coldly. "If someone is watching, we do not wish to alarm him by any deviation from our routine. I suggest you squat there in the corner, Peabody, where you will not be visible from the doorway. No one would ever believe, seeing you as you look just now, that I had invited you here for—er—amorous purposes."

I did not think it worthwhile to dignify this remark with a reply. Giving him a haughty look, I went to my corner.

The ensuing hours dragged tediously. At first I amused myself by watching Emerson, who continued to write as if I had not been there. He needed a haircut. Despite his illness his hair was healthy-looking—thick and black and a little wavy where it curled over his collar. The movement of the muscles of his back, under his thin shirt, was interesting to a student of anatomy.

After a time this occupation palled. I crawled across to the packing-case table, this maneuver winning an irritable growl from Emerson, and took one of the books that were scattered on its surface. It was a volume on the pyramids of Gizeh, by a certain Mr. Petrie. I remembered hearing Emerson mention this young scholar, if not with approval—for Emerson did not speak of anyone with approval—at least without the invective he directed toward most other archaeologists, so I began to read with considerable interest. I could see why Emerson approved of Mr. Petrie. The meticulous care with which his measurements were carried out, checked, and rechecked was most impressive. He had totally disproved the mystical theories of the people who think the Great Pyramid to be a great prophecy in stone; and his description of the methods used by the ancients in cutting and shaping stones with the most primitive tools was convincing and interesting. So I read on, in the dim light, the silence broken only by the whisper as I turned a page, and by the scratch of Emerson's pen. I suppose I must have presented a curious figure as I squatted there in my dusty black skirt and cloak, with my dirty face bent over the tome.

Finally Emerson laid down his pen and rose. He yawned and stretched ostentatiously. Then, without so much as a glance in my direction, he blew out the lamp. Darkness obliberated every object. As my eyes gradually adjusted, I made out the open entrance, a square of sky glittering with stars.

Placing the book carefully on the table, I crawled to the doorway. A whisper from Emerson told me of his position; I took up my post on the other side of the door.

An even more boring period of time followed. I had no book with which to beguile my time, and Emerson did not seem inclined for conversation. I believed it was safe to whisper; we could see some distance, and would have seen an intruder long before he could have heard low voices. Nor did I really believe Mohammed would get this far. He had no reason to expect an ambush, and would be trapped by Abdullah and Walter as soon as he betrayed himself by assuming his mummy attire.

But Emerson squelched my first attempt to discuss the theories of Mr. Petrie, so I did not try again.

The beauty of the night was unbelievable. I have never seen stars so thickly clustered as those that bestrew the night sky of Egypt; they blazed like a pharaoh's treasure against the dark. The cool, sweet air was as refreshing as water after a long thirst, and the silence was infinitely soothing. Even the distant howls of the jackals seemed fitting, a lonely cry that mourned the loss of past splendor.

I confess I was half asleep, leaning against the wall, when another sound broke the silence. I really did not expect it; I was so surprised and so stupid with sleep that I moved, and the brush of my sleeve against the stone sounded like an alarm. Emerson's arm moved in an abrupt warning gesture. My eyes were accustomed to the dark and the light from without helped me to see his movements; I was aware of the moment when his whole body stiffened and his head shifted forward as he stared.

From his side of the doorway he could see the far end of the ledge and the lower slope where the cooking tent, and the tent Abdullah occupied, were located. I saw the other end of the ledge, where it passed Evelyn's tomb. There was nothing to be seen there, although I thought the curtain before the doorway was pulled back just a little, where Michael stood watch.

Emerson put out his hand. We understood one another that night without the need of words. I grasped his hand and took two slow, silent steps to his side.

The thing was there. Pale in the moonlight, it stood motionless, not on the ledge, but on the lower slope. This time the moon shone full upon it, and there could be no mistake as to its nature. I could almost make out the pattern of the bandaging across its breast. The featureless head was wrapped all around with cloth.

It was bad enough to see this monstrosity when it stood motionless; but as I watched, the head turned. Its slow, weaving movement was appalling, like that of an eyeless creature of the abyss blindly seeking some source of attraction even more alluring than light.

Emerson's hand closed over my mouth. I let it remain; I had been about to gasp aloud, and he had heard the inspiration of breath that warned him of my intent. Insanely, the Mummy seemed to hear it too, although I knew that was impossible. The blind head turned up, as if looking toward the ledge.

Emerson's fingers were ice cold; he was not so impervious as he pretended. And as the creature's right arm lifted, in a threatening gesture, Emerson's self-control broke. Releasing me so abruptly that I staggered, he bounded out onto the ledge.

I was at his heels. Secrecy was useless now. I called out a warning as Emerson, disdaining the ledge path, plunged over the edge and slithered down the slope amid an avalanche of sliding pebbles. It was an imprudent thing to do, in the poor light, and it received the usual consequences of imprudence. Emerson lost his footing, slipped, and fell headlong.

The Mummy was in full flight. I watched it for a moment; its lumbering, stiff-kneed stride attained unexpected speed. I knew I should not be able to catch it up; nor, to be honest, was I anxious to do so. I followed the path down and picked my way through the fallen rocks to where Emerson was struggling to sit up. Evelyn and Michael were both on the ledge, calling out to me, and I shouted a brief synopsis as I went along.

"It was here; it has gone. Michael, don't come down. Don't stir from Miss Evelyn's side."

For, by this time, I was ready to grant the nocturnal horror any degree of slyness. This might be a diversion, to draw us away from its intended victim.

Why did I believe the creature meant to do more than frighten us? Emerson asked this very question, when we had all calmed down and were seated in his tomb discussing the event.

"I can't say for sure," I answered, in a tentative manner that was uncharacteristic of me. "In part, it is simply logic; for if we fail to be frightened by the mere appearance of the thing, it must resort to more drastic measures. Then there is Mohammed's statement—you recall, Emerson, when we went to the village—"

I had not told Evelyn of this, and I did not intend to. Emerson understood my reference, and nodded. He was looking very grim; the bloodstained bandages around his brow and hands added to the warlike atmosphere of our council meeting.

"Yes, I recall. I think that was an empty threat, however; not even Mohammed would dare. . . . Well, this has been a useless night. I will have something to say to young Walter when he wanders in; Mohammed diddled him and Abdullah very neatly."

"Should we not go out and look for them?" Evelyn asked anxiously. "Some accident may have befallen them."

"Not to both of them; that was why I sent two men, so that one might assist the other in case of misadventure. No, my two incapable friends are probably still hovering around the village waiting for Mohammed to come out. They may see him when he returns; but unless he has his disguise actually on his body, there is no use in apprehending him. No, Miss Evelyn, don't try to make me change my mind. Walter is perfectly safe, and we should only wander aimlessly in the dark if we went to search for him."

So far had the strangeness of our situation broken down formality that he actually addressed Evelyn by her first name. But then, I reflected in some surprise, we had all been informal, shockingly so. Several times, in the stress of emotion, I had so forgotten myself as to address Walter by his given name. I felt a genuine warmth toward the lad; it seemed as if I had known him a long time. Emerson, of course, could be called by no other name. His impertinence toward me did not allow me to address him respectfully, and I had no inclination to call him by his first name.

There was no sleep for us the rest of the night, although Emerson persuaded Evelyn to lie down on his cot. We had a long wait; the first streaks of dawn were red in the sky when the wanderers returned; and their astonishment, when they heard what had transpired, was equal to ours when we heard their report. Both were willing to swear that no one had left the village that night. Walter himself had watched the mayor's house, from an uncomfortable perch in a tree nearby. There was no possible way in which Mohammed could have been the Mummy.

7

I REMEMBER standing on the ledge, oblivious to the slow beauty of sunrise on the cliffs, as the impact of Walter's statement sank into my mind. None of us tried to argue with him; to believe that Mohammed had tricked both watchers, being unaware of surveillance, was really beyond the bounds of credibility.

Suddenly Emerson rose from his chair and ran off along the ledge. I knew where he was going. How I knew I cannot explain, but I did know; and I also knew what he would find. I followed him more slowly, my steps slowed by dread of the discovery. When I came up to him he was standing by the wooden shelter that had covered the painted pavement. The painting was no longer there. Only a broad expanse of broken shards covered the sand. The destruction had been vicious; some sections had been ground into powder.

So my work had gone for naught and the sacrifice of my skinned fingers had been in vain. This was not my first thought, however. The senseless, wanton loss of beauty miraculously preserved hurt like a physical blow.

Without conscious premeditation my hand reached out to Emerson's; his fingers closed bruisingly over mine and we stood for a moment with hands locked. After a moment Emerson seemed to realize what he was doing, and flung my hand away. The cut on his forehead was still oozing blood, but I knew his drawn, haggard expression was not caused by physical pain. I did not even resent his gesture.

"A vindictive apparition, our Mummy," I said.

"All part and parcel of the ridiculous story Mohammed is promulgating," Emerson said. "The priest of Amon wreaking his vengeance on Khuenaten's city. Peabody, has it occurred to you that this plot is too complex for a man of Mohammed's limited intelligence?"

"Perhaps you underestimate his intelligence."

"I think not. His motive is equally obscure to me. Why should he go to so much trouble for a petty revenge? Our presence brings income to the village—money these people badly need, however small it may seem to us."

"But if Walter is correct in claiming that Mohammed never left the village—"

"I cannot accept that. Who else could the Mummy be?"

"Then you think we must search for some power behind Mohammed. Who could *that* be?"

"That is equally difficult to understand. Unless some wealthy amateur excavator covets the site—"

"Oh, don't be ridiculous!" I exclaimed. "Next you will be accusing M. Maspero of planning this, in order to discredit you."

This injudicious remark ended the discussion. Emerson shot me a hateful look and started back toward camp.

Our spirits were at very low ebb that morning; if it had not been for Emerson's stubbornness, I think we would have taken our leave of Amarna. Only Evelyn's intervention prevented a full-scale battle at breakfast, and it was she who insisted that we all get some sleep before discussing the matter again. All our tempers were strained by fatigue, she said; we could not think clearly. This was, of course, Evelyn's tact; her temper was never strained, and I am rational under all circumstances. It was Emerson who needed rest in order to be sensible, although I doubted that sleep would improve his disposition very much.

We were all sleeping, then, when a shout from Abdullah, on guard below, roused us to the realization that some new factor had entered the scene. Stumbling out of the tomb and blinking against the brilliant sunlight, I made out a procession approaching us from the direction of the river. The leading figure was mounted on a donkey. It was soon clearly identifiable.

I turned to Evelyn, who stood shading her eyes with her hand. "Reinforcements have arrived," I remarked. "It will be interesting to see what Lord Ellesmere makes of our little mystery."

"Lucas!" Evelyn exclaimed.

Walter, followed by his brother, came out in time to hear our exchange. At Evelyn's exclamation he gave her a piercing look. The surprise in her voice might well have been taken for another emotion; and Walter turned to view the newcomer with a frown. Lucas had seen us; he raised his arm and waved vigorously. We could see the flash of his white teeth against a face that was now tanned almost as deeply as the skin of the natives. Walter's frown became a scowl.

"So you are acquainted with this infernal intruder?" Emerson inquired. "I might have expected he would be a friend of yours, Peabody."

"After all, Emerson, this site is not your private property," I replied spiritedly. "It is surprising that we have not had more visitors."

This reasonable comment seemed to strike Emerson; he nodded thoughtfully. I went on to give the explanations I felt were his due.

"Lord Ellesmere is a distant relative of Evelyn's. We met him in Cairo just as we were about to sail, and he told us of his intention to take the same trip. We were expecting to meet in Luxor. No doubt he recognized the *Philae* at her moorings, and inquired as to our whereabouts."

I was rather pleased with this account, which seemed to me to convey the necessary information without adding any extraneous facts. I intended to caution Lucas not to betray his real relationship with Evelyn, or hers with the late Lord Ellesmere. Neither of the Emersons were interested in scandal, unless it concerned the love affairs of ancient Egyptian pharaohs, so it was unlikely that they should have heard of the escapade of the late Lord Ellesmere's young heiress; but there was no point in taking chances.

Then I looked at Evelyn; and my heart sank down into my scuffed boots. How could I try to shield her, when she was fully determined to expose the whole affair if it became necessary? She had paled a trifle as she watched her cousin's advance; her lips were set in an expression I had come to know very well. Young Walter's face, as he looked from Evelyn to the newcomer, gave his own feelings away more clearly than speech.

I experienced a revelation in that moment. I wanted Walter for Evelyn. They were ideally suited; he was an honorable, lovable young fellow, who would treat her well. If I had to give her up, I would not repine seeing her in the tender care of a man like Walter. I determined, in that instant, that it should come to pass. But I foresaw that it would take some effort, even for me.

Lucas was now close. Waving and laughing and shouting greetings, he came on. Walter turned to Evelyn.

"Will you not go down to meet this relative of yours?"

His tone was positively spiteful. I smiled to myself.

142

Evelyn started. "Yes, of course," she said.

"I will meet him," I said, taking her by the arm. "Stay here; I will have Michael bring tea."

Lucas fell on me with shouts of joy. The fellow would have embraced me if I had not fended him off with a well-placed shove. I interrupted his babble with the caution I had intended to give; and he shot me a reproachful look.

"No such warning was necessary, Miss Amelia, I assure you. But tell me, what are you doing here? Your reis informed me that you have been here almost a week. Who are your friends, and why—"

Explanations and introductions followed, slowly, since Lucas kept interrupting. The interruptions ceased, however, when I—for of course it was I who was telling the story—reached the part of the narrative involving the Mummy. Lucas listened in silence. A grin spread slowly over his face, and when I concluded my story he burst into a shout of mirth.

"Excellent! Splendid! Little did I think when I set out for Egypt that I would have such luck. This is like one of Rider Haggard's tales; or the novels of Herr Ebers. How I look forward to meeting the Mummy!"

"I don't know that such an encounter will ever take place, Lord Ellesmere," Walter said. "There is no reason why you should concern yourself with our problems. If you will escort the ladies into safety, we—"

Lucas leaned forward; impetuously he placed a hand on the other young man's arm.

"But, my dear fellow, you would not deprive me of a part in this adventure? I don't claim any noble intentions; I'm sure you can manage quite well without me. My motives are purely selfish, and therefore you must give way to me!"

Watching his beaming face, hearing his jovial tones, I could understand why Mr. Dickens' Scrooge found his jolly nephew so

143

irritating. I was also struck by the contrast between the two young men. They were almost of an age, I thought. Walter's slim height looked boyish next to Lucas' breadth of chest and shoulders. His tumbled dark hair and thin cheeks made him appear even younger. Lucas was dressed with his usual elegance; his pith helmet shone like snow in the sun, his light suit was tailored like a uniform and fit him like a glove. Walter's shirt was open at the throat, displaying reddened, peeling skin. His boots were shabby and dusty, his hands calloused from hard labor.

At that, he looked relatively respectable next to his brother, whose bandaged brow and hand added to his look of a battered warrior just come off the battlefield. Emerson was contemplating Lucas with an expression that made me think we might become allies in this, if in nothing else. When he spoke, it was in the rasping growl that was more dangerous than his shouts.

"You should appeal to me, my lord, for permission to join our group. I confess I cannot think of any means of preventing you from pitching a tent anywhere you choose."

From Emerson this was positively a gracious speech. Lucas seemed to realize it; he turned his considerable charm on Emerson, who continued to study him with all the enthusiasm of a gruff old mastiff watching the gambols of a puppy. When Lucas expressed interest in the antiquities of the area, he unbent a trifle and offered to show Lucas some of the tombs.

"We have uncovered very little of the city," he explained. "The ruins that remain are not interesting to a layman. The carvings in the tombs have a certain appeal, however."

"I regret that I have not had time to examine them more closely," I interrupted. "I meant to ask you, Emerson, whether there might not be more tombs to be discovered. What of the king's own tomb, for instance? He of all people must have had a sepulcher here."

"That is one of the projects I had hoped to undertake this

season," Emerson replied. "The royal tomb has never been properly cleared out, although these villainous villagers removed anything of salable value some time ago. There was not much; the reliefs in the tomb were never finished, and I question whether Khuenaten was ever buried there, although fragments of a sarcophagus may still be seen in the burial chamber. Hmmm. Yes, Peabody, I would like to have another look at it. Suppose we go this afternoon."

"The royal tomb is not to my taste today," Lucas said, stretching out his booted feet lazily. "It is quite a distance, I am told, and the path is rugged."

"It would mar the finish of your boots," Emerson agreed gravely. "You seem to know something about Amarna, Lord Ellesmere. The royal tomb is not on the ordinary traveler's list of sights."

"Oh, I have become an interested student of all things Egyptian. Already I have made a splendid collection of antiquities, and I hope to acquire more along the way. I intend to set up an Egyptian gallery at Ellesmere Castle."

Emerson had been keeping himself under tight rein—for what reason I could not imagine—but this was too much for him.

"Another amateur collection, ignorantly displayed and isolated from scholars," he burst out. "Of course you are collecting your antiquities from the dealers, my lord—which means that they have been wantonly pilfered from their original places, with no records kept—"

"I seem to have struck inadvertently at a tender spot," Lucas said, smiling at Evelyn.

She did not return the smile; instead she said seriously, "Mr. Emerson's feelings are more than justified, Lucas. It is vital that excavations should be carried out only by trained archaeologists. Some objects are fragile and can be damaged by unskilled hands. More important, the provenance of an object can sometimes tell

145

us a great deal—where it was found, with what other objects, and so on. If visitors would not buy from dealers and peasants, they would stop their illicit digging."

"Dear me, you are becoming quite an enthusiast yourself," Lucas exclaimed. "That is what I shall need for my Egyptian gallery—an expert who will tend and classify my collection. Then perhaps Mr. Emerson will not despise me."

Evelyn's eyes fell under his meaningful regard.

"Emerson will despise you in any case," I said. "The only steps you can take to redeem yourself are, one, to cease buying antiquities, and two, to present the ones you have to the British Museum. The scholars there will take proper care of them."

Emerson muttered something which, though indistinct, was clearly uncomplimentary to the British Museum.

Lucas laughed. "No, I cannot give up my collection. But perhaps Mr. Emerson will read my papyrus for me."

"You have a papyrus?" I inquired interestedly.

"Yes, quite a good one—brown with age, crumbling, covered with those strange little scratches which were, I am told, developed from the hieroglyphic picture writing. When I unrolled it—"

An ominous moaning sound emerged from Emerson.

"You unrolled it," he repeated.

"Only the first section," said Lucas cheerfully. "It began to break apart then, so I thought. . . . Why, Mr. Emerson, you look quite pale. I gather I have done something reprehensible."

"You might as well confess to a murder," Emerson exclaimed. "There are too many people in the world as it is, but the supply of ancient manuscripts is severely limited."

Lucas seemed subdued by the reproof.

"I will give it to you, then, if you feel so strongly. Perhaps it will count as my payment of admission to this charming group," he added more cheerfully. "I must send back to my dahabeeyah

146

for supplies, if I am to spend the night. Let us just have a look around, shall we? I can hardly wait to see the scenes of the Mummy's appearance, and select a tomb for myself."

Emerson acquiesced with no more than a mumble. I was at a loss to account for his amiability at first. Then two explanations occurred to me. I was ready to believe either or both, since neither reflected any credit on Emerson.

Money for excavation was hard to come by; a wealthy patron could relieve Emerson's anxieties in this area. Furthermore, it was as clear as print that Lucas was interested in Evelyn. His eyes seldom left her face, and he made no attempt to conceal his tender concern. Emerson must realize that Walter also loved the girl. He would not be pleased to lose his devoted acolyte; perhaps he meant Walter to marry well, in order to supply more funds for the gaping maw of his research. By encouraging a rival to his brother, he kept that brother under his calloused thumb.

My suspicions were confirmed when Emerson waxed positively jovial as he showed Lucas the camp. As for Lucas, he bubbled with enthusiasm and admiration. Nothing could be more charming! He could not imagine anything more delightful than camping out in an ancient tomb! The scenery was magnificent, the air was like wine, and—in short, you would have thought our meticulous lordship was rhapsodizing over a modern luxury hotel and a vista of wooded grandeur. He plied Emerson with questions; shook his head over the perfidy of Mohammed and the superstitions of the visitors; insisted on pressing the hand of the faithful Abdullah, who looked askance at this demonstration. The only thing he expressed doubt about was Michael.

"Are you certain you can trust him?" he asked in a low voice, as we walked past the cook tent where Michael was preparing a simple lunch. The devoted fellow had taken over menial duties that would ordinarily have been below his dignity, since the villagers had abandoned us. We had decided not to involve any of our servants from the boat; there was no telling how they would react to the story, much less the sight, of the Mummy.

"I trust him implicitly," Evelyn replied firmly. "Amelia saved the life of his child; he would die for her, I think."

"Then there is no more to be said," said Lucas. But he did say more—a good deal more. Michael was, after all, a native. Was he not just as superstitious as the villagers? Could he be trusted to risk, not only his life, but his immortal soul, as he believed, with a demon of the night?

"I have considered that," Emerson replied shortly. "You need not concern yourself about it, your lordship."

His tone brooked no argument. Even Lucas recognized this, and he abandoned the subject.

Of the tombs in our immediate vicinity only a few were habitable; some were blocked by rock falls or heaps of debris. They were similar in plan, having a large hall with columns beyond the entrance corridor, from which another corridor led on to more rooms, including the burial chamber.

Evelyn and I occupied a tomb that had once belonged to a royal craftsman who bore the engaging title Washer of Hands of His Majesty. The title delighted me because it was a reminder of the constancy of human nature; I could not help recalling our own Tudor and Stuart monarchs, who were served by high noblemen who considered it an honor to be the official holders of the royal trousers.

But I digress.

Lucas was with difficulty dissuaded from moving into the most grandiose of the nearby tombs, that of one Mahu, who had been chief of police of the city. Clearing it out would have taken days. So Lucas's servants were set to work on another, smaller tomb, and one of them was sent back to the dahabeeyah with a long list of Lucas's requirements for the next day or two.

After luncheon we separated, Evelyn to rest, Walter to work at recording some pottery fragments which had been found on

148

the last day of digging, and Lucas to explore. He went jogging off on his little donkey, looking sufficiently ridiculous with his long legs trailing. When he was out of sight, Emerson turned to me.

"Come along, Peabody."

"Where to?"

"You said you wanted to see the royal tomb."

"What, now?"

"Now is as good a time as any."

I looked up at the broiling sun, now near the zenith; then I shrugged. If Emerson thought to subdue me by such tactics, he would soon find out that I could keep up with any project he proposed. I went to my tomb to assume my rationals. They were dreadfully creased and dusty, and I wished I had purchased several similar costumes.

When I emerged, Emerson was pacing up and down and glaring at his watch.

"Will Walter come?" I inquired, deliberately dawdling.

"Walter had better remain here. There must be someone on guard; I have told Abdullah to go after his lordship, in case the fool breaks a leg trying to climb the cliffs or tumbles off his donkey. Come, come, Peabody; if you don't hurry I will go alone."

I went—not because he had ordered me to do so, but because I suspected he wanted a private discussion with me.

However, no such development ensued. The walk was too difficult for leisurely conversation. We turned into a long rocky wadi, or canyon, and followed its course for several miles. It was the most desolate area I had seen yet. The steep, barren walls of the wadi were streaked and cracking; not a single blade of grass or hardy weed found sustenance in the sunbaked soil. The floor of the valley was covered with rocks of all sizes, from enormous boulders to pebbles, which had fallen from the cliffs. The silence was absolute. It was like being in another world; a world in which life was an intrusion.

After about three miles the rock walls closed in and smaller

149

wadis opened up to left and right. We turned to the northeast and picked our way through a narrow valley. As we stumbled along, Emerson began to ask questions, but they were not the questions I had expected. Instead he interrogated me about Lucas. I answered as shortly as I could. The drift of Emerson's curiosity convinced me that I had been correct in both my assumptions; he was immensely curious about the extent of Lord Ellesmere's fortune and the degree of his interest in Evelyn. I found it increasingly difficult to avoid his inquiries and finally put an end to them by picking a quarrel. That was never difficult with Emerson. He stalked along in offended silence until we reached the isolated tomb which had been prepared for the heretic king and his family.

In an effort to protect it from thieves seeking the rich treasures buried with the dead, the royal tomb had been situated in a remote part of the cliffs. The attempt at security had failed; the tomb had been robbed again and again. If Khuenaten had ever been buried there, the royal mummy had vanished centuries ago.

I shivered, even in the breathless heat, as I looked up the slope at the high dark hole that marked the entrance to the tomb. An air of brooding desolation hung over the spot. Disappointment and failure haunted it. Toward the end of his life, the royal reformer must have known that his religious revolution would not succeed. After his death his very name had been obliterated. I thought I would not like to come here after dark; it would be too easy to hear, in the jackals' howls, the lament of a starving, nameless ghost.

Emerson, unaffected by the aura of the place, was already scrambling up toward the entrance. Before it was a little plateau, about fifteen feet off the ground. I followed him, unassisted. He had brought candles; we lighted two of them and went in.

The tombs of Egyptian royalty were not the simple structures their subjects built. This one had long corridors, steep stairs, turns and curves, designed to frustrate the cupidity of thieves. These devices had succeeded as well as such devices usually do—that is to say, not at all. The royal tomb had been roughly cleared, probably by the experienced thieves of Haggi Qandil. Otherwise we would not have been able to penetrate its interior at all, and even so, it was a breathless, dusty, uncomfortable trip. We were unable to reach the burial chamber, because a deep pit, like the one in the other tomb I had seen, cut straight across the corridor. There was nothing to bridge it with. Emerson's suggestion that we run and jump was probably not to be taken seriously. *I* certainly did not take it seriously.

We retraced our steps to the top of the second flight of stairs, where three small rooms were located off the main corridor. Here crumbling reliefs showed the death and burial of a princess, one of Khuenaten's daughters. She had died young, and had been laid to rest in her father's tomb. The little body, stretched out stiffly on its bed, looked very pathetic, and the grief of the parents, holding one another's hands for comfort, was strangely moving. Almost one could hear a thin moan of anguish echoing down the deserted corridors. . . .

And then there was a moan—or at least, a faint sound of some kind. The reader can only faintly imagine the horrific effect of such a sound—of sound of any sort—in those dark, musty rooms that had never been inhabited except by the dead. Before my scalp had time to prickle, the fainter sound was followed by another, less ghostly, but even more alarming. It was a loud crash of falling rock. Whatever the sound lost by reason of distance was regained by the rolling echoes. I started and dropped my candle.

Using language no lady could possibly remember, much less reproduce, Emerson scrabbled around in the debris that littered the floor until he found the candle. He relighted it from his own. Then he looked directly at me and spoke in the quiet voice he employed in moments of emergency.

151

"You are no fool, Peabody, if you are a woman. You know what that sound may mean. Are you prepared? You will not swoon, or scream, or become hysterical?"

I gave him a look of withering scorn, and in silence started out of the room.

With Emerson breathing heavily behind me, I made my way along the corridor. I did not expect that we would meet with any obstruction there. The walls and floors were carved from the living stone of the mountains. No; the difficulty would be at the entrance, and long before we reached that spot I knew that my surmise was unhappily correct. From the foot of the final stair I saw that the light which should have been apparent at the entrance was—not apparent.

We made our way up the stairs, not without difficulty, for rocks littered the steps, and stood at last before the entrance. The narrow opening was closed by stones—some as small as pebbles, some as large as boulders.

I blew out my candle. It was obvious that we had better conserve what little light we had. I was stooping to pluck at the rocks when Emerson turned to stick his candle onto a ledge in a pool of its own grease.

"Take care," he said curtly. "You may start another landslide that will sweep both of us down the stairs."

We dug for a long time; not as long as it seemed, perhaps, but the first candle was almost burned out when there came a sound from without. It was, to say the least, a welcome event. At first the words were indistinguishable. Then I realized that the person was speaking Arabic. I recognized the voice and, in the stress of the moment, understood what was being said. The voice was Abdullah's. He demanded to know if we were within.

"Of course we are within," shouted Emerson angrily. "Oh, son of a blind, bowlegged mule, where else should we be?"

A howl, which I took to be one of delight, followed this question. The howl was followed by a shout in quite another voice: "Hold on, Miss Amelia! Lucas is on the job!"

All at once Emerson threw his arms against me and pushed me against the wall, pressing his body close to mine.

Although I am now alone as I write, my Critic having gone off on an errand, I hesitate to express the thoughts that flashed through my mind at that moment. I knew Emerson was no weakling, but I had not fully realized his strength until I felt the rigid muscles of his breast against mine and felt my bones give under the strength of his grasp. I thought . . . I expected. . . . Well, why not admit it? I thought he was embracing me—relief at our unexpected rescue having weakened his mind.

Luckily these absurd notions had no time to burgeon in my brain. A horrible rattling crash followed, as the barricade gave way, and great rocks bounded down the stairs and banged against the walls. I felt Emerson flinch and knew he had been struck by at least one rock, from whose impact his quick action had saved me; for my body was shielded by his and his big hand pressed my face into the shelter of his shoulder.

I was quite out of breath when he released me, and gulped air for several seconds before I realized it was the clean, hot air of the outer world I breathed, and that sunlight was streaming into the vault.

The sunlight was too bright for my dazzled eyes, accustomed to darkness. I could just make out the silhouettes of the heads and shoulders of two men above the heap of rock that still lay on the threshold.

Emerson leaned back against the wall, his left arm hanging at an odd angle. As Abdullah and Lucas came scrambling in over the rocks, Emerson turned his head toward his foreman. Rivulets of perspiration were streaming down his face, turning the dust that covered it into a muddy mask.

"You d—— fool," he said.

"You are hurt," said Abdullah intelligently.

"Words fail me," said Emerson.

But of course they did not; he went on, though he spoke in gasps. "An experienced foreman . . . knows better . . . shoving like a battering ram. . . ."

"I tried to tell him to go slowly," Lucas broke in. "Unfortunately my Arabic is nonexistent."

He looked so guilty, and Abdullah so particularly enigmatic, that I realized who was probably responsible for the accident. There was no point in pressing the matter, however.

"He was anxious to get us out," I said. "Let us eschew recriminations and act. Is your arm broken?"

"Dislocated," said Emerson, between his teeth. "I must get back . . . Walter knows how. . . ."

"You cannot walk so far," I said.

This was patently true, and anyone but Emerson would have admitted the fact at once. His knees were buckling, and only the wall at his back kept him upright.

"I can do . . . what I must," he replied.

"No doubt; but there is no need. I saw our local surgeon perform this operation once, on a farmer whose shoulder had been put out of place. If you will direct me—"

The idea seemed to revive Emerson. His eyes rolled toward me; I swear, I saw a flash of enjoyment.

"You won't like it," said Emerson.

"Neither will you," I replied.

I think I prefer not to describe the procedure that followed. Emerson was not in any mood to make jokes when it was over, but I was the one who had to sit down on the ground and put my head between my knees. Fortunately Abdullah had brought water; we both had been thirsty from the heat and dust even before the accident. A long drink revived me and helped Emerson. I then tore up my petticoat in order to fasten his arm to his body so that it would not be jarred unnecessarily. He had his wicked temper back by then, and made a rude remark.

"As you would say, my lord, it is just like one of Mr. Haggard's romances. The heroine always sacrifices a petticoat at some point in the proceedings. No doubt that is why females wear such ridiculous garments; they do come in useful in emergencies."

The way to the royal tomb had seemed long; the road back was interminable. Lucas's strength was of great assistance, and Emerson did not disdain the help of his arm. As we walked along, Lucas explained how he had happened to find us.

He had had a little adventure of his own. Riding not far from the village, he had been accosted by the owner of his donkey, who had abandoned animal and rider when they first approached the camp. Now the donkey owner demanded his animal back.

"It occurred to me," Lucas explained, "that you had probably been deprived of donkeys as well as workers, so I determined to keep that one, if I could. If the villagers had realized I was acquainted with you, I never should have gotten it in the first place. I offered to buy the wretched little beast—thinking of Evelyn's using it, of course. But it was no use; when I insisted, I was set upon by a howling horde of villagers and forcibly removed from my steed. They offered me no violence, but I was shaken up and very angry. I was on my way back to camp when I met Abdullah. He said you had gone to the royal tomb; and after my adventure, I was somewhat concerned about you. So we came here—fortunately!"

"You did not see the rockfall, then?" Emerson asked.

"No."

"It couldn't have been an accident," Emerson grunted. "Too fortuitous. Why that one spot, while we happened to be inside the tomb?"

"We were fortunate that it was not a more extensive landslide," I said, stumbling into a thornbush.

155

"Hmmph," said Emerson, trying not to groan.

A mile or two from camp we were met by Walter and Evelyn, who, alarmed at our prolonged absence, had set out to look for us. Walter went quite pale when he saw Emerson's faltering steps and bandaged body, but he knew better than to commiserate.

"It is most unfortunate," he said thoughtfully. "Another accident, just now, will merely confirm the villagers' superstitions."

"We need not tell them, surely," said Lucas.

"They will know," I said. "I suspect one of them has good reason to know what has occurred."

"Aha!" Lucas exclaimed. "You think it was no accident?"

He was altogether too pleased about the whole affair. I knew it was unfair of me to blame him for enjoying the adventure; his acquaintance with Emerson and Walter was of the slightest, so he could not be expected to feel for them as Evelyn and I did. And certainly the wild events of those days would have appealed to the adventurous spirit of any young gentleman. Nevertheless, his grin annoyed me.

"It was no accident," I said curtly. "This was a foolish expedition. From now on we must stay in the camp and close to one another. Perhaps no real harm was intended—"

"We cannot know that," Walter interrupted. "If the rock had struck my brother's head instead of his shoulder—"

"But his injury *was* an unfortunate accident. It was incurred during our release, not during the rockfall, which could hardly have been designed to murder us. You knew our destination; you would have searched for us if we had not returned, so that even if Abdullah had not happened to go after us, we would not have been incarcerated long. No; the attempt could not have been at murder. I believe it was only another harassment."

"And if Peabody says so," remarked Emerson, "that is the Word of the Prophet."

We finished the journey in cool silence.

156

However, we had much to be thankful for. Evelyn pointed this out as we prepared for dinner in our homey tomb. She was not looking well that evening; I noticed her pallor and sober looks all the more because it contrasted so strikingly with her appearance during the preceding week. She had been frightened, weary, and uncomfortable, as we all were; but under the strain there had been a quiet happiness, a kind of bloom. The bloom was now gone. And of course I knew the reason.

"Has Lucas been annoying you?" I inquired, with my usual tact.

Evelyn was doing her hair in front of the mirror. Her hands faltered; a bright lock of golden hair tumbled down her back.

"He asked me again to marry him."

"And you said . . .?"

Evelyn turned. The disordered masses of her hair flowed out with the force of her movement and fell about her shoulders. She had never looked lovelier, for the nobility of her purpose and the strength of her emotion transformed her face.

"Amelia, how can you ask? You know my feelings; I have never tried to conceal them from you, my cherished friend. I cannot marry the man I love; but I will never be the bride of another."

"You are wrong," I said forcefully. "Walter loves you. I know it; you must know it. You are being grossly unjust to him, not to give him the chance—"

"To know my shame—my folly? Never fear, Amelia; if he *should* ask me to marry him, I will tell him the truth."

"And why do you assume he will recoil? Oh, I agree; you must be candid, he would hear the story sooner or later, and he would have cause for resentment at hearing it from another than yourself. But he is a splendid lad, Evelyn; I like him more with every day that passes. He would not—"

"He is a man," said Evelyn, in a tone of weary wisdom that would have made me laugh, had I not been so distressed for her.

"What man could forget or forgive such a thing in his wife?"

"Bah," I said.

"If I had anything to offer him," Evelyn went on passionately. "The fortune I once despised would be a godsend to him and his brother. If only—"

"You don't suppose that splendid boy would refuse you for your misstep and forgive you for a fortune, do you?" I demanded indignantly.

Evelyn's eyes narrowed.

"Amelia, why do you speak as if you were a hundred years old? Walter is only a few years younger than you, and you are still in your prime. In the last week you seem to have drunk from the fountain of youth; you are looking younger and more attractive every day."

I stared at her in astonishment.

"Come, now, Evelyn, don't let your fondness for me destroy your aesthetic sense. I have been scoured by windblown sand, dried out and burned by the sun, and I have ruined every decent dress I own. Forget me, and let us settle your problem once and for all. If you would only listen to me—"

"I honor and love you," she interrupted, in a low voice. "But in this matter I cannot follow anything but my own conscience."

"But it is such a waste," I lamented. "You love this life. Your seeming fragility conceals a will of iron; you could be a helpmate as well as a wife to Walter."

"You are the one who loves this life," Evelyn said, watching me curiously. "What an archaeologist you would make, Amelia!"

"Hmmm," I said. "That is true. It is most unfortunate that I was not born a man. Emerson would accept me then as a colleague; my money would support his work; what a splendid time we would have, working and quarreling together. Oh, it is a pity that I am a woman. Emerson would agree."

"I am not so sure," said Evelyn. There was a faint smile on her lips.

158

"You are distracting me again," I complained. "You cannot avoid the issue, Evelyn. Suppose I were to finance—"

"No, Amelia," Evelyn said. I knew that gentle tone. It was as final as Emerson's growl.

"Then accept Lucas's offer. No, no, I mean his offer of money. Half of your grandfather's fortune is yours, morally. If you really believe Walter would accept—"

"Amelia, that is not worthy of you. Could I accept Lucas's generosity and use it to buy the affection of Lucas's rival?"

"You put things in such a cold-blooded way," I muttered.

"It is the honest way." Evelyn's animation had faded; she was pale and sad. "No, Amelia. I cannot—will not—marry Lucas, nor will I accept a penny from him. Are you so anxious to rid yourself of me? I had dared to let myself envision a life together. . . . Growing old with you, winding wool and keeping cats and tending a garden somewhere in the country. We could be content, could we not? Oh, Amelia, don't cry! I have never seen you weep; don't do it on my account. . . ."

She threw her arms around me and we clung together, both sobbing violently. I did not often cry, it is true; I don't know why I was crying then, but I found it soothing to do so. So I let myself go, wallowing in the luxuriance of openly expressed emotion, and Evelyn made me cry even harder by the fond expressions she choked out.

"I do love you, Amelia; you are dearer to me than any sister. Your kindness, your sense of humor, your saintly temper . . ."

The last phrase appealed too strongly to the sense of humor she had just mentioned; I stopped crying and began to laugh feebly.

"Dearest Evelyn, I have a temper like a fiend's, and the disposition of a balky mule. How beautiful is friendship, that it blinds one to the friend's true nature! Well, child, don't cry anymore; I know why you weep, and it is not because of my saintly nature. I suppose the Almighty will order our lives as He sees fit, and there is no reason for us to worry. I have not altogether decided to accept His decrees; but whatever happens, you and I will not part until I can give you up to a man who deserves you. Here, wipe your eyes, and then give me the handkerchief so I can wipe mine. I did not expect to need more than one handkerchief this evening."

We mopped our wet faces and went on with our dressing. Evelyn had one more comment to make.

"You speak as if I would be the one to leave you. Will you keep me on, Amelia, to wind wool and wash lapdogs, after *you* are married?"

"That is the most ridiculous remark you have made as yet," I said. "And many of your remarks have been extremely silly."

8

WHEN we came out of the tomb, wearing fresh garments and rather red eyes, we found the men assembled. Lucas had brought enough articles to stock a shop; there were flowers on the table, and a glittering array of silverware and crystal. The look on Emerson's face as he contemplated the elegantly set table was almost enough to compensate for the absurdity of the business.

Lucas was attired in a fresh suit, spotless and expensively tailored. He sprang to his feet when we appeared and held a chair for Evelyn. Walter held one for me. Lucas offered us sherry. He behaved as if he were the host. Emerson, who was now staring at the toes of his deplorable boots, said nothing. His arm was still strapped to his side, and I concluded that he felt too ill to be as objectionable as he usually was.

"Such elegance," I commented, as Lucas handed me a delicate

goblet. "We are not accustomed to luxury here, your lordship."

"I see no reason for depriving oneself of the amenities," Lucas replied, smiling. "If asceticism is necessary, I venture to say that you will find me ready to accept the most stringent measures; but while Amontillado and crystal are available, I will make use of them."

He lifted his own glass in a mock salute. It did not contain Amontillado, although the liquid was almost as dark a shade of amber. My father never drank spirits, but my brothers were not so abstemious. I looked critically at the glass, and remarked, "Do you think it wise to imbibe? We must be on the *qui vive* tonight. Or have you abandoned your intention of lying in wait for our visitor?"

"Not at all! I have a strong head, Miss Amelia, and a little whiskey only makes my senses more acute."

"That is the common delusion of the drinker," said Walter. His tone was offensive. Lucas smiled at him.

"We are appreciative of your luxuries, Lucas," Evelyn said. "But they really are not necessary. How heavily laden your daha-beeyah must be!"

"It would have been more heavily laden if I had had my way," Lucas replied. "Your boxes have arrived in Cairo, Evelyn. I intended to bring them along; but that old curmudgeon, Baring, refused to hand them over."

"Indeed?" I said. "He was an acquaintance of my father's."

"I am well aware of that. You should be complimented, Miss Amelia, that the new master of Egypt has taken the trouble to look after your affairs personally. The boxes were sent to you, since it was your address the Roman consul had for Evelyn. Baring took charge of them in Cairo and guards them like the dictator he is. I explained my relationship to Evelyn, but he was adamant."

"Perhaps your reputation has preceded you," I said mildly.

It was impossible to offend Lucas. He laughed heartily.

"Oh, it has. I went to university with a young relative of Baring's. I am afraid certain—er—escapades reached the distinguished gentleman's ears."

"It does not matter," Evelyn said. "I am grateful for your efforts, Lucas, but I need nothing more than I have."

"You need nothing except yourself," Lucas said warmly. "That is treasure enough. But your needs and your desserts are two different things. One day, Evelyn, you will be persuaded to accept what you deserve; although all the treasure houses of the pharaohs could not hold its real value."

Evelyn flushed and was silent; she was too gentle to reproach him for his remarks, which were, to say the least, out of place at that time and in that company. I felt quite exasperated with the girl; could she not see that her response to Lucas's florid compliments only inflamed poor Walter's jealousy? With a lover's excessive sensibility he misinterpreted every blush, every glance.

Emerson removed his gaze from the toes of his boots and glowered at me. "Are we to sit here all evening exchanging compliments? No doubt you have planned the evening's entertainment, Peabody; enlighten us as to what we must do."

"I had not given the matter much thought."

"Really? And why not?"

I had found that the surest way of annoying Emerson was to ignore his provocative remarks and reply as if he had spoken in ordinary courteous exchange.

"I was thinking of the royal tomb," I explained. "Of the relief of the little princess and her grieving parents. Evelyn should copy it. She would do it beautifully."

"I am surprised at the suggestion," Lucas exclaimed. "After what happened today—"

"Oh, I don't mean she should do it now; but one day, when the situation has been cleared up. Since your connection with Evelyn has been so distant, Lucas, you may not know that she is a splendid artist. She has already done a painting of the pavement that was destroyed."

Lucas insisted on seeing this painting and exclaimed over it quite excessively. The conversation having turned to matters archaeological, he was reminded of the papyrus scroll he had mentioned.

"I had the bearers fetch it," he said, reaching into the box at his side. "Here you are, Mr. Emerson. I said I would hand it over, and I keep my word."

The papyrus was enclosed in a carved and colored wooden case, except for a single section—the one Lucas had unrolled.

"I put it between two squares of glass," he explained. "That seemed the best method of keeping it from crumbling any further."

"At least you had that much sense," Emerson grumbled. "Hand it to Walter, if you please, your lordship. I might drop it, having only one good hand."

Walter took the framed section, as gently as if it had been a baby, on the palms of his two hands. The sun was setting, but there was still ample light. As Walter bent over the sheet of papyrus, a lock of hair tumbled down over his brow. His lips moved as if in silent prayer. He seemed to have forgotten our presence.

I leaned forward to see better. The papyrus seemed to me to be in fairly good condition, compared with others I had seen in antiquities shops. It was brown with age and the edges were crumbling, but the black, inky writing stood out clearly on the whole. An occasional word was written in red, which had not fared so well; it had faded to a rusty brown. Of course I had no notion whatsoever what the writing said. It resembled the hiero-glyphic writing; one could distinguish the shape of an occasional bird or squatting figure, each of which represented a letter in the ancient picture alphabet of the Egyptians. But the majority of the

164

letters were abbreviated forms and resembled a written script such as Arabic more than it resembled hieroglyphic writing.

"It is splendid hieratic," said Emerson, who was leaning over his brother's shoulder. "Much closer to the hieroglyphs than some I have seen. Can you make it out, Walter?"

"You don't mean that Master Walter can read that scribble?" Lucas exclaimed.

"Master Walter," said his brother drily, "is one of the world's leading experts on the ancient language. I know a bit, but I am primarily an excavator. Walter has specialized in philology. Well, Walter?"

"Your partiality makes you praise me too highly," Walter said, his eyes greedily devouring the crabbed script. "I must show this to Frank Griffith; he is with Petrie at Naucratis this season, and unless I miss my guess, he is going to be one of our leading scholars. However, I believe I can make out a few lines. You are right, Radcliffe; it is splendid hieratic. That," he explained to the rest of us, "was the cursive script used on documents and records. The hieroglyphic signs were too ornate and cumbersome for the scribes of a busy kingdom. The hieratic was developed from the hieroglyphic, and if you look closely, you will see how the signs resemble the original pictures."

"I see!" Evelyn burst out. We were all bending over the papyrus now, except Lucas, who sipped his whiskey and watched us all with his patronizing smile. "Surely that is an owl—the letter 'm.' And the following word much resembles the seated man, which is the pronoun 'I.' "

"Quite right, quite right." Walter was delighted. "Here is the word for 'sister.' In ancient Egyptian that might mean. . . ." His voice faltered. Evelyn, sensitive to the slightest change in his feelings, quietly returned to her chair.

"Sister and brother were terms of endearment," said Emerson, finishing the sentence his brother had begun. "A lover spoke of

165

his sweetheart as his sister."

"And this," said Walter in a low voice, "is a love poem."

"Splendid," exclaimed Lucas. "Read it to us, Master Walter, if you please."

Lucas had insisted that we be informal; but his address of Walter by the childish title was certainly meant to provoke. On this occasion it had no effect; Walter was too absorbed in his studies.

"I can only make out a few lines," he said. "You ought not to have unrolled it, Lord Ellesmere; the break goes through part of the text. However, this section reads:

> I go down with thee into the water
> And come forth to thee again
> With a red fish, which is—beautiful on my fingers.

"There is a break here. The lovers are by the water; a pond, or the Nile. They—they disport themselves in the cool water."

"It doesn't have the ring of a love poem to me," Lucas said skeptically. "If I offered a fish, red or white, to a lady of my acquaintance as a love offering, she would not receive it graciously. A diamond necklace would be more welcome."

Evelyn moved slightly in her chair. Walter went on, "This is certainly a lover speaking. He is on one side of the river—

> The love of the sister is upon yonder side;
> A stretch of water is between
> And a crocodile waiteth upon the sandbank.

> But I go down into the water, I walk upon the flood;
> My heart is brave upon the water.
> It is the love of her that makes me strong."

There was a brief silence when he stopped speaking. I don't know which impressed me more—the quaint charm of the lines

166

or the expertness with which the modest young man had deciphered them.

"Brilliant, Walter," I cried, forgetting propriety in my enthusiasm. "How inspiring it is to realize that noble human emotions are as ancient as man himself."

"It seems to me not so much noble as foolhardy," said Lucas lazily. "Any man who jumps into a river inhabited by crocodiles deserves to be eaten up."

"The crocodile is a symbol," I said scornfully. "A symbol of the dangers and difficulties any true lover would risk to win his sweetheart."

"That is very clever, Miss Amelia," Walter said, smiling at me.

"Too clever," growled Emerson. "Attempting to read the minds of the ancient Egyptians is a chancy business, Peabody. It is more likely that the crocodile is a typical lover's extravagance —a boast that sounds well, but that no man of sense would carry out."

I was about to reply when Evelyn fell into a fit of coughing.

"Well, well," Lucas said. "How happy I am that my little offering has proved to be so interesting! But don't you think we ought to make plans for tonight? The sun is almost down."

It was one of the most stunning sunsets I had ever beheld. The fine dust in the atmosphere produces amazing conditions of light, such as our hazy English air does not allow. There was something almost threatening about the sunset that evening; great bands of blood-red and royal purple, translucent blue like the glaze on ancient pottery, gold and amber and copper streaks.

I asked Lucas whether his crew might not help us guard the camp, but he shook his head.

"Evidently they met some of the villagers today. Your crew has also been infected, Miss Amelia. I would not be surprised if all of them fled."

"They cannot do that," I exclaimed. "I am paying them! Nor

167

do I believe that Reis Hassan would abandon his trust."

"He would have some excellent excuse," Lucas said cynically. "Adverse winds, threatening weather—any excuse for mooring elsewhere."

I was aware, then, of someone beside me. Turning, I beheld Michael, whom I had not seen all day.

"Sitt Hakim"—for so he always addressed me—"I must speak to you alone."

"Certainly," I said, although I was surprised at his request and at his interruption of our conversation.

"After dinner," Lucas said, giving the poor fellow a sharp look. Michael shrank back, and Lucas added, "Michael, or whatever your name is, you are not needed. My men will serve the meal. I promised them they might return before dark. Miss Peabody will speak with you later."

Michael obeyed, with a last pleading glance at me. As soon as he was out of earshot I said, "Lucas, I really cannot have you reprimanding my servants!"

"My first name!" Lucas exclaimed, with a broad smile. "You have broken down at last, Miss Amelia; you have done me the honor of addressing me as a friend. We must drink to that." And he refilled his wine glass.

"We—to use the word loosely—have drunk too much already," I retorted. "As for Michael—"

"Good heavens, such a fuss over a servant," Lucas said contemptuously. "I think I know what he wants to speak to you about, Miss Amelia, and if I were you I should not be in a hurry to hear it."

He held up his glass as if admiring the sparkle of the liquid in the fading light.

"What do you mean?" I asked.

Lucas shrugged.

"Why, the fellow means to be off. My men tell me that he is

168

in a complete funk. It is to his babbling, in no small measure, that I attribute their cowardice. No doubt he will have some specious excuse for leaving you, but leave you he will."

"I cannot believe it," Evelyn said firmly. "Michael is a fine man. Loyal, devoted—"

"But a native," Lucas finished. "With a native's weaknesses."

"And you are quite familiar with the weaknesses of the—er— natives," Emerson put in. He had not spoken much; for once his grating purr, like the throaty emanation of a very large, angry cat, did not offend my ears.

"Human beings are much the same the world over," Lucas replied negligently. "The ignorant always have their superstitions and their fondness for money."

"I bow to your superior knowledge," Emerson said. "I had been under the impression that it was not only the ignorant who are corrupted by money."

"I cannot believe Michael will desert us," I said, putting an end to the bickering. "I will speak to him later."

But later I was forced to admit, little as I liked it, that Lucas had been right. Michael was nowhere to be found. At first, when he did not seek me out, I assumed he had changed his mind about wanting to speak to me. It was not until we began thinking of our plans for the night that we realized he was missing. A search produced no trace of him. Lucas's servants—a shabby-looking group if I had ever seen one—had long since departed, so we could not ask if they had seen him.

"He had not even the courage to make his excuses to you," Lucas said, "Depend upon it, he has crept away."

Michael's defection left us in rather serious condition, I thought, but when I expressed the idea, Lucas pooh-poohed my concern.

"We ought to get to our posts," he continued. "With all due respect to your measures, I do not believe you went about the

169

business very sensibly."

"Let us hear your plans," said Emerson humbly.

I could not imagine what ailed the man. Except for brief outbursts of irony he adopted an attitude of subservient meekness toward Lucas, a man considerably his junior in age and certainly his inferior in experience. Nor could I believe that it was physical weakness that curbed his tongue. Emerson would criticize Old Nick himself when that individual came to bear him away as he lay dying.

"Very well," said Lucas, expanding visibly. "I see no reason to watch the village. If your villain means to frighten you away he will come here, and it is here that we must concentrate our forces. But we must not show force. You frightened him away the other night—"

"Oh, do you think that is what happened?" Emerson asked seriously.

"Only look at the sequence. The first time he came he ventured as far as the entrance to the ladies' residence and stood there for some time, if Miss Amelia's evidence is to be believed—"

"It is," I said, snapping my teeth together.

"Certainly, I did not mean. . . . Very well, then; on the next night, when Evelyn saw him, we do not know how far he progressed. He may have come no farther than the spot, down below, where she saw him. But on the third occasion he was definitely wary; he never came onto the ledge at all, and it was as if he knew you were awake and waiting for him."

Even in the dark I could sense Walter's increasing anger. The tone Lucas adopted was really quite insufferable. I was not surprised when the lad interrupted Lucas's lecture in a voice that shook with his efforts at self-control.

"You mean to imply, Lord Ellesmere, that the miscreant saw Abdullah and myself. I assure you—"

"No, no, my dear fellow," Lucas exclaimed. "I mean to imply

that your friend Mohammed was warned in advance!"

There was a muffled exclamation from Emerson. It sounded to me as if he were strangling on an oath he did not dare speak aloud. Lucas took it for an expression of chagrin, and he nodded graciously at the older man.

"Yes; Michael. I am convinced that he has been in league with the villagers. No doubt they promised him part of the loot."

"Loot!" Evelyn exclaimed, with unusual heat. "What reward could they offer, when they are so poor they cannot clothe their own children?"

"I see you have not reasoned it out," Lucas said complacently. "Perhaps I can see more clearly because I am removed from the terror that has haunted you in recent days."

"Enlighten us," said Emerson, through his teeth. I saw them gleaming in the dark, like the fangs of a wolf.

Lucas leaned back in his chair. He stretched out his long legs and gazed admiringly at his boots.

"I asked myself," he began, "what motive these people could have for driving you away. Malice is not a sufficient explanation; they need the money you were paying them. Does not the answer seem obvious to you? For generations these fellahin have been robbing the tombs of their remote ancestors. Their discoveries fill the antika shops of Cairo and Luxor, and you archaeologists are always complaining that whenever you find a tomb, the natives have been there before you. I suggest that the villagers have recently discovered such a tomb—a rich one, or they would not be so anxious to drive you away before you can find it."

The explanation had occurred to me, of course. I had discarded it, however, and now I voiced the objection aloud.

"That would mean that all the villagers are in league with Mohammed. I do not believe that. If you had seen the trembling fear of the old mayor—"

"You ladies always trust people," Lucas said. "These villagers

171

are congenital liars, Miss Amelia, and expert at dissimulation."

"If I really believed such a tomb existed, it would require an earthquake to make me leave," said Emerson.

"Naturally," Lucas said cheerfully. "I feel the same. All the more reason for catching our Mummy before he can do any serious damage."

"If your explanation is correct, my lord, catching the Mummy will not solve the problem." It was Walter who spoke. "According to you, the entire village knows that the Mummy is a fraud. Exposing him will not change their intention of forcing us to leave."

"But it will give us a hostage," Lucas explained tolerantly. "The mayor's own son. We will force him to lead us to the tomb and then dispatch a message back to Cairo for reinforcements. Also, once we have exposed the supposed curse we may be able to enlist the crews of our boats to help guard the tomb. They consider the villagers savages; the only thing they have in common is their superstitious terror of the dead."

"Another objection," I said. "If Michael is a traitor—though I still find it hard to believe—he will have warned the village of our plans for tonight. The Mummy again will be on his guard."

"What a splendidly logical mind you have," Lucas exclaimed. "That is quite true; and it prompts my next suggestion. We must appear to be off *our* guard, and we must offer the Mummy a lure, in order to entice it into our clutches."

"What sort of lure?" Walter asked suspiciously.

"I had not thought," Lucas said negligently. "I have appeared to drink more than I really have, in order to give the impression that I will sleep heavily. I wish you two gentlemen had done the same, but evidently you failed to follow my reasoning. Have you any suggestions, along the lines I have indicated?"

Several suggestions were made. Walter offered to take up his post at some distance, and then pretend to fall asleep. Emerson proposed to stand out in the open and consume an entire bottle of wine, and then collapse upon the sand as if overcome by intoxication. This last idea was received with the silent contempt it deserved, and no one spoke for a time. Then Evelyn stirred.

"I think there is only one object that may attract the creature to venture close enough to be seized," she said. "I shall steal out for a stroll after midnight. If I am far enough from the camp—"

The remainder of her sentence was drowned out by our cries of protest. Lucas alone remained silent; when Walter's voice had died, he said thoughtfully,

"But why not? There can be no danger; the villain only wants to catch one of us alone in order to play some silly trick."

"Do you call this a silly trick?" Emerson asked, indicating his bandaged shoulder. "You are mad, my lord, to consider such a thing. Walter," he added sternly, "be quiet. Do not speak if you cannot speak calmly."

"How can anyone speak calmly of such a thing?" Walter bellowed, in a fair imitation of his brother's best roar. "Under any circumstances it is an appalling idea; but remembering what that swine Mohammed said, when we were in the village . . ."

He broke off, with a glance at Evelyn.

"Lucas does not know that, Walter," she said steadily. "But I do. I overheard Amelia and Mr. Emerson speaking of it. Surely that makes my plan more practical."

Walter sputtered speechlessly. Lucas of course demanded to know what we were talking about. Seeing that Evelyn already knew the worst, I saw no reason not to repeat the statement to Lucas, and I did so, adding, "After all, Evelyn, you are being vain in assuming that the Mummy is only interested in you. Mohammed looked at *me* when he spoke; and I think if you are going to take a stroll, I will make myself available also. We will give him his choice of prey. Who knows, he may prefer a more mature type of lady."

This time the outcry was dominated by Emerson's bull-like voice.

"Why, Emerson," I said. "Do you mean to suggest that the Mummy will not be intrigued by me? You must not insult me."

"You are a fool, Peabody," said Emerson furiously. "And if you suppose I am going to allow any such idiotic, imbecilic, stupid—"

The plot was arranged as I had suggested. As we discussed it, it became more complex. By 'we,' I refer to Evelyn, Lucas, and myself. Emerson's contribution took the form of a low rumble rather like the sound of a volcano about to erupt. Walter's tense silence was almost as threatening. He took Evelyn's behavior as evidence of an understanding between her and Lucas, and reacted accordingly; it was not at all difficult to feign a quarrel, which was part of our plan, in case any spy should be watching. We parted acrimoniously. Walter tried to make a last protest, and Lucas responded by producing a pistol.

"I shall be within ten feet of Evelyn the entire time," he said in a thrilling whisper, holding the gun so that no one outside our group could see it. "I think our bandaged friend will be deterred by the mere sight of this. If not, I have no scruples about using it."

"And what about me?" I asked.

Emerson was unable to ignore the opportunity.

"God help the poor mummy who encounters you, Peabody," he said bitterly. "We ought to supply *it* with a pistol, to even the odds."

So saying, he stalked away. He was followed by Walter. Lucas chuckled and rubbed his hands together.

"What an adventure! I can hardly wait!"

"Nor I," said Evelyn. "Amelia, will you not reconsider?"

174

"Certainly not," I said in a loud voice, and walked off with my head held stiffly. I did not like leaving them alone together, but I felt it wise to add to the impression of ill will. It would be helpful later, when Evelyn and I staged our quarrel.

It was a one-sided argument, for Evelyn could not even pretend to shout at me. I made up the deficiency, and ended the argument by storming out of our tomb with my pillow and counterpane under my arm. I carried them down the ledge and into the little tent Michael had been occupying. Any watcher might readily assume that Evelyn and I had had a falling out, and that I had refused to share our sleeping quarters.

I could not strike a light, since it would have been visible through the canvas walls of the tent. It was not an honest English tent, only a low shelter of canvas; I could not stand erect in it. Squatting on the sand which was the floor of the shelter, I thought seriously of the man who had been its occupant. I was not at all convinced that Michael had left of his own free will. Men are frail creatures, of course; one does not expect them to exhibit the steadfastness of women. All the same, I did not like having my judgment of Michael disproved, and I determined to search the tent in the hope of finding some clue.

There was just enough light from without to show me that Michael's scanty possessions had been removed; but as I wriggled around, my fingers touched an object buried in the sand. I dug it out. I did not need to see the moonlight sparkling off its metallic surface to comprehend what it was. A crucifix. Part of the chain was still there, but only part. It had been snapped, not unfastened in the usual way.

My fingers closed tightly over the small object. Michael would never have left it; it was the only thing of value he owned, as well as an amulet against evil. The breaking of the chain confirmed my dread. It must have been snapped during a struggle.

Heedless of possible watchers, I crawled around the confined space searching for further clues, but found nothing. I was relieved; I had feared to find bloodstains.

So absorbed was I in the conjectures and suspicions which followed my discovery that time passed swiftly. A sound from without brought me back to myself. Stretching out flat, I lifted one edge of the canvas and peered out.

There was nothing to be seen—literally nothing. I had miscalculated, and I cursed my stupidity. The tent was behind a low ridge of tumbled stones that extended out from the cliff; I could not see the ledge, or the tomb entrances. This would never do. I must be in a position to assist Evelyn if the Mummy pursued her; and, in spite of my boasts, I did not really think it was after me. Squirming out from under the tent, I began to crawl forward. Before long I had reached the end of the rocky ridge and, rising to my knees, peered cautiously around it.

I pride myself on my self-possession; but I confess I almost let out a cry when I saw what stood beyond the ridge, only a few feet away. I had never seen it so close before. We claim to be rational, but there is a layer of primitive savagery in all of us. My brain sturdily denied superstition, but some deeply hidden weakness inside whimpered and cowered at the sight of the thing.

It was a grisly sight in the cold moonlight. In that clear, dry air the moon gives a queer, deceptive light; small details are visible in it, but shadows distort and deceive the eyes; the pallid glow robs objects of their real color and gives them a sickly grayish-green shade. The Mummy stood out as if faintly luminescent. The bandaged hands resembled a leper's stumps. The hands were raised as if in invocation; the creature stood not twenty feet away, with its back toward me. It faced the ledge, and the blind head was tilted back as if the eyeless sockets could see.

If Evelyn carried out our plan, she would shortly emerge from the tomb and start along the ledge. I expected her; I knew that there were four strong, alert men hidden nearby. But when the slight white form appeared in the dark mouth of the tomb, I started as violently as if I had seen an actual spirit.

Evelyn stood for a moment staring up at the stars. I knew she was trying to gather her courage to leave the security of the ledge, and my heart went out to her. She could not see the Mummy. At the moment she emerged it had moved with horrid swiftness, sinking down behind a rock at the cliff's foot.

I have written that there were four defenders close at hand; but I was not absolutely certain of that fact. Despite Emerson's sneers, I am not a stupid woman. I had already considered an idea that must have occurred to my more intelligent readers, and as Evelyn turned and slowly began to descend, my brain rapidly reviewed this reasoning.

I had been impressed by Walter's insistence that Mohammed had not left the village on one occasion when we were visited by the Mummy. Moreover, much as I disliked agreeing with Emerson on any subject, I felt as he did, that the plot was un-Egyptian —if I may use that term. Not only was it too sophisticated for the crafty but uneducated mind of Mohammed, but it smacked quite strongly of European romanticism. It might have been invented by a reader of gothic novels, inspired by *An Egyptian Princess* and other fictional horrors.

If Mohammed was not the Mummy, who was? It is no wonder that a certain name came immediately to mind; for he had the shallow but fertile intelligence, the bizarre sense of humor that suited the plot.

I was fully aware of the objections to my theory. The greatest was the question of motive. Why should Lucas, Lord Ellesmere, go to such absurd extremes in order to frighten his cousin? Or was it I he was trying to frighten? However, I was not worried about this; Lucas's motives were beyond my comprehension, and I thought it possible that he had some insane notion of terrifying Evelyn into leaving Egypt and accepting his protection. He would never suceed, but he might not have sense enough to know that.

The other objections were more difficult. Lucas might possibly have caught us up in time to play his role; we had dawdled and stopped along the way. But he could not have anticipated our stay at Amarna. It had been purely fortuitous, not known to him in advance.

Despite the objections, I clung to the notion of Lucas's villainy. The truth is, I wanted him to be a villain—a veritable crocodile, like the one in the ancient poem, that lay in wait for the lover seeking to win his sweetheart. A woman's instinct, I always feel, supersedes logic. So you may believe that I waited with considerable interest to see whether Lucas would appear to rescue Evelyn.

My heart beat in sympathy with the girl as she advanced along the path that led away from safety. She put on a good act of indifference; only once, as she passed the quarters of Walter and his brother, did she falter and glance aside. But she squared her shoulders and went on. She reached the bottom of the ledge and started out across the sand.

If she continued on the route she had chosen, she would pass too close to the Mummy for comfort. I wondered if I was the only one who knew the creature's precise location. I was not sure where the men lay concealed; perhaps they had not seen the thing. If so, it was incumbent on me to interfere before Evelyn went much farther. I did not know the creature's intentions. It would be shock enough if it merely jumped out and began moaning and waving its arms. But suppose it tried to touch her? The horror of that, to a girl of Evelyn's sensitive temperament, would be dreadful. And yet if I moved too precipitately I might frighten the thing away before the men could seize it. I hesitated, in an agony of doubt.

Evelyn was walking straight toward the boulder behind which the Mummy lay concealed. But—wait! It had been concealed there; it was there no longer. While my attention had been fixed on Evelyn it must have slid away. Where was it now? What was happening? And where were our stalwart defenders? Except for Evelyn's slim white figure, not a living soul moved in the moonlight. The silence was so intense I could hear the pounding of my heart.

A flash of pale color among the rocks at the foot of the path! How silently the creature had moved! It was between Evelyn and the ledge now; she could not retreat to that point of safety. I could endure the suspense no longer. I started to rise. At the same moment the Mummy stepped out into the open, emitting a low, moaning growl that brought Evelyn spinning around to confront it.

Thirty paces—not more—separated the grisly monster from its intended prey. Evelyn's hands went to her throat. She swayed. I tried to get to my feet—stepped on the folds of my dressing gown —tripped—fell prostrate, my limbs entangled—and saw, from that position, the next act of the drama.

With slow, measured steps the Mummy advanced on Evelyn, who did not move. Either she was paralyzed by terror or she was carrying out her part of the plot with what seemed to me excessive devotion. I would have been in flight by then, and I am not ashamed to admit it. The blank, featureless face of the thing was more frightening than any possible distortion or scarred countenance. Two dark hollows, under the ridges of the brows, were the only sign of eyes.

Scratching at the sand, kicking ineffectually, I shouted. Evelyn did not even turn her head. She stood as if mesmerized, her hands clasped on her breast, watching the thing advance. Then—just as I was about to explode with horror and frustration—rescue came! Walter was the first to appear. In a single great bound he burst out of the tomb and reached the edge of the cliff. He flung himself down, preparatory to sliding down the slope. At the same moment Lucas stepped out from behind the concealment of a

179

heap of rocks. I was not even disappointed at the collapse of my theory, I was so relieved to see him—and to see the firearm he held. He shouted and pointed the pistol.

The Mummy stopped. It stood still for a moment, its head turning from side to side, as if it were considering its next move. Its appearance of cool deliberation was maddening to me. I finally managed to struggle free of my encumbering skirts and stagger to my feet. Another shout from Lucas stopped me as I was about to run to Evelyn. His meaning was plain; he did not want me to get into the line of fire. The pistol was aimed straight at the Mummy's bandaged breast, but Lucas did not shoot; he meant only to threaten, and I could not help but admire his calm in that tense moment.

Lucas stepped slowly forward, his gun at the ready. The eyeless head turned toward him; from the creature came a horrible mewing cry. It was too much for Evelyn, whose nerves were already strained to the breaking point. She swayed and collapsed into a heap on the ground. With another ghastly moan, the Mummy lumbered toward her.

I felt sure then that the mummy wrappings did not conceal the form of Mohammed. These people knew firearms and had a healthy respect for them. Even as the thought passed through my mind, Lucas fired.

The explosion thundered through the silent night. The Mummy stopped and jerked back. One bandaged paw went to its breast. Holding my breath, I waited to see it fall. It did not! It came on, more slowly, emitting that low mewing growl. Lucas took careful aim and fired again. No more than a dozen yards separated the two; this time I could have sworn I saw the missile strike, full in the center of the creature's rotting body. Again it pawed at the place where the bullet had struck; again it came on.

Lucas stepped back a few paces. His face shone with sweaty pallor; his open mouth looked like a black wound. He fumbled in his jacket pocket. I deduced that his weapon held only two bullets and that he now had to refill it.

Walter had paused, poised on the edge of the drop, to see what would ensue. Needless to say, the actions which have taken so long to describe only occupied a few moments of real time. Now, with a shout of warning, Walter let himself drop. His booted feet struck the sloping heap of rocky detritus with a force that started a miniature landslide, but he did not lose his balance. Slipping, sliding, running, he reached the bottom and rushed on without a halt.

Lucas was shouting too, but I could not hear him because of the crash of falling rock. I would not have known he was speaking if I had not seen his lips move. He had finished loading the gun; he raised it. I cried out—but too late. Carried on by the impetus of his leap, Walter flung himself at the menace just as Lucas fired for the third time. And this time his bullet found a vulnerable target. Walter stood stock still. His head turned toward Lucas. His expression was one of utter astonishment. Then his head fell on his breast; his knees gave way; and he collapsed face down onto the sand.

For the space of a single heartbeat there was not a sound. Lucas stood frozen, the pistol dangling from his lax hand; his face was a mask of horror. Then, from the Mummy, came a sound that froze the blood in my veins. The creature was laughing—howling, rather, with a hideous mirth that resembled the shrieks of a lost soul. Still laughing, it retreated, and none of the horrified watchers moved to prevent it. Even after the thing had vanished from sight around the curve of the cliff, I could hear its ghastly laughter reverberating from the rocky walls.

9

WHEN I reached Walter's side I found Emerson there before me. Where he had been, or how he had come, I did not know; brain and organs of sight were hazy with horror. Kneeling by his young brother, Emerson ripped the bloodstained shirt away from the body. Then he looked up at Lucas, who had joined us and was staring down at the fallen man.

"Shot in the back," said Emerson, in a voice like none I had heard from him heretofore. "Your hunting colleagues in England would not approve, Lord Ellesmere."

"My God," stammered Lucas, finding his voice at last. "Oh, God—I did not mean. . . . I warned him to keep away, he rushed in, I could not help. . . . For the love of heaven, Mr. Emerson, don't say he is—he is—"

"He is not dead," said Emerson. "Do you think I would be

sitting here, discussing the matter, if you had killed him?"

My knees gave way. I sat down hard on the warm sand.

"Thank God," I whispered.

Emerson gave me a critical look.

"Pull yourself together, Peabody, this is no time for a fit of the vapors. You had better see to the other victim; I think she has merely fainted. Walter is not badly hurt. The wound is high and clean. Fortunately his lordship's weapon uses small-caliber bullets."

Lucas let out his breath. Some of the color had returned to his face.

"I know you don't like me, Mr. Emerson," he said, with a new and becoming humility. "But will you believe me when I say that the news you have just given us is the best I have heard for a long, long time?"

"Hmm," said Emerson, studying him. "Yes, your lordship; if it is any consolation to you, I do believe you. Now go and give Amelia a hand with Evelyn."

Evelyn was stirring feebly when we reached her, and when she learned what had happened to Walter she was too concerned about him to think of herself. It is wonderful what strength love can lend; rising up from a faint of terror, she walked at Walter's side as his brother carried him to his bed, and insisted on helping me clean and dress the wound.

I was relieved to find that Emerson's assessment was correct. I had not had any experience with gunshot wounds, but a common-sense knowledge of anatomy assured me that the bullet had gone through the fleshy part of the right shoulder, without striking a bone.

I had not the heart to send Evelyn away, but really she was more of a handicap than a help; whenever I reached for a cloth or a bandage she was supposed to hand me, I would find her staring bemusedly at the unconscious lad, tears in her eyes and her feelings writ plain on her face for all the world to see. I could hardly blame her; Walter reminded me of the beautiful Greek youth Adonis, dying among the river reeds. He was slight, but his muscular development was admirable; the long lashes that shadowed his cheek, the tumbled curls on his brow, and the boyish droop of his mouth made a picture that must appeal to any woman who is sensitive to beauty and pathos.

Walter was conscious by the time I finished bandaging the wound. He did not speak at first, only watched me steadily, and when I had finished he thanked me with a pallid smile. His first look, however, had been for Evelyn; and having assured himself that she was safe, he did not look at her again. As she turned away with her bowl of water, I saw her lips tremble.

Emerson had produced a new atrocity—a dreadful pipe that smelled like a hot summer afternoon on a poultry farm—and was sitting in a corner puffing out clouds of foul smoke. When I had finished with Walter, Emerson rose to his feet and stretched.

"The evening's entertainment is over, it seems," he remarked. "We may as well get some sleep for what is left of the night."

"How can you talk of sleeping?" I demanded. "I am so full of questions and comments—"

"More of the latter than the former, I fancy," said Emerson, puffing away at his pipe. "I don't think Walter is up to your conversation, Peabody. It takes a well man, in his full strength, to—"

"Now, Radcliffe, that will do," Walter interrupted. His voice was weak, but the smile he gave me was his old sweet smile. "I am not feeling too bad; and I agree with Miss Amelia that we have much to discuss."

"I, too, agree," said Lucas, breaking a long—for him—silence. "But first—may I suggest a restorative, all around? A little brandy might ease Walter's pain—"

"I do not approve of spirits for such injuries," I said firmly.

184

Emerson snorted through his pipe, producing a great puff of smoke.

"I am not in much pain," Walter said. "But perhaps brandy might help—the ladies. They—they have undergone a considerable shock."

So we had our brandy. Emerson seemed to enjoy his very much. Although I do not ordinarily approve of spirits, they are of use in some situations; I felt the need of stimulants myself, and the liquor lessened Evelyn's pallor. She was still wearing her nightclothes and dressing gown, not having had time to dress. They were embroidered lawn, of a pale blue, and I could see that Lucas admired them.

"Well, Peabody," said Emerson. "What is your first question?"

"Now that is not easy to say. The entire episode has been so bewildering. . . . First, though, I should like to know what has happened to Abdullah."

"Good heavens," exclaimed Lucas. "I had quite forgotten him. Where is the fellow?"

"Don't waste your suspicions on Abdullah," said Emerson. "He is probably following the Mummy. I told him to do so if we failed to apprehend it. But I fancy he will be returning soon. . . . Ah, yes, I believe I hear him now."

He beamed as complacently as if he had arranged Abdullah's opportune arrival. The tall, stately form of the foreman now appeared at the entrance to the tomb. His eyes widened as he beheld Walter, and some time was wasted on explanations before Abdullah told us his story. Again, I translate into ordinary English.

He had been stationed by Emerson some distance from the camp. He had heard the shots but of course had not known what they betokened. They had, however, alerted him, and thus he was able to catch sight of the Mummy when it left us. Its speed amazed him; he kept repeating, "It ran like a swift young man."

He had not tried to interfere with the creature. Indeed, I think he was afraid to do so. But he had summoned up enough courage to follow it, at a safe distance.

"Where did it go?" I demanded. "To the village?"

Abdullah shook his head.

"Not village. Into the wadi, to the royal tomb. I did not follow; I thought you need me, I come here."

Emerson laughed shortly.

"So it is the ghost of Khuenaten we have with us? Come, now, Abdullah, that does not make sense. Our ghost is an avenging Amonist priest, if you remember, not a follower of the heretic king."

"Oh, stop it," I said impatiently. "I cannot blame Abdullah for not following the thing. We agreed, did we not, that the villain, whoever he is, must conceal his grisly costume in some remote place. He was on his way there. Perhaps he went to the village later."

Emerson was about to reply when Evelyn's quiet voice broke in.

"I think we should end the discussion. Walter ought to rest."

Walter opened his eyes when she spoke, but I had seen the signs of fatigue too.

"Evelyn is right," I said, rising. "She, too, has had a nasty experience."

"I am all right," Walter muttered.

"Of course you are," I said, with a cheer I did not feel. Fever commonly follows such wounds, and infection is rampant in Egypt. But there was no point in anticipating trouble. "All you need is rest. Come along, Evelyn—Lucas—"

"I must say one thing first." Lucas bent over the pallet where the sick man lay. "Walter, please tell me you forgive my clumsiness. I had no intention—"

"It was very stupid, all the same," said Emerson, as Walter

made a feeble gesture of conciliation.

"You are right," Lucas muttered. "But if you had been in my place—you saw, I know, but you did not feel the recoil of the pistol, and then see that ghastly thing come on and on. . . ." With a sudden movement he pulled the gun from his pocket. "I shall never use this again. There is one bullet left. . . ."

His arm straightened, pointing the gun out the mouth of the tomb. His finger was actually tightening on the trigger when Emerson moved. The man was constantly surprising me; his leap had a tigerish swiftness I would not have expected. His fingers clasped around Lucas's wrist with a force that made the younger man cry out.

"You fool," Emerson mumbled around the stem of the pipe. Snatching the gun from Lucas's palsied hand, he put it in his belt. "The echoes from a shot in this confined place would deafen us. Not to mention the danger of a ricochet. . . . I will take charge of your weapon, Lord Ellesmere. Now go to bed."

Lucas left without another word. I felt an unexpected stab of pity as I watched him go, his shoulders bowed and his steps dragging. Evelyn and I followed. As soon as she had dropped off to sleep I went back onto the ledge, and somehow I was not surprised to see Emerson sitting there. His feet dangling over empty space, he was smoking his pipe and staring out at the serene vista of star-strewn sky with apparent enjoyment.

"Sit down, Peabody," he said, gesturing at the ledge beside him. "That discussion was getting nowhere, but I think you and I might profit from a quiet chat."

I sat down.

"You called me Amelia, earlier," I said, somewhat to my own surprise.

"Did I?" Emerson did not look at me. "A moment of aberration, no doubt."

"You were entitled to be distracted," I admitted. "Seeing your brother struck down. . . . It was not entirely Lucas's fault, Emerson. Walter rushed into the path of the bullet."

"In view of the fact that his lordship had already fired twice without result, I would have supposed he would have sense enough to stop."

I shivered.

"Get a shawl, if you are cold," said Emerson, smoking.

"I am not cold. I am frightened. Are none of us willing to admit the consequences of what we saw? Emerson, the bullets struck that thing. I saw them strike."

"Did you?"

"Yes! Where were you, that you did not see?"

"I saw its hands, or paws, clutch at its breast," Emerson admitted. "Peabody, I expected better of you. Are you becoming a spiritualist?"

"I hope I am reasonable enough not to deny an idea simply because it is unorthodox," I retorted. "One by one our rational explanations are failing."

"I can think of at least two rational explanations for the failure of the bullets to harm the creature," Emerson said. "A weapon of that type is extremely inaccurate, even in the hands of an expert, which I believe his lordship is not. He may have fired two clean misses, and the Mummy put on a performance of being hit in order to increase our mystification."

"That is possible," I admitted. "However, if I stood in the Mummy's shoes—or sandals, rather—I should hate to depend on Lucas's bad marksmanship. What is your other explanation?"

"Some form of armor," Emerson replied promptly. "I don't suppose you read novels, Peabody? A gentleman named Rider Haggard is gaining popularity with his adventurous tales; his most recent book, *King Solomon's Mines,* concerns the fantastic experiences of three English explorers who seek the lost diamond mines of that biblical monarch. At one point in the tale he

188

mentions chain mail, and its usefulness in deflecting the swords and spears of primitive tribes. I believe it would also stop a small-caliber bullet. Have we not all heard of men being saved from bullet wounds by a book—it is usually a Bible—carried in their breast pockets? I have often thought it a pity that our troops in the Sudan are not equipped with armor. Even a padded leather jerkin, such as the old English foot soldiers wore, would save many a life."

"Yes," I admitted. "The wrappings could cover some such protective padding. And I have read of Crusaders' armor being found in this mysterious continent, even in Cairo antique shops. But would such an ingenious idea occur to a man like Mohammed?"

"Let us abandon that idea once and for all. Mohammed was not the Mummy."

"How can you be so sure?"

"Its height," Emerson replied calmly. "For a moment Walter was close enough so that I could measure their comparative heights. It was as tall as he, or taller. Mohammed and the other villagers are small people. Bad diet and poor living conditions. . . ."

"How can you be so cool? Discussing diet, at such a time. . . ."

"Why," said Emerson, puffing away, "I am beginning to enjoy myself. Lord Ellesmere's sporting instincts have infected me; he reminds me that an Englishman's duty is to preserve icy detachment under any and all circumstances. Even if he were being boiled to provide a cannibal's dinner it would be incumbent upon him to—"

"I would expect that you would be taking notes on the dietary habits of aborigines as the water bubbled around your neck," I admitted. "But I cannot believe you are really so calm about Walter's injury."

"That is perceptive of you. In fact, I mean to catch the person

189

who is responsible for injuring him."

I believed that. Emerson's voice was even, but it held a note that made me glad I was not the person he referred to.

"You have left off your bandages," I said suddenly.

"You are absolutely brilliant tonight, Peabody."

"I am sure you should not—"

"I cannot afford to pamper myself. Matters are approaching a climax."

"Then what shall we do?"

"You, asking for advice? Let me feel your brow, Peabody; I am sure you must be fevered."

"Really, your manners are atrocious," I exclaimed angrily.

Emerson raised one hand in a command for silence.

"We had better take a stroll," he said. "Unless you want to waken Miss Evelyn. I don't know why you can't carry on a reasonable discussion without raising your voice."

He offered me a hand to help me rise; but the jerk with which he lifted me to my feet was not gentle; for a moment my weight dangled from his arm in an undignified manner. He set me on my feet and walked off. I followed, and caught him up at the bottom of the cliff. We strolled along in silence for a time. Even Emerson was moved by the beauty of the night.

Before us, the moonlight lay upon the tumbled desolation of sand that had once been the brilliant capital of a pharaoh. For a moment I had a vision; I seemed to see the ruined walls rise up again, the stately villas in their green groves and gardens, the white walls of the temples, adorned with brilliantly painted reliefs, the flash of gold-tipped flagstaffs, with crimson pennants flying in the breeze. The wide, tree-lined avenues were filled with a laughing throng of white-clad worshipers, going to the temple; and before them all raced the golden chariot of the king, drawn by a matched pair of snow-white horses. . . . Gone. All gone, into the dust to which we must all descend when our hour comes.

190

"Well?" I said, shaking off my melancholy mood. "You promised me the benefit of your advice. I await it breathlessly."

"What would you say to striking camp tomorrow?"

"Give up? Never!"

"Just what I would have expected an Englishwoman to say. Are you willing to risk Miss Evelyn?"

"You think the Mummy has designs on her?"

"I am unwilling to commit myself as to its original intentions," said Emerson pedantically. "But it seems clear that the Mummy is now interested in her. I am afraid it is not attracted by your charms, Peabody. It must have known you were in the tent; I was watching, and I thought for a time, seeing the walls bulge and vibrate, that you would have the whole structure down about your ears. What were you doing—physical knee jerks?"

I decided to ignore his childish malice.

"I was looking for evidence of what had happened to Michael," I explained. "I found this."

I showed him the crucifix, pointing out the break in the chain. He looked grave.

"Careless of the attacker, to leave such a clue."

"You believe Michael was forcibly abducted?"

"I am inclined to think so."

"And you do nothing? A faithful follower—a helper we badly need—"

"What can I do?" Emerson inquired, reasonably enough. "One result of these activities has been to keep us fully occupied; we have not had time, or personnel, for retaliation; we can barely enact defensive measures. I think Michael has not been harmed."

"I wish I could be so confident. Well, we can hardly march into the village and demand that he be delivered up to us. What a pity we could not apprehend the Mummy. We might have effected an exchange of prisoners."

"We could do a great deal more than that if we had the

Mummy," Emerson replied. He tapped out his pipe and put it in his pocket. "It does seem as if the stars are against us. Twice now we ought to have had our hands on it. But let us not waste time in vain regrets. I am concerned for Miss Evelyn—"

"Do you suppose I am not? I think I must take her away. She might at least sleep on the dahabeeyah, with the crew to guard her."

"The boat is only a few miles from here. Our mummified friend seems to have excellent powers of locomotion."

I felt as if a bucket of cold water had been dashed over me.

"It surely would not venture there! If its primary aim is to convince you to quit the site—"

"I am not in a position to state, unequivocally, what the aim of an animated mummy might be. But if that is its purpose, a serious threat to Miss Evelyn might accomplish it. Do you suppose Walter would remain here if he believed she was in danger?"

"Ah," I said. "So you have observed that."

"I am not blind, nor deaf, nor wholly insensible. I sense also that she is not indifferent to him."

"And, of course, you disapprove."

"Why, Peabody, you know my mercenary nature. I need money for my excavations. The aim is noble—to rescue knowledge from the vandalism of man and time. Walter might make an advantageous marriage; he is a handsome fellow, don't you think? You could hardly suppose I would allow him to throw himself away on a penniless girl. Miss Evelyn *is* penniless, is she not?"

As he spoke, in an insufferably sarcastic tone, I thought I detected a faint smell of singeing cloth.

"She is penniless," I replied shortly.

"A pity," Emerson mused. "Well, but if she is not good enough for Walter, she is too nice a child to be handed over to the Mummy. I propose that we test our theory. Let her sleep tomor-

192

row night on the dahabeeyah, and—we will see what happens. You will have to use trickery, Peabody, to induce her to stay there; she does not lack courage, and will not willingly leave Walter. I suggest we propose an expedition to the boat tomorrow, to fetch various necessities. I will leave Abdullah to guard Walter—"

"Why not carry Walter with us? He would be better on the boat."

"I don't think we should risk moving him."

"Perhaps not. But to leave him here alone, with only Abdullah. . . . He is not the most reliable of guards. I think he is increasingly fearful."

"Walter will only be alone for a few hours, in daylight. I will return as soon as I have escorted you to the dahabeeyah. You must counterfeit illness, or something, to keep Miss Evelyn there overnight."

"Yes, sir," I said. "And then?"

"Then you must remain on guard. I may be wrong; the Mummy may not come. But if it does, you and you alone will be responsible for Miss Evelyn's safety. Can you take on such a task?"

The smell of singeing cloth grew stronger. I have a very keen sense of smell.

"Certainly I can."

"You had better take this," he said, and, to my consternation, produced the revolver he had taken from Lucas. I shrank back as he offered it.

"No, don't be absurd! I have never handled firearms; I might injure someone. I can manage without a gun, you may be sure."

"So you do admit to some weaknesses."

There was definitely a small curl of smoke issuing from the pocket in which Emerson had placed his pipe. I had been about to point this out. Instead I remarked, "I have said that I can manage without a weapon. How many men can claim as much?

Good night, Emerson. I accept your plan. You need have no fear of my failing in my role."

Emerson did not reply. A most peculiar expression had come over his face. I watched him for a moment, relishing the situation with, I fear, a malice most unbecoming a Christian woman.

"Your pocket is on fire," I added. "I thought when you put your pipe away that it was not quite out, but you dislike advice so much. . . . Good night."

I went away, leaving Emerson dancing up and down in the moonlight, beating at his pocket with both hands.

II

To my infinite relief, Walter was better next morning. The dreaded fever of infection had not appeared, and I was optimistic about his prospects, so long as he did not aggravate the wound. I had only time for a quick exchange with Emerson that morning. We agreed that Walter should not attempt the trip to the dahabeeyah.

So the scheme we had arranged was carried out. We had great difficulty in persuading Evelyn to go, but finally she agreed, as she thought, to a quick journey to and from the river. Glancing back, as our caravan set forth, I saw Abdullah squatting on the ledge, his knees up and his turbaned head bowed. He looked like the spirit of an ancient scribe brooding over the desolate site of his former home.

The walk, through sand and under a broiling sun, was not an easy one. It was with considerable relief that I made out the mast and furled sails of the *Philae*, bobbing gently at anchor. Beyond, I saw Lucas's boat. It was called the *Cleopatra*. If that famous queen was as fatally lovely as history claims, her namesake did not live up to its model; the *Cleopatra* was smaller than the *Philae* and not nearly so neat. As we drew nearer I saw some members

194

of the crew lounging about the deck; they were as dirty and unkempt as their boat, and the sullen indifference with which they watched us contrasted eloquently with the enthusiastic welcome of my men. You would have thought we had returned from the jaws of death instead of a place only four miles away. Reis Hassan seemed to recognize Emerson; his white teeth gleamed in a smile as their hands met, and the two fell into animated conversation.

I did not need to follow the rapid Arabic to know that Emerson's first questions concerned our missing Michael; it had been my intention to investigate that matter immediately if he had not. The reis's response was equally intelligible—a firm negative.

And yet, despite my ignorance of the language, I felt there was something hidden behind the captain's steady look and quick reply—some reservation he did not care to state. I was ready, by that time, to believe that everyone around me was party to the plot, but I knew Hassan might be quite innocent and yet not quite candid. He might be concealing a shamed, fugitive Michael; he might have heard the tales of the villagers and be reluctant to confess his own fears.

Emerson's flashing glance at me indicated that he had similar doubts. He turned back to the reis with a barrage of questions, but got little satisfaction. Michael had not been seen. No doubt he had become bored, or lonely for his family, as "these Christians" were wont to do, and had deserted.

Emerson stamped impatiently as Hassan took his departure. He really did behave like a spoiled child at times; but now I could hardly blame him. He was on fire to return to Walter, and could not waste more time in interrogation; when an Egyptian decides not to speak, it requires a Grand Inquisitor to get a word out of him. Evelyn had gone below to pack the articles that were our ostensible reason for coming. Lucas had gone to his own dahabeeyah. Emerson and I stood alone on the upper deck.

"I must get back," he muttered. "Peabody, all is not well. The crewmen have been talking with the villagers. One of them has already run away, and I think Hassan is doubtful of his ability to control the others. Not that he would admit it—"

"I felt something was wrong. But you ought not to wait; I too am apprehensive about Walter. Go."

"You will not forget what I have told you?"

"No."

"And you will act as I have directed?"

"Yes."

The sun on the upper deck was burning hot, with the awning rolled back. Streaks of perspiration trickled down Emerson's face.

"The situation is intolerable," he exclaimed. "Amelia, swear to me that you will do precisely what I said; you will not take foolish chances, or expose yourself—"

"I have said I would. Don't you understand English?"

"Good God! You are the one who fails to understand; don't you realize there is not another woman living whom I would—"

He broke off. From the far end of the deck Lucas approached, his hands in his pockets, his lips pursed in a whistle. The strains of "Rule, Britannia" floated to my ears.

Emerson gave me a long, piercing look—a look that burned itself into my brain. Without another word he turned and vanished down the ladder to the lower deck.

I could not face Lucas just then. I followed Emerson. He was out of sight by the time I reached the lower deck, so I went on down, into the area where the cabins were located. My cheeks were tingling; I felt a foolish desire to imitate Lucas's whistling. It had been very hot on the upper deck; even those few moments had burned my face so that it felt warm and flushed.

In the narrow, dark corridor I ran full tilt into Evelyn.

"Amelia," she cried, clutching my arm. "I have just seen Mr. Emerson from my window. He is leaving—he is on his way back, without us. Stop him, pray do; I must go back—"

With a start of repugnance I remembered the role I must play.

Evelyn was trying to brush past me. I put my hands on her arms and leaned heavily against her.

"I am feeling ill," I muttered. "I really think I must lie down. . . ."

Evelyn responded as I had known she would. She assisted me to my cabin and helped me loosen my dress. I pretended to be faint; I am afraid I did not do a convincing job of it, what with shame at betraying her trust and the odd exhilaration that bubbled inside me; but poor Evelyn never suspected me of false dealing. She worked assiduously to restore me; indeed, she waved the smelling salts so ardently under my nose that I went into a fit of sneezing.

"Leave off, do," I exclaimed between paroxysms. "My head will fly off in a moment!"

"You are better," Evelyn said eagerly. "That was your old strong voice. *Are* you better, Amelia? Dare I leave you for a moment? I will run after Mr. Emerson and tell him to wait—"

I fell back on the pillow with a heartrending groan.

"I cannot walk, Evelyn. I think—I think I must stay here tonight. Of course," I added craftily, "if you feel you must go— and leave me here alone—I will not try to keep you. . . ."

I closed my eyes, but I watched Evelyn through my lashes. The struggle on the girl's face made me feel like Judas. Almost I weakened. Then I remembered Emerson's look, and his words. "There is not another woman alive whom I would—" What had he meant to say? "Whom I would trust, as I am trusting in your strength and courage?" Would the sentence, interrupted by Lucas, have ended in some such wise? If so—and there could hardly be any other meaning—it was an accolade I could not fail to deserve. The triumph of converting that arrogant misogynist into an admission that Woman, as represented by my humble

197

self, had admirable qualities. . . . No, I thought, if I must choose between Evelyn or Emerson—or rather, between Evelyn and my own principles—I must betray Evelyn. It was for her own good.

Still, I felt rather uncomfortable as I watched her fight her silent battle. Her hands were pressed so tightly together that the knuckles showed white, but when she spoke her voice was resigned.

"Of course I will stay with you, Amelia. How could you suppose I would do otherwise? Perhaps a quiet night's sleep will restore you."

"I am sure it will," I mumbled, unable to deny the girl that much comfort. Little did she know what sort of night I half expected!

I ought to have stayed in my bed, refusing food, to carry out my performance; but as the day went on, I began to be perfectly ravenous. Darkness fell, and I felt I was safe; not even Evelyn would insist that we make the journey by night. So I admitted to feeling a little better, and agreed that nourishment would do me good. I had a frightful time trying to pick at the food and not bolt it down like a laborer. The cook had outdone himself, as if in celebration of our return, and Lucas had fetched several bottles of champagne from his dahabeeyah.

He was attired in evening dress; the austere black and white became his sturdy body and handsome face very well. He had become exceedingly tanned. I felt as if he ought to be wearing the crimson sashes and orders of some exotic foreign emissary, or even the gold-embroidered robes of a Beduin sheikh.

We dined on the upper deck. The canopy had been rolled back, and the great vault of heaven, spangled with stars, formed a roof finer than any oriental palace could boast. As we sipped our soup, a feeling of unreality swept over me. It was as if the preceding week had never happened. This was a night like the first nights on the dahabeeyah, surrounded by the sights and sounds and

198

olfactory sensations that had so quickly become dear and familiar. The soft lapping of the water against the prow and the gentle sway of the boat; the liquid voices of the crewmen down below, as mellow and wordless as music to our untrained ears; the balmy night breeze, carrying the homely scents of burning charcoal and pitch and unwashed Egyptian; and under them all the indefinable, austere perfume of the desert itself. I knew I would never be free of its enchantment, never cease to desire it after it was gone. And although the strange events of past days seemed remote and dreamlike, I knew that in some indefinable way they had heightened the enjoyment of the journey, given it a sharp tang of danger and adventure.

Lucas was drinking too much. I must admit he held his wine like a gentleman; his speech did not become slurred nor his movements unsteady. Only his eyes showed the effect, becoming larger and more brilliant as the evening wore on; and his conversation became, if possible, quicker and more fantastical. One moment he declared his intention of returning to the camp, for fear of missing another encounter with the Mummy; the next moment he was ridiculing the whole affair—the Emerson brothers, their shabby way of life, the absurdity of spending the years of youth grubbing for broken pots—and declaring his intention to move on to the luxuries of Luxor and the glories of Thebes.

Evelyn sat like a pale statue, unresponsive to the jeers or to the increasingly soft glances her cousin directed at her. She had not dressed for dinner, but was wearing a simple morning frock, a faded pink lawn sprigged with tiny rosebuds.

Lucas kept looking at the gown; finally he burst out, "I don't mean to criticize your choice of costume, Cousin, but I yearn to see you in something becoming your beauty and your station. Since that first night in Cairo I have not seen you wear a gown that suited you. What a pity I could not bring your boxes with me!"

"You are too conscientious, Lucas," Evelyn replied. "It may relieve you to know that I am not looking forward to unpacking those boxes. I shall never wear the gowns again; their elegance would remind me too painfully of Grandfather's generosity."

"When we return to Cairo we will burn them unopened," Lucas declared extravagantly. "A grand auto-da-fé of the past! I want to supply you with a wardrobe fitting your station, my dear Evelyn—with garments that will have no painful memories associated with them."

Evelyn smiled, but her eyes were sad.

"I *have* the wardrobe befitting my station," she replied, with a loving glance at me. "But we cannot destroy the past, Lucas, nor yield to weakness. No; fortified by my faith as a Christian, I will look over Grandfather's gifts in solitude. There are trinkets, mementos I cannot part with; I will keep them to remind me of my errors. Not in any spirit of self-flagellation," she added, with another affectionate look at me. "I have too much to be thankful for to indulge in that error."

"Spoken like an Englishwoman and a Christian," I exclaimed. "But indeed, I have difficulty in hearing you speak, Evelyn; what is going on down below? The men are making a great deal of noise."

I spoke in part to change a subject that was clearly painful to Evelyn, but I was right; for some time the soft murmur of voices from the deck below had been gradually increasing in volume. The sound was not angry or alarming, there was considerable laughter and some unorganized singing.

Lucas smiled. "They are celebrating your return. I ordered a ration of whiskey to be served out. A few of them refused, on religious grounds; but the majority seem willing to forget the admonitions of the Prophet for one night. Moslems are very much like Christians in some ways."

"You ought not to have done that," I said severely. "We ought

200

to strengthen the principles of these poor people, not corrupt them with our civilized vices."

"There is nothing vicious about a glass of wine," Lucas protested.

"Well, you have had enough," I said, removing the bottle as he reached for it. "Kindly recall, my lord, that our friends at the camp are still in danger. If we should receive a distress signal in the night—"

Evelyn let out a cry of alarm, and Lucas glared at me.

"Your friend Emerson would not call for help if he were being burned at the stake," he said, with a sneer that robbed the statement of any complimentary effect. "Why do you frighten Evelyn unnecessarily?"

"I am not frightened," Evelyn said. "And I agree with Amelia. Please, Lucas, don't drink any more."

"Your slightest wish is my command," said Lucas softly.

But I feared the request had come too late. Lucas had already taken more than was good for him.

Soon after this Evelyn pleaded fatigue and suggested that I too retire, in order to build up my strength. The reminder came at an opportune time, for I had forgotten I was supposed to be ailing. I sent her to her cabin and then called the reis; the noise from below was now so great that I was afraid Evelyn would not be able to sleep. Hassan, at least, showed no signs of inebriation, but I had a hard time communicating with him, for, of course, he spoke very little English. How I missed our devoted Michael! Eventually I got the reis to understand that we were retiring, and we wished the noise kept down. He bowed and retired; shortly thereafter the voices did drop in tone.

Lucas had been sitting in sullen silence, staring at the wine bottle, which was at my elbow. I was of two minds as to whether to carry it with me when I retired. I decided against it. Lucas probably had plenty more.

As I rose, he jumped up and held my chair.

"Excuse my bad manners, Miss Amelia," he said quietly. "But indeed, I am not at all drunk. I merely wanted to convey that impression."

"It seems to be a favorite plan of yours," I said drily, walking toward the stairs. Lucas followed me.

"I am sleeping in one of the cabins below," he said, in the same soft voice. "I will be awake and ready in case I am needed."

Now I had said nothing to Lucas of my conversation with Emerson the preceding night. Emerson had not needed to caution me against it; I had no particular confidence in Lucas myself. His comment meant that, independently, he had arrived at the same conclusion we had reached, and this fact both alarmed and interested me.

"I trust I will not need you," I replied.

We descended the narrow stairs and went into the cabin area. Lucas took my arm and brought me to a halt.

"This is the cabin I am occupying," he whispered. "Will you wait a moment, Miss Amelia? I want to show you something."

I waited in the dark corridor while he stepped into the cabin. He was back in a moment, carrying a long object, like a stick. I peered through the gloom before I was able to identify it; and then I started to expostulate.

"Never fear," said Lucas, holding up the rifle—for such it was. "It is not loaded. I would not make that mistake again."

"Then why carry it?"

"Sssh!" Lucas put a finger to his lips. "Only you and I know it is not loaded. Perhaps the Mummy has reason not to fear a small-caliber handgun; he will not be so nonchalant about a shell from an express that can bring down a charging elephant. And if all else fails, it makes an admirable club!"

He raised the rifle above his head.

"I think it is a foolish idea," I snapped. "But if you are determined on it. . . . Good night, Lucas."

I left him brandishing the weapon, an idiotic grin on his face.

Ordinarily Evelyn and I occupied separate cabins, but I had no intention of leaving her alone that night. I feigned a return of weakness, in order to persuade her to share my room without alarming her, and she helped me into bed with sweet solicitude. She soon joined me. Darkness fell as she blew out the lamp, and before long her soft, regular breathing told me that fatigue had overcome the anxieties that still distressed her.

I did not sleep, but I found it more difficult than I had expected to overcome Morpheus. I had taken only a single glass of wine, despite Lucas's attempts to induce me to drink more. Ordinarily such a small amount does not affect me in the slightest, but as the minutes went on and the voices of the crewmen faded into silence, I fought sleep as if it had been a bitter enemy. Finally I arose—with care, so as not to waken Evelyn—and went into the adjoining cubicle, which served as our bathroom, where I splashed water on my face and even slapped it as vigorously as I dared. I was finally driven to pinching myself; and a foolish figure I would have made, if anyone had been there to see—standing bolt upright in the center of the room, applying my nails to the flesh of my arm at regular intervals.

The night was very silent. The men were asleep, I assumed. The soft night sounds of the Nile were as soothing as a lullaby. My knees kept bending, and I kept jerking myself erect. I had no idea how much time had passed. It seemed like hours.

At last, feeling slightly more alert, I went back into the sleeping chamber and approached the window. It was not the porthole sort of window one finds on regular sailing ships, but a wide aperture, open to the air but covered by a curtain in order to keep out the light. It opened onto the lower deck, not quite level with the flooring, but easily reached from it. I knew that if danger should approach, it must come this way. Our door was locked and bolted securely, but there was no way of locking the window without shutting out the air and making the room too stifling for comfortable sleep.

My hand went to the window frame all the same. After some internal debate I decided to leave it open. The increasingly stuffy air might waken Evelyn, and the window creaked, as I remembered from before. Instead I drew the curtain back just enough to see out, and remained standing, my elbows on the sill, my hands propping my drowsy head.

I could see a section of the deck from where I stood, and beyond it the silvered reaches of the river, with the night sky overhead. The moon's rays were so bright I could make out details like the nails in the planking. Nothing moved, except the rippling silver of the water.

How long I stood there I cannot calculate. I fell into a kind of waking doze, erect, but not wholly conscious. Finally I became aware of something moving along the deck to my right.

Lucas's cabin was in that direction, but I knew it was not Lucas. I knew what it was. Had I not expected it?

It kept to the shadows, but I made out the now familiar pale shape of it easily enough. I cannot explain why, but on this occasion I felt none of the superstitious terror that had paralyzed me on its earlier visits. Perhaps it was the skulking surreptitious movement of the thing; perhaps it was the familiarity of the surroundings. In any case, I began to feel enormous exasperation. Really, the Mummy was becoming ridiculous! Its repertoire was so limited; why didn't it do something different, instead of creeping around waving its arms?

I was no longer sleepy, and I calculated, quite coolly, what I should do. How I would crow over Emerson if, single-handedly, I could capture our mysterious adversary! I quite forgot his admonitions. I would not be satisfied with driving the Mummy away, as we had planned; no, I must catch it!

The only question was: Should I call for help, or should I attack the creature myself? I was reluctant to follow the former course. The crewmen were at the far end of the deck and were, no doubt, sleeping off their unaccustomed debauch so heavily that a cry would not waken them in time to prevent the creature's escape. As for Lucas, I did not doubt that he was snoring heavily. No, I thought; I would wait, to see what the Mummy did. If it tried to enter our room through the window—then I had it! My right hand already clasped the handle of the pitcher which, filled with water, stood beside the bed. It was a heavy earthenware jug and would raise a good lump on the head of anything it struck.

As I debated with myself, the Mummy stepped out into the moonlight. It had to do so, in order to reach our room; and as it did, my feelings underwent a sudden alteration. It was so large! It seemed bigger than a grown man, and although I told myself that the appearance of gigantism was the result of the bulky bandaging, my nerves were not quite convinced. Would the jug be sufficient to render the thing unconscious? I had forgotten that its head was padded. Suppose I struck and failed? I have considerable faith in my powers, but I was not mad enough to suppose that I could engage in hand-to-hand struggle with a creature of that size and come out victorious. Even if it were a mere man, and not a monster endowed with supernatural strength, it could overcome me; and then. . . . Evelyn lay sleeping and helpless in the bed. No—no, I could not risk that. I must wake her; better that she should be frightened than—the unspeakable alternative. I must call out; better that the thing should escape than . . .

I drew a deep breath.

"Lucas! Lucas!" I shrieked. "*Á moi*, Lucas! Help!"

I cannot imagine why I shouted in French. It was a dramatic moment.

To my taut nerves the results of my cry seemed long in coming. The Mummy stopped its stealthy advance. I had the decided impression that it was surprised to hear my voice. Behind me, Evelyn stirred and began to mutter sleepily. And then, with a loud thump and crash, Lucas jumped through the window of the next cabin onto the deck.

Even in that moment of danger I was glad Evelyn could not see him as he rushed to her rescue. He was fully dressed, but his shirt collar was open and his sleeves were rolled up, displaying muscular, rather hairy arms. His face was set in an expression of grim resolve; his right hand clasped the rifle. He was a sight to thrill any romantic girl; I felt a mild thrill myself as he threw the rifle to his shoulder and aimed it at the gruesome form that confronted him.

"Stop," he ordered, in a low but compelling voice. "Do not take another step, or I fire! D——it," he added vexedly, "does the monstrosity understand English? How absurd this is!"

"It understands the gesture, at least," I called, thrusting head and shoulders through the window. "Lucas, for pity's sake, seize it! Don't stand there deriding its linguistic inadequacies!"

The Mummy's head swung around until the featureless face looked directly at me. Oh, yes, it could see; I swear I caught a flash of eyes amid the darkness under its brows. It raised its arms and began to emit the mewing, growling cry that seemed to characterize its angry moods.

Evelyn was awake and calling out. I heard the bedsprings creak as she tried to rise.

"Stay where you are, Evelyn," I ordered. "Don't move. Lucas" —I disliked giving him the credit, but honesty demanded I should—"Lucas and I have the situation under control."

"What do I do now?" Lucas asked, addressing me. "It does not seem to understand me; and you know, Miss Amelia—"

"Strike it on the head," I shouted. "Rush at it and strike! Good Gad, why are you standing there? I will do it myself!"

I started to climb through the window. Evelyn had disregarded my orders; she was standing behind me, and as I essayed to move she caught me around the waist, crying out in alarm. Lucas was grinning broadly; the man had no sense of the proprieties. His smile did not endure, however. As I struggled with Evelyn, the Mummy moved. It lowered its arms; then one, the right arm, shot out with the force of a man throwing some object. Nothing left its hand. It did not step forward. But Lucas's body jerked violently. The rifle fell, as if his arms had suddenly lost their strength; it struck the deck with a metallic clatter, and Lucas fell upon it, face downward.

I stopped struggling. Evelyn and I stood with our arms wrapped around one another, frozen with horror. The Mummy's hideous laughter resounded through the quiet night. It turned to face our window.

Then, at long last, from the deck to the left came the sound of voices. The crewmen were awake. The Mummy heard. It raised one bandaged arm and shook a paw menacingly in the direction of the approaching men. I could not see them, but I knew they had seen the Mummy; they had probably seen the entire incredible performance, which had been played out on the open deck.

With a series of acrobatic bounds, the bandaged figure left. Evelyn was limp in my grasp. I shook her, none too gently.

"Lie down," I ordered. "You are safe, Evelyn; I must go to Lucas."

She slumped down onto the floor, and I scrambled through the window—no easy task in my voluminous night garments. I am afraid I displayed some part of my limbs as I crawled out onto the deck, but I was past worrying about that, and the crewmen were in no condition to notice my lack of dignity. I saw them as I got to my feet; they were clustered in a dark mass at the end of the deck, huddling together like silly sheep afraid of a wolf.

Lucas was still motionless.

I turned him over, not without difficulty; he was a heavy man, and would one day be fat, if he continued to indulge himself. He did not appear to be injured; his pulse was strong, if a little too quick, and his color was good. But his breath came and went in the oddest whistling gasps, and from time to time his whole body quivered in a kind of muscular spasm.

At first the men would not approach, and when they finally crept forward they refused to touch Lucas, even to carry him to a cabin. Reis Hassan finally came; his whiplash voice roused the men. I fancied they were almost as afraid of him as they were of the supernatural—but not quite. As soon as they had placed Lucas on his bed, they fled.

Hassan remained, standing just within the doorway, with his arms folded across his broad chest.

Never had I so regretted that I had not learned Arabic instead of Latin, Greek, and Hebrew. Hassan was not anxious to explain himself, and my incoherent questions were probably as unintelligible to him as his answers were to me. I thought he was rather ashamed of himself, but the cause of his shame was not easy to ascertain. He had slept too soundly, that much I was able to understand. All the crew had slept. It was not a natural sleep. It was like a spell—like magic. Otherwise they would, of course, have rushed to answer my call for help.

That much I grasped, or thought I grasped. It did not reassure me. I dismissed Hassan, after ordering him, as well as I could, to keep a man on watch for the remainder of the night. Lucas demanded my attention; and I was uneasily aware of the fact that I could no longer rely on my crew, not even my captain. If they had not already been frightened by tales of the Mummy, the night's adventure would have done the job.

Lucas was still unconscious. I did not dare consider the nature of the force that had struck him down so mysteriously; after examining him for a wound, and finding none, I decided to treat his condition as I would an ordinary faint. But none of my mea-

208

sures succeeded. His eyes remained closed; his broad chest rose and fell in the strange, stentorious breathing.

I began to be frightened. If this was a faint, it was an unnatural one. I rubbed his hands, slapped cold cloths on face and breast, elevated his feet—to no avail. Finally I turned to Evelyn, who was standing in the open doorway watching me.

"He is not . . ." She could not finish the sentence.

"No, nor in any danger of dying," I replied quickly. "I don't understand what is wrong with him."

"I can't bear it," Evelyn whispered; and then, as I started to speak, she added, "No, Amelia, it is not what you think; I admire, I like Lucas; after his courage tonight, I can hardly help but respect him. But my grief at his illness is that of a friend and cousin. Only—I am beginning to feel as if I brought disaster on all those who love me. Am I somehow accursed? Must I leave those I love, lest I infect them, as my coming brought harm to Walter—and now to poor Lucas? Must I leave you, Amelia?"

"Don't talk nonsense," I replied brusquely. Harshness was the only proper response to the rising hysteria in the child's voice. "Go and fetch my smelling salts. If they are as strong as I remember, they ought to bring Lucas to his senses. They almost deprived me of mine."

Evelyn nodded. I could always command her by appealing to her sense of duty. As she turned, I was electrified by the first sign of life I had seen in my patient. His lips parted. In a low, sighing voice, he enunciated a single word.

"He calls your name," I said to Evelyn, who had paused. "Come quickly; answer him."

Evelyn knelt down by the bed. "Lucas," she said. "Lucas, I am here. Speak to me."

Lucas's hand moved. It groped feebly. Evelyn put her hand on his; the fingers closed around hers and clung.

"Evelyn," Lucas repeated. "My darling . . ."

209

"I am here," Evelyn repeated. "Can you hear me, Lucas?"

The sick man's head moved slightly. "So far away," he murmured, in a failing voice. "Where are you, Evelyn? Don't leave me. I am all alone in the dark. . . ."

Evelyn leaned over him. "I won't leave you, Lucas. Wake up, I implore you. Speak to us."

"Take my hand. Don't let me wander away. . . . I am lost without you. . . ."

This banal exchange continued for some time, with Lucas's weak voice pleading and Evelyn reassuring him. I shifted impatiently from one foot to the other. I suspected that Lucas was now fully conscious. He was certainly not delirious in the ordinary sense of the word. Only congenital stupidity could have produced such inane dialogue. Finally Lucas got to the point. His eyes were still closed.

"Don't leave me," he moaned. "Never leave me, my love, my hope. Promise you will never leave me."

Evelyn was bending so close that her unbound hair brushed his cheek. Her face was transformed by pity, and I rather hated to disillusion her, but I was not sure what she might promise in the heat of her innocent enthusiasm. If she made a promise, she would keep it. And I was determined that matters should proceed according to the plan I had conceived. So I said briskly, "He is coming around now, Evelyn. Are you going to promise to marry him, or shall we try the smelling salts first?"

Evelyn sat back on her heels. Her face was flushed. Lucas opened his eyes.

"Evelyn," he said slowly—but in his normal, deep tones, not the moaning whisper he had been using. "It is really you? I dreamed. God preserve me from any more such dreams!"

"Thank God," Evelyn said sincerely. "How do you feel, Lucas? We were so frightened for you."

"A little weak; otherwise, quite all right. It was your voice that

210

brought me back, Evelyn; I seemed to be disembodied, lost and alone in a dark without a single spark of light. Then I heard your voice and followed it as I would follow a beacon."

"I am glad I could help you, Lucas."

"You saved my life. Henceforth it is yours."

Evelyn shook her head shyly. She was trying to free her hand; and after a moment Lucas let it go.

"Enough of this," I interposed. "I am not so much interested in your dreams, Lucas, as I am in what produced them. What happened? I saw you stumble and fall, but I could swear the creature did not throw any missile."

"Nothing struck me," Lucas answered. "Nothing physical. . . . You found no bruise, no mark, I suppose?"

He glanced down at his bared chest. Blushing still more deeply, Evelyn got to her feet and retreated from the bed.

"There was no mark I could see," I replied. "What did you feel?"

"Impossible to describe it! I can only imagine that a man struck by a bolt of lightning might have a similar sensation. First a shocking thrill, electrical in intensity; then utter weakness and unconsciousness. I felt myself falling, but did not feel my body strike the deck."

"Splendid," I said sarcastically. "We now have a creature with the power to hurl thunderbolts. Emerson will be delighted to hear it."

"Emerson's opinions are of no interest to me," Lucas snapped.

III

I slept soundly for what remained of the night. I believe Evelyn did not sleep at all. When I awoke it was to see the exquisite pink flush of dawn staining the sky, and Evelyn silhouetted against it. She was standing at the window; she was fully dressed, in a

211

businesslike serge skirt and blouse. The moment I moved, she spoke.

"I am going to the camp," she announced firmly. "You need not come, Amelia; I will be back soon, I will hurry. I hope to persuade Mr. Emerson to bring his brother here, and to set sail at once for Luxor. But if they will not come, then—then I think we should go. I know you will not want to leave, Amelia; I have seen how interested you are in—in archaeology. But I think Lucas will go, if I ask him; and I shall leave, with him, if you want to remain here."

The sight of her pale, resolute face checked the remonstrance that had risen to my lips. I saw that I must speak with careful consideration. The girl believed the awful idea that had come to her the previous night! It was both pitiful and amusing to note that she had no qualms about burdening Lucas with her deadly presence, as she thought it, when it came to a choice between endangering Lucas or Walter.

"Well," I said, getting out of bed, "you will not go without breakfast, I hope. It would be silly to faint, from inanition, in the middle of the desert."

Evelyn unwillingly consented to partake of breakfast. As she restlessly paced the upper deck, I sent a servant to summon Lucas. It was easy to see how the events of the night had affected the crew. Young Habib, our smiling waiter, was not smiling that morning; and the usual cheerful babble of voices from the lower deck was not to be heard.

Lucas joined us while we were drinking our tea. He looked perfectly fit, and said he felt the same. Evelyn immediately told him of her plan. Lucas was not fool enough to fail to understand her agitation. His eyebrows climbed alarmingly as she spoke. In case he should miss the point I kicked him under the table. And when he turned to me indignantly, I semaphored warning as well as I could. He took the hint.

212

"My dearest," he said gently, "if you wish to leave this place, you shall leave. I told you that your slightest wish was my command. But I must make one small reservation. You can ask me for my life, but not for my honor as a gentleman and an Englishman! You cannot ask me to abandon our friends. No, do not speak; I will order the crew to be prepared to leave at a moment's notice, and to carry you and Miss Amelia to Luxor, or wherever you wish to go. But I will remain. You would not respect me if I fled now."

Evelyn sat in silence, her head bowed. I decided to intervene. I could hardly take exception to Lucas's sentiments but he managed to create an atmosphere of sticky sentimentality that disgusted me.

"I have no intention of leaving unless the Emersons join us," I said firmly. "And I will deal with my own crew, if you please, Lucas. You may give yours whatever orders you like."

"I will," Lucas replied huffily.

And he went off to do so, while I summoned Reis Hassan and made another effort to break through the language barrier. I had thought of asking Lucas for the loan of his dragoman as interpreter; but what I had seen of that shifty-eyed personage did not impress me, and if Emerson had not been able to induce Hassan to speak openly, I thought no one could.

Hassan managed to convey one concept unequivocally. He kept repeating the word "go," and pointing upstream.

"Emerson?" I asked, and gestured toward the camp.

Hassan nodded vigorously. We were all to go. Today.

That was one Arabic word I understood, although the word for "tomorrow" is even more commonly used. I repeated it now.

Hassan's face fell. Then he gave the queer Arab shrug.

"Tomorrow," he said soberly. *"In'shallah."*

I knew that word too. It means, "God willing."

10

Soon after breakfast we set out. The sun was well up; the sands shone palely gold, and the glare, even at that early hour, was hard on the eyes. There was little conversation during the walk. Evelyn had not spoken at all since she made her declaration; I was worried about her, and—which is not usual for me—uncertain as to how I might best relieve her strange fears. Not that I blamed her for being distracted; most girls of her protected station in life would have been prostrate after the experiences she had undergone.

The first person to greet us was no other than Walter. He wore a sling, to support the injured arm, but otherwise he seemed well enough, and I was delighted to see him on his feet. He came to meet us, not quite running, and grasped my hand. But he looked at Evelyn.

"You cannot conceive how relieved I am to see you," he exclaimed. "I was furious with Radcliffe when he told me you had gone."

"I don't know why you should have been worried," I replied, returning his hearty handclasp. "It was you we worried about. How do you feel? And where is your brother?"

"You won't believe it," Walter said, smiling. "Guess."

"I don't need to guess," I replied. "Emerson has taken advantage of my absence to continue his excavations. He is totally without conscience! I suppose he has made another discovery. What is it? Another fragment of painting?"

Walter's eyes were wide with surprise.

"Miss Amelia, you astound me! You seem to read minds. How did you know?"

"I know your brother very well," I replied angrily. "He is capable of any stupidity where his precious antiquities are concerned. At such a time as this, to waste his time and energy. . . . Where is he? I want to speak to him."

"The pavement is not far from the other one that was destroyed," Walter replied. "But—"

"But me no buts," I said. "The rest of you return to camp. I will fetch Emerson."

I set off without another word, not waiting to see whether they obeyed me. By the time I found Emerson I had worked myself up into quite a state of anger. He was squatting on the ground, his tan clothing and dusty helmet blending so well with the hue of the sand that I did not distinguish his form until I was almost upon him. He was so preoccupied that he failed to hear my approach. I struck him, not lightly, on the shoulder with my parasol.

"Oh," he said, glancing at me. "So it's you, Peabody. Of course. Who else would greet a man by beating him over the head?"

215

I squatted down beside him. This posture, so difficult at first, had become easier. My knees no longer cracked when I knelt.

He had cleared a patch of pavement some three feet square. I saw the blue undersurface which denoted water, and upon it three exquisitely shaped lotus flowers, with green leaves framing the pure-white petals.

"So this is the explanation of your plot," I remarked. "Sending me off with Evelyn in order to distract the Mummy, so that you could work in peace. Thank you, Emerson, for your concern! You are the most despicable, selfish. . . . That is a great waste of time, you know, scooping at the sand with your bare hands. You will never clear the pavement that way. The sand trickles down as fast as you pull it away."

Emerson grinned unpleasantly at me over his shoulder.

"Tsk, tsk, Peabody, you are losing track of what you were saying. I am despicable, selfish—"

"Aren't you even curious?" I demanded angrily. "Don't you want to know what happened last night?"

"I know what happened." Emerson sat back on his haunches. "I went to the boat just before dawn this morning and had a talk with Hassan."

Now that I looked at him, I realized he appeared weary. There were dark circles under his eyes, and new lines around the firm mouth. I was momentarily deflated by this, and by his calm statement. But only momentarily.

"You did, did you? And what do you make of it all?"

"Why, matters transpired as I expected. The Mummy appeared, and was duly routed by you—"

"By Lucas," I interrupted.

"His lordship does not appear to have been particularly useful. His collapse threw the crew into a complete panic. Even Reis Hassan—who is far from being a coward, I assure you—is afraid. I trust his lordship is fully recovered this morning from what

216

Hassan described as a personally delivered curse?"

"I don't know what was wrong with him," I admitted. "If he were not such an intrepid fellow, I would suspect he simply fainted."

"Ha," said Emerson.

"Jeer as much as you like, you cannot deny the man's courage. He is no coward."

Emerson shrugged and began to scoop away more sand.

"Have you taken leave of your senses?" I asked. "You have had one painting destroyed; uncover this, and it will meet the same fate. Its only safety now lies in obscurity."

"Perhaps its survival is not my chief concern," Emerson replied, still scooping. "We must have some lure for our mysterious visitor; better to lose this than Miss Evelyn."

I studied him in silence for several minutes.

"I cannot believe you mean that," I said finally.

"No, I am sure you have the lowest possible opinion of me and all my works. It is true, nevertheless."

There was a new note in his voice, one I had not heard before. Anger he had displayed, contempt, disgust; but never such weary bitterness. I felt peculiarly affected.

"I do not have a low opinion of you," I said—mumbled, rather.

Emerson turned.

"What did you say?"

We presented a ridiculous picture. Half kneeling, half squatting, Emerson was leaning forward to peer into my face. His hands rested on the ground, and his posture rather suggested that of an inquisitive orangutang. My own position, squatting on my heels with my skirts bunched up around me, was no less ludicrous. I was not conscious of absurdity or incongruity, however; I was only conscious of his eyes, blue and glittering as sapphires, holding my gaze with a strange intensity. Their look was too much to endure; my eyes fell, and my face felt uncomfortably warm.

And then the sound of a voice shattered the spell. Looking up, I saw Walter coming toward us. Emerson sat back.

"Radcliffe," Walter began, "what do you suppose has—"

He stopped speaking, and looked from one of us to the other. "Is something wrong? Have I interrupted—"

"Nothing," Emerson said coldly. "You have not interrupted. What is it, Walter? You appear agitated."

"Agitated? I am, indeed! And so will you be, when you hear what transpired last night."

"I know what transpired," Emerson said, in the same cool voice.

I looked at him from under my lashes. His face was as impassive as one of the stone pharaohs in the Boulaq Museum. I decided I must have imagined the fleeting look of passionate inquiry. I was tired, after a sleepless night, and subject to fancies.

"Then Miss Amelia has told you," Walter said innocently. "Radcliffe, something must be done, this is frightful! You must persuade the ladies to leave—now—today! Come back to camp, I beg, and use your powers of persuasion. I cannot seem to prevail with either Miss Evelyn or his lordship."

"Oh, very well," Emerson grumbled, rising to his feet.

Walter extended his hand to me. His brother stalked away and we followed. When we caught him up, Walter continued to express his horror and alarm. Finally Emerson interrupted.

"Walter, you are babbling, and I don't believe you have thought the matter through. Suppose we do succeed in sending Miss Evelyn away; will that solve the difficulty? If the Mummy is a supernatural agent, which all you fools seem to believe, it can follow her wherever she goes. It can equally well follow her if it is not supernatural! Since you seem to be more concerned with her safety than with the success of our work here, perhaps you would agree that we ought to bend all our efforts on ascertaining the creature's motives, and apprehending it."

218

Walter looked distressed. The reasoning made some impression on his intellect, but all his protective instincts were at war with his brain; he wanted to see Evelyn out of danger.

"Indeed," I put in, "we really have no reason to suppose that the creature means Evelyn any harm. Both of you, and Lucas as well, have taken injury, but Evelyn has not been touched. She is the only one who has not been harmed—except for me."

"Ah," said Emerson, giving me a long, thoughtful look. "I assure you, Peabody, that point has not escaped me."

We finished the trip in silence. Walter was too worried, and I was too furious, to speak. I understood Emerson's implication. Could he really suspect *me* of being behind the diabolical plot? Surely not even Emerson was capable. . . . But, I told myself—he was! Such a cynic, who has never had an altruistic thought in his life, is always projecting his own failings on to other people.

Evelyn and Lucas were waiting for us, and we sat down for a discussion which at first proved fruitless. The fault was mine; ordinarily I have no difficulty in making up my mind, nor in convincing others of the correctness of my decision. On this occasion I could not come to a decision.

The safest course would have been for all of us to pack up and abandon the site. This I knew Emerson would never consider, and I had a certain sympathy for his point of view. Equally impossible to me was the idea of abandoning the Emersons and sailing away. Neither of them was in perfect health; they would be helpless if the villagers should turn from passive resistance to active hostility. They had no means of summoning help. Even in busy years the remote ruins of Amarna attract relatively few visitors, and the unsettled conditions in the Sudan had frightened away many travelers.

An alternative was for me to remain with my dahabeeyah, in case of emergency, while Lucas and Evelyn returned to Cairo for assistance. It would be improper for them to travel unchaperoned;

but by that time I was ready to consign the proprieties to perdition, where they belonged. However, the plan had a number of difficulties. Evelyn would refuse to leave me, and Emerson would howl like a jackal at the idea of my remaining to protect him. He had the lowest possible opinion of Maspero and the Antiquities Department; the notion of appealing to them for help would offend his masculine pride.

Nevertheless, I thought it my duty to propose the scheme. It was received with the unanimous, negative outcry I had expected. Did I say unanimous? I am incorrect. The only one who did not object was the one I had expected to be most vehement. Emerson sat with his lips pressed tightly together.

Lucas was the most outspoken.

"Abandon our friends?" he exclaimed. "And you, Miss Amelia? It is not to be thought of! Furthermore, I cannot possibly agree to allowing Evelyn to risk her reputation traveling alone with me. There is only one circumstance under which such a scheme would be feasible. . . ."

And he looked significantly at Evelyn, who flushed and turned her head away.

His meaning was clear. If Evelyn traveled as his affianced bride, the ceremony to be performed immediately upon their arrival in Cairo. . . . In our conventional times the proprieties might be shaken by such an arrangement, but they would not be unalterably shattered.

Walter caught the meaning as soon as I did. His ingenuous young countenance fell. Emerson had produced his pipe and was puffing away with every appearance of enjoyment; his eyes gleamed maliciously as he looked from one of us to the other.

"Oh, this is absurd," I said, jumping to my feet. "We must make some decision. The day is passing, and I am worn out."

"Of course you are," Evelyn exclaimed, immediately concerned. "You must have rest, that is more important than any-

220

thing else. Go and lie down, Amelia."

"We have not yet made a decision," I began.

Emerson took his pipe from his mouth.

"Really, Peabody, this strange indecisiveness is not like you. Indeed, I am surprised at all of you. You are acting like impulsive children, ready to run from a shadow."

"A shadow!" I exclaimed indignantly. "It was a shadow, I suppose, that struck you down with a rock; a shadow that wounded Walter!"

"To be precise, it was an avalanche that injured me," Emerson replied coolly. "An equally unfortunate accident"—he stressed the word, glancing at Lucas as he did so—"an accident caused Walter's wound. Come, come, Peabody, use your head. To date, there is nothing to suggest that any of these mishaps were the result of deliberate malice. As for his lordship's strange collapse last night—the body is subject to inexplicable weaknesses. Fatigue, excitement—a trifle too much wine. . . ."

He paused, cocking his head and peering at Lucas with quizzical blue eyes. Lucas flushed angrily.

"I deny the allegation!"

"The only alternative is to believe in the supernatural powers of the Mummy," Emerson replied drily. "That I refuse to do. I will continue to seek a rational explanation until reason leaves me altogether; and unless one of you can suggest a motive, unknown to me, why any of us should be in danger. . . ."

Again he paused, raking us in turn with his cool stare. No one spoke.

"No vendettas, nor feuds?" Emerson asked mockingly. "No desperate lovers, or enemies burning for revenge? Very well, then; we return to the only sensible explanation for all this; it was suggested, I believe, by his lordship. The villagers wish to drive us away from here because they have made a valuable discovery. I will not be driven away. It is as simple as that."

221

I could not help but be impressed by the man's irrefutable logic. And yet in my innermost soul a strange uneasiness lingered.

"Then what do you propose that we do?" I asked.

"I propose that we take the aggressive," Emerson replied. "So far we have not done so; we have been preoccupied with defending ourselves against fancied dangers. And that, I believe, is precisely what our opponents wish us to do. If the villagers can find a tomb, we can find it. Tomorrow I will begin searching. We will enlist the assistance of your crews. It will not be easy to do that; the men have been told by the villagers that we are under a curse. Yet I fancy that a judicious blend of flattery, appeal, and bribery will win them over. We must have sufficient manpower to protect the ladies and to conduct a thorough search. Well? What do you say? Is the scheme a good one?"

I had nothing to say. The scheme was a good one, but I would rather have died than admit it aloud. The others were clearly impressed. Evelyn's somber face had brightened.

"Then you really believe that the Mummy is only trying to frighten us? That no one is in danger?"

"My dear girl, I am convinced of it. If it will make you feel safer, we will damn the conventions and spend the night huddled together in a single room. But I feel sure no such discomfort is necessary. Are we all agreed? Excellent. Then Peabody had better retire to her bed; she is clearly in need of recuperative sleep, she has not made a sarcastic remark for fully ten minutes."

II

I thought I would not sleep. My mind was in a state of confusion such as I seldom permit in that organ; but on this occasion the methods I normally apply to resolve it were not effective. Something kept me from ratiocination. Mental fatigue, as well as physical exhaustion, finally sent me into heavy slumber, filled with bewildering fragments of dreams. The common theme of them all seemed to be light—bright beams of illumination that flashed on and then went out, leaving me in deeper darkness than before. I groped in the dark, seeking I knew not what.

It was such a beam of light that finally woke me. When the curtain at the mouth of the tomb was lifted, the rays of the setting sun struck straight into the shadowy gloom. I lay motionless, struggling against the bonds of sleep that still clung to me; my uneasy slumber had twisted the bedclothes about my limbs and loosened my hair from its net. Damp with perspiration, the thick coils weighted my heavy head.

Then I heard the voice. I did not recognize it at first; it was a harsh whisper, tremulous with fear and warning.

"Don't move! For your life, remain motionless!"

The tones woke me like a dash of cold water. I opened my drowsy eyes. The first object to meet my gaze was a coil of what appeared to be thick brown rope, resting on the foot of my couch. As I stared, the coil moved. A flat head lifted from the mass; two narrow orbs, sparkling with life, fixed themselves on mine.

The whisper came again.

"Be still. Not a breath, not a movement. . . ."

I did not need that injunction. I could not have moved, even if waking intelligence had not warned me that the slightest movement might rouse the serpent to strike. The small obsidian eyes held me. I had read that snakes paralyze their intended prey thus; and I knew how the trembling rabbit must feel when its murderer glides toward it.

With a desperate effort I wrenched my eyes from the hypnotic glare of the snake. I rolled them toward the door. I dared move no farther.

Emerson's face was streaked with rivulets of perspiration. He did not look at me. His eyes were fixed on the flat reptilian head, which was now weaving slowly back and forth. His hand, half lifted, shook with strain. It moved slowly, inch by inch. It touched his pocket and, with the same agonizing deliberation, reached inside.

Before and after that time I have made efforts that were not easy to make, but never have I done anything more difficult than remaining motionless. Lively terror had replaced my paralysis; every nerve in my body shook with the desire for action. I wanted to scream aloud, to fling myself from the deadly couch. Every ounce of my will was occupied in fighting this instinct. The strain was too much. A fog descended over my staring eyes. I knew that in another moment I must move.

When it finally came, the act was too quick for my failing eyes to see it. Emerson's arm flashed in a blur of motion. Simultaneously, or so it seemed, the heavens fell. Blinding light, a crash of sound that rolled like thunder. . . . Merciful oblivion overcame me.

I was not unconscious for long. When I awoke I could not remember, at first, what had happened. My head rested against a hard, warm surface that vibrated erratically. My ears still rang with the echoes of that final thunderclap. I decided, drowsily, that the rapid beating sound was that of my own blood rushing through my veins with the rapidity of terror; for a normal heartbeat was never so fast. I felt surprisingly comfortable—limp and boneless as a baby in its mother's arms. Then something began to touch my face—lips, closed eyes, cheeks—with a light pressure like the brush of fingers, only warmer and softer. That odd, fleeting touch had the strangest effect on me. I had been about to open my eyes. Instead, I closed them tighter. I decided I must be dreaming. Similar sensations had occurred, occasionally, in dreams; why should I dismiss such pleasurable experiences for a reality which would not be so enjoyable? I remembered everything now. The snake must have struck its fangs into me. I was poisoned—delirious—dreaming.

I genuinely resented the sounds that finally broke the spell. Voices crying out in alarm, running footsteps, streaks of light that irritated my closed eyes—yes, the dream was over. I felt myself being lowered to a flat surface, being shaken, and—crowning indignity—slapped smartly across the cheek. I opened my eyes, and then narrowed them in a frown as I recognized Emerson's face hovering over me like a nightmarish mask. It was he who had slapped me, of course. Beyond, I saw Evelyn, her face as white as her dress. She pushed Emerson away, with a strength and rudeness quite foreign to her nature, and flung herself down on the cot beside me.

"Amelia! Oh, my dear, dear Amelia—we heard the shot and came running—what has happened? Are you wounded? Are you dying?"

"Not wounded, not dying, merely enjoying a ladylike swoon," said Emerson's familiar, detestable voice. "Allow me to congratulate you, Peabody; it is the first time I have seen you behave as a lady is supposed to do. I must make a note of it in my journal."

I tried to think of something sufficiently cutting to say in reply, but was too unstrung to do so; I simply glared at him. He had stepped back and was standing beside the cot, his hands in his pockets. A low cry from Walter interrupted Evelyn's agitated questions. He rose from the foot of the bed, holding the limp body of the serpent in his hand.

"Good God," he exclaimed, his voice shaking. "It is a hooded cobra—one of the deadliest serpents in Egypt. Radcliffe—it was you who fired the shot? Are you certain it did not strike before you killed it?"

I thought for a moment Evelyn was going to faint. She roused herself and began to fumble around in the bedclothes, trying to examine my lower limbs. I pulled them away. I felt perfectly well now; Emerson's rudeness had the effect of rousing me.

"Don't fuss, Evelyn," I said irritably. "The snake did not touch me; it is a slow-witted creature and took so long making up its mind whether to bite me that Emerson had ample time to shoot it. He took plenty of time, too, I must say; I could have dealt with ten snakes during the interval he required to take out his pistol."

"You know better, Miss Amelia," Walter exclaimed. "It was necessary to move with deliberation; a rapid movement might have startled the snake into striking. To think that it was just here, at the foot of your bed! It turns me quite cold to think of it. Thank God you had a weapon, Radcliffe."

"My weapon, I suppose," said Lucas from the doorway. He came slowly into the room. "What a fortunate chance that you were carrying it with you."

"There was one bullet left," Emerson said. His lips curled in a frightful grimace; abruptly he turned his back.

"It was an extraordinary shot," Lucas said, his eyes on the other man's rigid shoulders. "A lucky shot, I should say. You might have struck Miss Amelia."

"It had to be attempted, whatever the risk," Walter exclaimed. The implied criticism of his brother brought a flush of anger to his face.

"Of course," cried Evelyn.

She was still pale with agitation, but she arose with her usual grace and, going to Emerson, placed her hand timidly on his arm.

"God bless you, Mr. Emerson. Your quick wits and keen eye saved Amelia's life. How can I ever thank you?"

Emerson's stiff, haughty pose relaxed. He turned and looked down at the girl. Some of the color returned to her face under his steady regard. Then he smiled faintly.

"I will let you know," he replied enigmatically.

"In the meantime, perhaps Master Walter might consider getting rid of his souvenir," said Lucas. "It cannot be a pleasant sight for the ladies."

Walter started. He was still holding the snake's body at arms' length. He crossed the room, brushing past Lucas, and went out the door.

"And," Lucas continued, "let us all leave this room, which reeks of gunpowder and holds unpleasant associations. Come, Miss Amelia, let me offer you my arm."

"Thank you," I replied. "I need no assistance. Perhaps a cup of tea . . ."

Evelyn and I had tea. The gentlemen had something stronger. Lucas was the only one who seemed normal; he kept speculating as to how the serpent got into the tomb.

"No doubt it crawled within during the night," he said.

"I wonder why I didn't see it earlier," I said. "I must have disturbed it when I flung myself down to sleep."

"Because it was not on the cot then," Lucas replied. "It was curled in a corner, and crept onto your bed later. It was fortunate that Emerson came in when he did; if you had awakened and moved about—"

"Enough of this," I interrupted. "The thing is over and done with. In the meantime, the sun is setting. We have yet to decide what we are going to do tonight."

"I have decided." It was Evelyn who spoke. We all turned to look at her as she rose slowly from her chair. Her face was as white and set as that of a marble statue; but unconquerable resolution shone in her eyes.

"I accept Lord Ellesmere's proposal of marriage," she went on. "He and I will leave here now—this moment. Tomorrow at dawn we will sail for Cairo."

Utter silence followed. It was broken by Walter. He leaped to his feet with an unintelligible cry; dark, dusky color stained his cheeks. Lucas also rose. His slow, deliberate movements and the smile that spread across his face had an insolent triumph that infuriated me.

"I am, of course, the happiest man in the world," he said coolly.

227

"Although I could have wished, my darling, that you had not chosen to accept me quite so publicly. However, if that is what you prefer . . . ."

Before any of us suspected what he meant to do, he had caught Evelyn's hands and pulled her roughly to him. I honestly believe the rascal would have embraced her, there before us all, if Walter had not intervened. With another wordless cry, he struck his rival's hands away. For a moment the two young men stood facing one another in open enmity. Walter's breast rose and fell with his agitated breathing; the sling supporting his wounded arm rose and fell with it.

Lucas's eyes narrowed. I saw, as never before, the hot Latin blood of his sire.

"So," he said softly. "You dare. . . . You will answer for this, Emerson, I promise you."

Evelyn stepped between them.

"Lucas—Walter—for shame! I have said what I must do. I *will* do it. Nothing can change my mind."

"Evelyn!" Walter turned to her, ignoring the other man. "You cannot do this! You don't love him—you are sacrificing yourself because of some absurd notion that you are the cause of our troubles—"

"She could not possibly be so stupid." Emerson's calm voice broke in. He had not moved during the little scene; sitting at ease, his legs stretched out, he was smoking his pipe and watching like a spectator at a play.

"Sit down, all of you," he went on, his voice taking on a sharp tone that forced obedience. "Now let us talk like reasonable human beings. If Miss Evelyn decides to become Lady Ellesmere, that is her right; but I cannot allow her to take that step under a misapprehension."

He turned to Evelyn, who had dropped into a chair, where she sat with one trembling hand over her eyes.

228

"Young woman, do you really believe that you are the jinx, the Jonah, who brings evil upon us? That is unbecoming a sensible woman."

"Amelia, today," said Evelyn in a faint voice. "It was the final warning. Danger to all those I love—"

"Nonsense!" The word burst from Emerson's lips. "Simple nonsense, my girl. Have you forgotten what we decided, at the beginning of this obscene charade? The only possible motive for it all is the desire of some unknown to force us away from this site. How will your departure accomplish this, if Walter and I remain? While you sail safely down the river toward Cairo, in the arms of your betrothed—"

There was a wordless protest from Walter at this. Emerson gave him a sardonic look before proceeding, in a tone that seemed designed to provoke the young fellow even more.

"As you sail along in soft dalliance under the moon, we may be beleaguered here. No; if your motive truly is to benefit us, your flight cannot accomplish that. If, on the other hand, you yearn to be alone with his lordship—"

It was Lucas's turn to protest.

"Emerson, how dare you take that tone? You insult a lady—"

"Quite the contrary," said Emerson, maddeningly cool. "I pay the lady the compliment of assuming that she has a brain and is capable of using it. Well, Evelyn?"

Evelyn sat motionless, her hand still shading her eyes.

I do not know what had kept me silent so long. Emerson's motives eluded me; that he had some ulterior purpose, however, I did not doubt. I decided it was time to add my opinion.

"Emerson states the facts with his usual boorishness, yet he is basically correct. We are still in the dark as to the motive for this charade, as he rightly terms it. Precipitate action may be fatal. You may ignorantly do precisely what our unknown adversary wants you to do."

Lucas turned to look at me, and I knew that if I had not been a woman he would have threatened me as he had Walter. I cared not at all for his opinion. Anxiously I watched Evelyn.

"I don't know what to do," she whispered. "I must be alone —let me think. Don't follow me, please."

Slowly, her face averted, she passed along the ledge and began to descend.

Lucas started to follow.

"Your lordship!" Emerson's voice cracked like a whip.

"Don't interfere with me, Emerson," Lucas said tightly. "You are not my master."

"Interfere?" Emerson's eyes widened in honest indignation. "I never interfere. You are, of course, too much of a gentleman to lay hands on the young lady again; I need not caution you as to that. I was merely about to remind you not to wander out of sight."

"Very well," Lucas said shortly.

Evelyn had reached the bottom of the path and was walking slowly across the sand, away from camp. The poor child looked infinitely weary and sad as she proceeded with dragging steps and bowed head. The setting sun struck off her golden head like a flame.

Lucas's pace was quicker; he soon caught her up and they walked on together. Naturally I could not hear what they said, but I felt sure he was pressing his suit. The weary shake of her head gave me some hope, but not enough.

I turned to Walter, who was sitting beside me. His eyes were fixed on the distant couple. He looked ten years older than his real age.

"They make a pretty pair," said Emerson, who was outdoing himself in obnoxiousness that afternoon. "My lord and my lady; it will be an excellent match."

"Oh, do be still," I snapped.

"Why, I thought ladies enjoyed matchmaking. You may be proud if you bring this off. He is rich, titled, handsome; she is poor. A brilliant match for a girl like that."

My self-control, ordinarily excellent, suddenly snapped. I was utterly disgusted with the lot of them—with Evelyn and her morbid love of martyrdom, with Lucas and his arrogance, with Walter's hang-dog suffering acceptance—and most of all with Emerson. He thought he had won, and I feared he had; by handing Evelyn over to Lucas he kept his brother bound to his selfish wishes and now he was twisting the knife in the wound, convincing Walter that the girl was marrying Lucas out of the desire for wealth and worldly position. His smile maddened me; I could no longer hold my tongue.

"Bring it off!" I cried. "I would rather see Evelyn in a—in a monastery than married to that wretch. She does not love him. She loves—someone else, and thinks she will save him by accepting Lucas. Perhaps she is right after all. The man she loves is a poor-spirited wretch, who will not even take the trouble to declare himself!"

Walter grasped my hands. His face was transfigured.

"You can't mean it," he whispered. "You can't mean that I—"

"Yes, you young fool." I gave him a shove that sent him staggering. "She loves you; why, I cannot imagine, but she does. Now go and stop her!"

Walter gave me a look that made me tremble. He bounded off down the ledge; and I turned to face his brother, throwing my shoulders back defiantly. I had done a foolhardy thing; I did not know what would come of it. But at that moment I was prepared to face a whole horde of Mummies, much less Emerson, to defend my act.

He was rocking back and forth in his chair, shaken by silent spasms of laughter.

"My dear Peabody," he gasped. "You amaze me. Can it be that you are a secret romantic after all?"

He was impossible. I turned my back on him and watched the tableau down below.

Walter ran like a deer; he soon reached the others, and the three stood talking. It was only too easy to follow the conversation; Walter's impassioned gestures, Evelyn's startled response, and Lucas's angry interruption.

"I am going down," I said uneasily. "I may have acted a trifle precipitately. . . ."

"Intervention might be advisable," Emerson agreed calmly. "His noble lordship is not above striking a wounded man; and Walter is no match for him with only one arm. Damnation! I have waited too long!"

He *had* waited too long; and he had been correct in his assessment of Lucas's character. He struck; Walter went staggering back. Emerson was already halfway down the path, leaping along like a mountain goat. I followed; I dared not go quickly, for I could not remove my eyes from the little drama below.

Evelyn tried to intervene; Lucas shook her off. Walter had been shaken but not felled; he returned to the fray. Ducking his head under the other man's flailing blows, he returned them with interest; and I could scarcely repress a cheer when his clenched fist struck Lucas's outthrust jaw with a solid smack. Lucas fell just as Emerson came running up. He seized his brother's arm— unnecessarily, for Walter was not the man to take advantage of a fallen opponent. Running as fast as I could with the handicaps of full skirts and drifted sand, I came up to them as Lucas was rising to his feet.

He stood swaying unsteadily, his hand rubbing his chin. The fall had scarcely rumpled his elegant attire, but there was little of the English gentleman about him as he glared at Walter, his liquid black eyes hot with Latin rage.

"Two against one?" he inquired with a sneer. "Very sporting, gentlemen!"

"You are a fine one to talk of sportsmanship," I exclaimed. "To strike an injured man—"

"He used terms I allow no man to use to me," Lucas interrupted.

"I regret the terms," Walter said in a low voice. "But not the emotion that prompted them. Miss Amelia—Radcliffe—if you had heard the things he said of Evelyn—the implications he was vile enough to make—"

"They were true," Evelyn said.

All eyes turned toward Evelyn.

White as the lace at her throat, straight as a young birch tree, she faced the staring eyes without flinching. She stepped back— not in retreat, but in a deliberate movement that separated her from support. She waved me back with an irresistible gesture of command as I started toward her, expostulations rising to my lips.

"No, Amelia," she said, in the same quiet voice. "I had, for a time, the cowardly hope of avoiding this. But in justice to Lucas —and to all of you—I cannot remain silent. In the heat of anger Lucas spoke the truth. Not only have I lost a woman's most priceless jewel, I gave it up to a profligate, a wastrel, and a ruffian. I acted of my own free will. I abandoned an old man who loved me, and was only saved from the ultimate sin of taking my own life by Amelia's charity. Now that you know the worst, you will no longer seek to detain me. And you will accept my thanks for saving me, in the nick of time, from the despicable act I was about to commit. I see now that I cannot injure Lucas by taking advantage of his noble offer of marriage. That would be a fine way to repay his kindness, would it not?"

"Evelyn, my dearest," Lucas began.

She shook her head. It was a mild enough gesture, but even Lucas was convinced by the unalterable firmness of her expression. His outstretched hand fell to his side.

"I shall never marry. By devoting my life to good works and charitable undertakings I may one day partially redeem my ruined character."

She had intended to say more; she was proceeding in fine dramatic style, poor young thing, carried away by the tragedy of it all, as the young are. But her emotions were too genuine, too painful; her voice broke in a sob. She continued to stand pilloried under the astonished gaze of—Walter. She had spoken as if to all of us; but it was Walter she had really addressed.

He looked like a man who has received a mortal wound and does not yet realize that he ought to fall down. Emerson's countenance was as blank as the rock cliff behind him. Only his eyes were alive. They moved from Evelyn's ashen face to the equally corpse-like countenance of his brother; but that was the only movement he made; he did not speak.

Suddenly the color rushed back into Walter's face, so hecticly that he looked fevered. His dull, blank eyes came alive. Stepping forward, he dropped to his knees before Evelyn.

I thought that the long-expected collapse was about to occur. It was with an indescribable thrill of emotion that I realized he had grasped Evelyn's limp hand in his and was pressing his lips against it. I did not need to hear his words to know he had risen to heights I never really expected a man to reach.

"You are the noblest girl I have ever met," he cried, raising his eyes to Evelyn's astonished face. "The truest, the most courageous, the loveliest. . . . I don't know many men who would have the strength to do what you have just done! But my dearest, sweetest girl. . . ." He rose, still holding her hand and looking down at her with tender reproach. "Do you think so little of me that you suppose I would not understand your tragic story? Evelyn, you might have trusted me!"

For a moment she returned his gaze, her eyes wide, wondering,

234

unbelieving. Then, with a tired little sigh, she closed her eyes and let her golden head fall upon his breast. His arm around her waist, Walter held her close.

I watched them with the most thorough satisfaction I had ever felt in my life. I did not even wipe away the tears that rained down my face—although I began to think it was just as well Evelyn was leaving me. A few more weeks with her, and I should have turned into a rampageous sentimentalist.

"Thank goodness that is settled," said Emerson. "It took long enough, heaven knows, and became sickeningly maudlin toward the end. Come, Walter, kiss your fiancée, and let us all go back to camp. I am hungry; I want my dinner."

I don't think Walter heard a word of this speech. It struck just the right note for me; I needed some vent for my overflowing emotions.

"No one would ever accuse you of being sentimental," I said angrily. "Are you trying to suggest, you dreadful man, that you expected this development? Will you allow your brother to throw himself away on a penniless girl?"

"Not only penniless," said Emerson cheerfully, "but ruined. Although why 'ruined,' I cannot make out; she seems to be quite undamaged in all meaningful respects. A capable artist will be a useful addition to the staff. And I shan't have to pay her a salary —just think of the saving!"

"This is a trick."

The voice spoke just behind me. I started, and turned. Incredible as it seems, I had quite forgotten Lucas.

His passions were under control; only the intense glitter of his eyes betrayed his feelings as, ignoring me, he walked up to Emerson.

"A trick," he repeated. "You cannot mean to encourage this, Emerson. You don't mean it."

"Your lordship fails to understand my character," said Emerson smoothly. "Who am I to stand in the path of true love? I honestly believe," he added, looking intently at Lucas, "that this is the best of all possible arrangements for all of us. Don't you agree, my lord?"

Lucas did not reply immediately. I felt a faint stir of pity for him as he struggled with his emotions. They were intense; I wondered if, after all, he did love Evelyn, as much as a man of his limited capacity was capable of love. And when he finally spoke, I had to admire his attitude.

"Perhaps you are right. Perhaps this is how it was meant to be. 'There is a fatality that shapes our ends,' as Shakespeare has put it. . . ."

"If not precisely in those words," Emerson agreed. "May I congratulate you, my lord, on behaving like a true British nobleman. Will you heap coals of fire on our heads by joining us in a toast to the engaged couple? Walter—come, Walter, wake up, Walter—"

He joggled his brother's elbow. Walter raised his face from where it had been resting on Evelyn's bowed head; he looked like a man waking from an ecstatic dream to find that the dream is reality.

Lucas hesitated for a moment, looking at Evelyn. She didn't see him; she was gazing up into Walter's face like an acolyte adoring a saint. Lucas shrugged, or perhaps he shivered; the movement rippled through his body and was gone.

"I am not so noble as that," he said, with a faint smile. "Excuse me. I think I want to be alone for a while."

"Off into the sunset," said Emerson, as Lucas's retreating form was silhouetted against the west. "How theatrical these young persons are! Thank God for our sober, middle-aged common sense, eh, Peabody?"

I watched Evelyn and Walter walk away. His arm was about

her waist; her head still rested on his shoulder, and if he felt pain, where it pressed against the bullet wound, he showed no signs of it.

"Yes, indeed," I replied sourly. "Thank God for it."

11

I NEVER expected I would be concerned about Lucas, but as the hours passed and he did not return, I began to worry.

We had eaten one of the vilest dinners imaginable. It had been cooked by Abdullah; he explained that Lucas's cook and the waiter who had accompanied us to camp that morning were not to be found. I found this alarming, but Emerson, who was in an inexplicably good mood, shrugged it away.

We were all sitting on the ledge together, watching the moon rise; but Emerson and I might as well have been alone, for all the conversation we got out of the other two. They didn't hear a word anyone said to them. I was therefore forced to confide my worries about Lucas to Emerson, although I did not expect to find much concern in that quarter. In this assumption I was correct.

"He has probably gone with his men," Emerson said calmly.

"I think, Peabody, that we have seen the last of his lordship."

"You mean—he has deserted us? He would not be so cowardly!"

"I fancy he might. But let me do him justice; he has not abandoned us to danger. Indeed, I think it possible that we have also seen the last of the Mummy."

"Nonsense," I said irritably. "Lucas could not have been the Mummy. We saw them together on more than one occasion."

"I may be wrong," said Emerson—in a tone that contradicted the false modesty of his words. "His suggestion—which had also occurred to me—may be the correct one: that there is an unrobbed tomb back in the hills which the villagers hope to exploit. In any case, it must be obvious even to you, Peabody, that the instigator of the plot is not an Egyptian; it contains too many features that could have been invented only by a European or an Englishman. Or perhaps an American; they have their share of unscrupulous collectors. . . ."

"What are you talking about?"

"Professional jealousy, Peabody. No doubt it seems incredible to you that any reasonable man would act so, but I assure you, there are colleagues in my field who would go to any extreme to exploit a sensational discovery such as a royal tomb. I have the concession at Amarna; I had a devil of a time wringing it out of Maspero, but not even he would dare take it away now. The man is quite capable of employing such tricks to make me abandon my excavation and leave the field open to him. Another feather in his cap! Not that Maspero is the only one—"

"Of all the absurd ideas!"

"What is the alternative? If not the place, it is a person who is under attack. I have no enemies—"

"Ha," I said.

"A few individuals may resent my justified criticism," Emerson said meditatively. "Yes; I daresay there are some individuals so degraded that they might respond to my well-intended suggestions with rancor—"

"If anyone murders you," I interrupted, "which seems quite likely, it will be in the heat of anger, with a club or some other convenient blunt instrument. I am only surprised it has not happened before this."

"My enemies are professional, not personal," Emerson insisted. "Walter has none, of either kind. His character is regrettably mild. Are you sure there are no discarded lovers pursuing you?"

The question did not deserve an answer.

After a moment, Emerson went on, "Then it must be Miss Evelyn who inspires such agitated activity on the part of our unknown enemy. If that is the case, the events of this evening must settle the question. His lordship, having received his *congé*, has departed—"

The rattle of pebbles on the path below disproved his words as soon as they were spoken. I knew the step.

The moon was a spectacular silver orb, almost at the full, shedding a silvery radiance over the silent desert, the river, the cliffs. The light was not quite bright enough for me to distinguish Emerson's expression. I much regretted that.

"Lucas," I said, turning to welcome the newcomer with a warmth I had not heretofore displayed. "I am relieved you are back. I was worried about you."

"How kind of you." Lucas looked, betrayingly, into the shadows behind us, where Evelyn and Walter were sitting. Receiving no greeting from that quarter, his eyes returned to me. "I felt the need of a walk. I have walked; I have accomplished my purpose. You did not suppose I would desert you?"

"I felt sure you would not," I said.

From Emerson, beside me, came no comment.

"Of course not. Tomorrow I will endeavor to forget certain . . . personal griefs in hard work; it will be delightful to explore

240

the cliffs for buried treasure. In the meantime, I remembered Emerson's suggestion; I have brought a bottle of wine, in which to drink to my cousin."

I could not help shooting a triumphant glance at Emerson. He sat in glum silence, his face in shadow; only his hand was visible, clenched whitely on the arm of his chair. I don't know why I should have been so pleased to see Lucas behaving like a gentleman for a change. I never liked the man. . . . But of course I do know why. I would have defended Satan himself if he had been in disfavor with Emerson.

Lucas was as good as his word; it was as if he had determined to humble himself as thoroughly as possible. He carried a tray with glasses and a bottle; putting this down, with a flourish that struck me as rather pathetic, he began to work at the cork.

"Won't you persuade Evelyn to join us?" he asked in a low voice. "I dare not; to be candid, I am ashamed of myself for my behavior this afternoon. I am of a passionate nature; I suppose dear old Grandfather would say it was my Latin blood."

So I called Evelyn, and she came out of the deep shadow where she had been sitting, holding Walter by the hand and smiling shyly at her cousin. I found his excuses inadequate. Nothing could possibly excuse his reference to her misfortune in front of Walter. But, on the other hand, this very reference had brought about the present happy state of affairs, and I must say that Lucas made his apologies like a man and a Briton. Walter received them in the same spirit; to see the two young fellows clasp hands, there in the moonlight, was a touching sight.

Then Lucas handed us each a glass and raised his own.

"To Evelyn's future!" he cried. "May it bring all that her closest kinsman could desire!"

We drank. Even Emerson took a sip. He made a face, like a nasty little boy taking medicine. He had moved his chair out near the table, and I could see him quite well; his expression of sour disapproval pleased me no end. Seeing that he was in no mood to do the proper thing, and realizing that it was a little too much to expect of Lucas, I proposed the next toast.

"To Walter! May he make Evelyn as happy as she deserves—or I will deal with him!"

"Spoken with characteristic tact," said Emerson under his breath.

Walter leaned forward and put his hand on mine.

"You may deal with me as you see fit, Miss Amelia," he said warmly. "Don't think I shall ever forget that it is to your encouragement, in large measure, that I owe my present happiness. I hope you will be often with us; you may keep your eye on me that way and make sure I measure up to your expectations."

Emerson rolled his eyes heavenward.

"I may take advantage of your invitation," I said cheerfully. "I have developed quite a taste for archaeology."

I suppose it was the wine that made me feel so giddy. We all waxed cheerful under its benign influence—all but Emerson, who sat brooding like a hard stone statue. Finally, when the bottle was empty, Lucas concluded the fete.

"If all goes well, we shall have a busy day tomorrow. Rest is advisable. I suggest, gentlemen, that we stand watch tonight. Tomorrow may bring an end to the mysteries that surround us; let us make sure no mishap occurs tonight."

"Just what I was about to suggest," muttered Emerson, shooting a piercing glance at Lucas. "Which watch would you prefer, my lord?"

Lucas replied with a shrug. It was arranged that he should remain on guard for the first three hours of the night, Emerson for the second watch, and Walter for the remainder. I carried Evelyn off to our sleeping chamber; she was in such a fog her feet seemed not to touch the ground, and after a few incoherent exclamations of gratitude and joy, she quickly fell asleep.

I was drowsy myself, unusually so, for the hour was still early; yet my drooping eyelids obstinately refused to remain shut. Some indefinable nagging discomfort kept forcing them open. The discomfort was purely mental; I had become inured by then to the hard mattress and the other rugged accompaniments to camping out. There is nothing more abominable than being in a state of bodily exhaustion and mental irritation; I was too lethargic to get up and seek some means of occupying my mind, but I was too uneasy to fall asleep. Try as I might, I could not pin down the cause of my uneasiness. We were, of course, in danger of a nocturnal visit from a singularly unpleasant apparition, but that was not what bothered me; I was becoming accustomed to that worry, it was like a familiar ache in a particular tooth. I thought if it continued much longer I should probably become quite accustomed to it. No, this was another sort of twinge; I could not locate it. I ought to have been in a state of peaceful triumph; I had won out over Emerson and attained what I most desired for the girl who was so dear to me. . . .

Had I won out, though?

The more I recalled Emerson's behavior and speech that day, the more I wondered. It was almost as if he had been working to attain the same end; everything he had said was a spur, a prick, a goad, to urge his brother on to a declaration.

I ground my teeth together. If Emerson wanted Evelyn for his brother, he must have some ulterior motive that escaped me.

There came a sound, at the entrance to the tomb chamber. The curtain was lifted.

I rolled over. The rough mattress crackled.

"Who is it?" I whispered. "Lucas, is that you?"

"Yes. What is wrong, Miss Amelia? Can't you sleep?"

With a gigantic effort I dragged myself from bed and assumed my dressing gown. Evelyn was still sleeping sweetly. I tiptoed to the doorway.

"I can't sleep," I said softly. "Perhaps I am too tired. And you, Lucas? Did you have some reason for looking in just now?"

"I don't know. . . . I am strangely uneasy tonight. I heard you stirring, and was afraid. . . ."

"I am uneasy too."

I joined him on the ledge. The night was perfect. The world dreamed peacefully under the moon. The air felt cool; I shivered, and drew my dressing gown close around my throat.

"You ought to sleep," Lucas said. "Perhaps another glass of wine is what you need."

"Lucas, you are not drinking more wine? Surely that is unwise."

"I am not made of iron," Lucas said; his voice was so savage I recoiled. "I will do what must be done; but allow me something with which to fortify myself. Come; I insist that you join me."

Fool that I was! I felt sorry for him. His genuine emotion seemed more pathetic to me than the theatrics he had shown earlier. He was pouring the wine when Emerson came out of his chamber and advanced upon us.

"A party, and you did not invite me?" he said. "Or am I interrupting a more personal meeting?"

"Don't be any more foolish than you can help," I said. My last words were muffled in a huge yawn. "Oh, dear, I am so tired. I don't know why I can't sleep."

"Evelyn seems to be the only one with a clear conscience," said Lucas, snapping his teeth together. "Or is the lucky man sleeping too?"

"Yes," Emerson said. "Walter is asleep."

"And why not you? It is too early for you to relieve me."

"Still, you may as well retire now that I am here. There is no point in all of us being awake. Sometimes I never go to bed at all. This seems to be one of those nights. I don't know why they happen," said Emerson musingly. "It is unaccountable. But I feel just now as if I should never want to sleep again."

I knew then that something was badly wrong; and that Emerson was aware of it. His idiotic speech was an unconvincing lie; his lids were half closed, his shoulders drooped; and now that I looked at him more closely, I saw that his thick black hair was damp, as if he had been pouring water on it . . . to keep awake? I had employed a similar trick myself, the preceding night. All my senses prickled in alarm.

"Oh, very well," Lucas said sulkily. "Since I am of no use, I may as well remove myself and finish my bottle in private—unless I can persuade you two to join me in a glass? No? Good night, then. I have no desire to go into that stifling hole of a tomb; I shall sleep in the tent down below, and you, my gallant Emerson, can waken me with a shout if we have unexpected visitors."

Cradling the wine bottle in his arms, he staggered down the path. I had not realized he was so intoxicated. Was that what Emerson feared—that Lucas would fail as a guard because of his drinking?

The moment he was out of sight, Emerson turned on me and dragged me up out of the chair into which I had slumped. He shook me till my head rolled and my hair came loose from the net.

"Wake up, Peabody! If you fall asleep, I shall slap you till you howl. Curse it, don't you understand that we have been drugged?"

"Drugged?" I repeated stupidly.

"I have been fighting sleep myself for an hour, and a hard fight it was. Have you nothing in that medicine box of yours to counteract the effects of laudanum?"

I tried to think. Something was certainly dulling my mind.

"My smelling salts," I said, with an effort. "They are extremely strong. . . ."

"Oh, damnation," said Emerson. "A pretty picture that will be! Well, it's better than nothing. Go fetch them. Hurry."

To hurry was impossible. I could barely drag myself along. But

I found the smelling salts, and then had a look at Evelyn. A single glance told me Emerson was right. She was sleeping too soundly. I shook her, without effect. Either she had received a larger dose of the drug, or her delicate constitution was more susceptible to it than mine. It would be difficult to awaken her.

I applied the bottle to my own nose. It was certainly effective. Feeling much more alert, I hastened back to Emerson, who was leaning up against the cliff with his arms and legs at strange angles and his eyes slightly crossed. I thrust the bottle at him. He started back, banging his head against the rock, and made several profane remarks.

"Now tell me what is wrong," I said, recapping the bottle. "What is it you fear will happen? If your reasoning is correct—"

"My reasoning was damnably, stupidly, fatally wrong," Emerson replied forcibly. "I am missing a vital clue—a piece of information that would make sense of the whole business. I suspect you hold that clue, Peabody. You must tell me—"

He stopped speaking; I suppose the expression on my face struck him dumb. I felt the hairs on the back of my neck rising. I was facing the lower end of the path; and there, barely visible, around the corner of the cliff, something moved. A low moan echoed through the air.

Emerson spun around. The moaning cry came again.

It was a frightening sound, but I knew, after the first moment, that it did not come from the throat of the Mummy. This cry held human anguish and pain; I could not have resisted its appeal if a thousand gibbering, gesticulating Mummies had stood in my way.

Quickly as I moved, Emerson was before me. He went more cautiously than I would have done, his arm holding me back, and when we reached the bottom of the path he thrust me away while he went on to investigate. The object I had seen, whatever it was, had disappeared from sight; Emerson followed it into invisibility, and for a moment I held my breath. Then I heard his low exclamation—not of fear, but of horror and distress. Rounding the rock corner, I saw him kneeling on the ground beside the prostrate body of a man. I knew the man, although, God forgive me, I had almost forgotten him. It was our vanished servant—the dragoman, Michael.

"Oh, heavens," I cried, flinging myself down beside the recumbent form. "Is he dead?"

"Not yet. But I fear . . ."

Emerson raised his hand, which had been resting on the back of Michael's head. The stains on his fingers looked like ink in the moonlight.

Michael was wearing the same faded blue-and-white-striped robe that he had worn the day of his disappearance. It was now torn and crumpled. I reached for his wrist, to feel his pulse, but a closer sight of his outflung arm made me exclaim aloud. The bared wrist was swollen and bloody.

"He has been a prisoner," I said, forcing my fingers to touch the torn flesh. "These are the marks of ropes."

"They are. How is his pulse?"

"Steady, but feeble. He must have medical attention at once. I will do what I can, but my skill is so small. . . . Can we carry him up to the tomb? Perhaps Lucas will help."

"I can manage."

Emerson turned Michael over; with a single heave of his broad shoulders he lifted the dragoman's slight form into his arms, and rose.

And then—dear Heaven, I can scarcely write of it now without a reminiscent shudder. Screams—the high, agonized shriek of a woman in the extremity of terror! They died in a long, wailing moan.

Emerson bounded forward, carrying the unconscious man as if

he weighed no more than a feather. I followed; and as we came around the corner of the cliff, the whole hideous tableau burst upon our eyes, like a scene from the worst conceptions of Madame Tussaud.

On the ledge above us stood the Mummy. The blind, bandaged head was turned toward us; one stubby leg was lifted, as if our sudden appearance had stopped it in midstep. To the crumbling, rotting bandages of its breast, the horror clasped the unconscious form of Evelyn.

Her tumbled golden curls hung down over its arm; her little white feet peeped pathetically out of the folds of her nightdress. After the first scream of terror she had fainted dead away, as any girl might, finding herself in the arms of such a suitor.

I began pounding on Emerson's back. He was barring the entrance to the narrow path, and I was frantic to pass him and attack the thing. I remembered poor Evelyn's exclamation on that far-off day, when a ghoulish peddler had tried to sell us a mummified hand. She would die, she said, if the withered flesh should touch her. . . . Well, we had it trapped now. If it had supernatural powers, it would need them all to escape *me.*

The passage of time seemed to halt; I felt like one trapped in quicksand, or the slow, floating motion of a dream, where enormous effort is required to make the slightest movement. Then all sorts of things happened at once.

Lucas came out of the tent, which was not far from us. I assumed he had been asleep, had been wakened by Evelyn's screams, and, his senses dulled by wine, had been slow to respond. He took in the situation at a glance, and moved more quickly than I would have expected. In his haste, he collided with us. Emerson kept his feet with difficulty, falling back against the cliff face with the body of the dying man still in his arms; I was thrown to the ground. While we were tumbling about, the Mummy took advantage of our confusion. Flexing its stiff knees, the creature jumped

248

—actually leaped from the ledge. Such was my state of mind, I half expected to see it take wing and soar through the air like a giant bat. Alighting, still erect, amid the tumble of rocks at the base of the cliff, it scrambled down the slope and ran. Evelyn's fair hair streamed out behind.

"Pursue it!" I shrieked. "Do not let it escape!"

At least that is what I believe I shrieked. Emerson informs me that my language was less coherent, and so inflammatory that he positively blushed, despite the urgency of the moment. He, of course, was in a dreadful predicament; encumbered by the injured man, he could hardly fling him to the ground. I was so entangled in the abominable garments forced on women by the decrees of fashion that I could not arise. It all depended on Lucas; and after the first confused moments, he rose to the occasion.

"Never fear," he cried, leaping up. "It will not escape me! Remain here—we must not all abandon the camp—I will rescue Evelyn—"

Running fleetly, he was already several yards away as his last words reached my ears.

An echoing cry came from above. Looking up, I saw Walter, who had just emerged from his sleeping chamber. If he had been drugged, the vision before his eyes woke him with a vengeance; with another shout of mingled rage and horror, he flung himself down the slope and followed Lucas.

As I started after them, Emerson kicked me in the shin. I must confess he could not have stopped me in any other way, since his arms were occupied.

"This is madness," he groaned. "Keep your head, Peabody; someone must act sensibly—follow me, you must remain with Michael."

The advice was excellent; the difficulty was in following it. The folly of pursuit was manifest; if the young men could not catch up with the mummified miscreant, it was futile for a woman,

249

hampered by her skirts, to try and do so. I could still see the pale shape of the Mummy, as it flitted in and out among the rocks. Walter stumbled along behind, waving his arms and shouting. All this happened, of course, in far less time than it takes to write it down.

I ran after Emerson, who was ascending the path in great leaps. If I was not wringing my hands, it was because I needed them to keep my balance. Emerson was correct; it was necessary for one of us to tend Michael's wounds, but I really did not see how I could bear to remain there, in ignorance and forced inactivity.

Emerson laid his burden gently upon his couch. To do him justice, he had not wasted a moment, nor did he waste time now in unnecessary directions to me. Instantly he turned back to the entrance. I reached for the lamp, meaning to light it. As I did so, there came a crack and a whine from without. Emerson's tall form, silhouetted in the doorway, staggered and fell.

12

It is vain to attempt to describe my sensations at that moment. I had recognized the sound as that of a bullet. I dropped the lamp; I forgot my injured servant; for an instant I even forgot Evelyn and her deadly peril. I started toward the spot where I had seen Emerson fall.

My heart had not missed more than a few beats, however, when a hand caught my ankle and brought me crashing to the ground. I fell on top of Emerson, and heard him grunt with pain. My hands, fumbling at his face, encountered a wet, sticky flow.

"You are wounded," I exclaimed. "My God, Emerson—"

Emerson sneezed.

"I beg that you will leave off tickling me," he said irritably. "The region around the chin and jaw is particularly sensitive. For God's sake, Peabody, stop sniveling; it is only a cut from a bit of flying rock."

251

"Oh," I said. "But the shot was aimed at you! In heaven's name, what are you doing now? Don't go out there—"

He was crawling toward the entrance.

"The shot was meant as a warning," he said over his shoulder. "We are safe enough—for the moment—unless we try to leave the tomb. Hand me that shirt of Walter's, if you please—it is lying across his bed—and my walking stick. Thank you. Now let us see—"

A second shot rewarded his demonstration when he draped the shirt over the stick and extended it out the doorway. Emerson withdrew it.

"He is there, among the rocks," he said calmly.

"He? Who?"

"You sound like one of the villagers' donkeys," said Emerson. "Who else could it be? You must have deduced his identity by now. I have known it for some time; but his motive still eludes me. What the devil ails the fellow, to seek to win a wife by such means? I would not have thought him capable of the insane passion that prompts such acts."

Once—even a few hours earlier—his calm, drawling voice would have driven me wild. Now I was seized by the same icy calm. We had already delayed too long; even if we could escape from this ambush uninjured, Evelyn and her abductor would be out of sight. It was up to Walter now. At least he had only one enemy to face. The other was below, with a rifle in his hands.

"There is motive," I said. "I am only now beginning to see. . . . No, no, it is impossible. From the first I too suspected Lucas. But he was not here. He did not arrive until long after we did, long after the Mummy made its first appearance. He did not know we would stop here—"

"I think it is high time we compared notes," said Emerson, recumbent before the entrance. "You might give Michael a little water, Peabody; I fear that is all we can do for the poor fellow now, since we dare not strike a light, and your medical supplies are in your sleeping chamber. Then come here and join me."

I did what I could for Michael. It was little enough. He was still breathing, but that was about all I could say. I then crawled to the entrance and lay down flat, next to Emerson, who was peering out across the moonlit plain, his chin propped on his folded arms.

"You and I have been at cross purposes since we met, Peabody," he said. "It is a pity; for we might have prevented this unfortunate business if we had taken the trouble to be civil to one another. You see, I have known for some days that his lordship has been lying. Reis Hassan talked to the reis of the *Cleopatra*, and passed some of the gossip on to me. His lordship's payments to his crew have been princely. By means of exorbitant bribes, he got underway the very day after you left. He was moored downriver, at Minieh, the day you landed here.

"But that is not the important thing. His lordship has a confederate—not a hired native, but a man as dedicated to evil as he is. That confederate is the man who is playing the role of the Mummy. This man's whereabouts, prior to his public appearance here, are unknown. I believe he came here some time ago and set the scene for the drama—bribing Mohammed, introducing the mummy Walter found into an empty tomb. His costume, his role were planned well in advance—probably in Cairo, where, I imagine, young Lord Ellesmere arrived earlier than he led you to believe. Do you have an idea who this confederate might be?"

"No. Lucas must have bribed him well. Of course it could be a friend of Lucas's—one of his companions in vice. I do not know them. But, Emerson, there is one great flaw in your argument. How could they know where to set the scene? We did not plan to stop here—"

"Then Reis Hassan is a liar. He informs me that you laid out your itinerary while still in Cairo, and that he tried several times to dissuade you from it."

"Oh, that. I did mention the possibility of visiting Amarna—along with a number of other sites. But how could Lucas know?"

"From Michael, I imagine. Did he have an opportunity to speak with him before you left Cairo?"

"He did indeed," I said grimly. "And to think that we introduced them, so that Michael might assist Lucas in the selection of a dragoman. . . . Good God, what a fool I was!"

"You had no reason to suspect any danger. Nor did Michael. His lordship was your friend, Evelyn's relation. It was not until developments here became serious that Michael began to wonder about his harmless indiscretion. He is an intelligent man, and devoted to you body and soul; on the day of his disappearance he asked to speak to you alone—"

"And Lucas heard him! He struck him down and spirited him away."

"Not Lucas, but one of his men. He kept the poor fellow prisoner in one of the caves that are so common in these cliffs, and when we obstinately refused to succumb to the laudanum he had placed in our wine, he carried Michael here to distract us while his confederate reached Evelyn.

"I must admit that the fellow has imagination; he acts brilliantly and unhesitatingly in emergencies, and makes good use of any fortuitous circumstances that can be turned to account. My illness was one such lucky accident—lucky for him—but I feel sure he and his confederate had planned some means of detaining you here—damage to the dahabeeyah, or to one of us. At that point in time, his lordship had not determined to commit murder. He hoped to attain his ends by less drastic means, although it seems clear he prepared for the worst, in case it should become necessary. And I was misled. Not until you were attacked this afternoon did I fully realize that Evelyn was the real object of the attentions we have been receiving, and even then I was fool enough to suppose that once she had accepted Walter, his lordship would give up his idiotic and dangerous games."

Emerson extended his stick once again out the entrance. Another shot rang out, followed by the splintering of rock.

"Still there," he said. "I wonder how long he means to keep us here. We are safe so long as we do not confront him. He will have some specious excuse to explain why he failed to rescue Evelyn; I think the fellow is actually vain enough to suppose he can get away with it. Shall we save our skins, Peabody, and sit still?"

"While Evelyn is in the clutches of that monster?" I demanded. "Don't bait me, Emerson; you have no more intention of accepting this than I do. Do you think Walter—"

"I am extremely concerned about Walter," said Emerson; I knew him well enough now to hear the controlled agony under his calm tones. "But at the moment we can do nothing to help him or Evelyn until we understand what is behind this affair. There is some more desperate motive behind his lordship's acts than frustrated love. Think, Peabody; if you have ever used your brain, now is the time."

"I have a faint inkling of the truth," I said, in a stifled voice. "I hate to contemplate it; for if I am right. . . . Emerson, you and I have behaved like fools. If I had known what you knew about Lucas's movements; and if you had known what I am about to tell you—"

"Speak, then. That is the trouble with women, even the best of them," Emerson added. "They *will* indulge in vain cries of 'if only' and 'had I but known.' "

"The criticism is justified," I said; my pride was thoroughly leveled by the magnitude of the disaster. "Listen, then, while I narrate Evelyn's story."

He listened. Only his eyes moved, so intent was he on what I had to say.

255

"Yes," he said, when I finished. "The clue is there, somewhere. A vast amount of money may be an inducement to violence. But how? I cannot see it, even now. Is it possible that his lordship lied to you about the old man's death? If he still lives, and contemplates restoring Evelyn as his heiress—"

"No, he is dead; one of my acquaintances in Cairo knew of it."

Emerson struck his fist against the floor.

"The conclusion is inescapable, Peabody; in some way we do not comprehend, Evelyn must have control of the fortune his lordship so ardently desires. He has done everything a man could do to induce her to become his wife. I believed his sole motive was passionate love of his cousin. But in this day and age an English girl cannot be forced into marriage, and a forced marriage is the only kind that could come out of this night's work. Nothing the wretch could do now would induce Evelyn to marry him of her own free will. No; it is the lady's money that is being sought, not the lady's person. If we only knew how—"

"I believe I do know," I interrupted. "I told you that before the late Lord Ellesmere died he gathered all Evelyn's belongings and sent them to her. Lucas told me—good heavens, he actually boasted of it—that he was in full control at Ellesmere Castle while the old gentleman lay ill. If Ellesmere had softened toward Evelyn and wished to restore her to favor, Lucas would make certain he did not reach his lawyers in order to make a new will. But he might write a new will—a holograph will, I believe it is called. Knowing Lucas as he did, the poor old man saw only one way to ensure that such a document would survive. He could send it to Evelyn—packed in with her other possessions. He hoped to escape arousing Lucas's suspicions that way."

"By Gad, Peabody, I think you've got it!" Emerson exclaimed.

"I think so too. Lucas has tried every possible means of getting to those boxes of Evelyn's, or of having them destroyed unopened. He must have missed them in Rome; and when they arrived in

Egypt they went into the safekeeping of Baring, who is the most powerful man in the government. He was a friend of father's, and he knows of Lucas's unsavory reputation; from such a man Lucas had no chance of extracting the precious boxes. Alas; for if he had—"

"Evelyn would not now be in danger," Emerson's quick wits supplied the conclusion. "He may not be certain that such a will exists, but he must have reason to suspect that it does. If he could destroy it he would be safe. Failing that, he pursued Evelyn. As her husband he would have control of her fortune in any case, and he would have a good excuse to take charge of her baggage. But the marriage plan failed as well; thanks to our strenuous efforts, his lordship has now only one means left of gaining his ends. . . . Peabody, you must not blame yourself. How could you possibly have suspected this?"

"I don't blame myself," I said, wiping away the tears that were stealing down my face. "As you say, I could not have suspected. It is the most farfetched scheme I have ever encountered; only a frivolous, amoral man, who had been reading too many wild romances, would think of such a thing. And vain regret is useless. I will not indulge in it. I will get out of here and go after Evelyn, and I will kill his lordship if he has harmed her."

I rose to my knees. Emerson put his hand in the center of my back and pushed me down again.

"I am in complete agreement with your program. But let us try to think of some safer way to do it."

"Can we expect no help from anyone? What of Abdullah? And the crewmen on the boat—surely they heard the shots."

"I have grave suspicions of Abdullah," Emerson said grimly. "You forget, Peabody, that these people are desperately poor."

"And Reis Hassan too? I thought he looked strange the other day when you were questioning him."

"Hassan is one of the few honest men I know. Unfortunately

he is also superstitious. He was ashamed to admit to me that he had been terrorized by Mohammed's tales of ghosts and curses. No; he will come, I believe, if he can overcome his fears and persuade his crew. But we cannot count on that. Then there is the crew of his lordship's dahabeeyah to be considered. What if they have been paid to prevent a rescue attempt? No, Peabody, if we are to get out of here in time, it must be by ourselves. And I think we had better set about it."

"But how . . .?"

"There are pebbles and rocks on the threshold. When I give the signal, begin rolling them down. Meanwhile, I will creep along the path in the other direction and try to get behind him."

"It is a foolhardy scheme," I said. "He will surely see or hear you."

"From below he has a poor chance of hitting me if I keep low. You must cover any sounds I make by the exuberance of your performance and, if possible, induce him to empty the magazine of his repeater. Come, come, Peabody; if you have any more practical suggestion, I will be happy to hear it. I have never had the inclination to be a hero. But we must do something, and soon."

I had nothing to say—nothing practical, that is. There were many things I wanted to say. I wanted to say them so badly that I had to bury my teeth in my lower lip to keep it from forming the words. I turned my head away.

Emerson took me by the shoulders and rolled me over. He had lifted himself upon his elbows; I lay between them, like an unfortunate mouse under a cat's paws. His face was so close I could see the bristles of his whiskers.

"It seems possible that we shall not live through the night," he remarked. "I would hate to die without having. . . . Damnation! I *will* do it, even at the risk of surviving to face the consequences!"

Whereupon he bent his head and kissed me full on the mouth.

At first I was too stupefied by surprise to do anything. Afterward, I was simply too stupefied to do anything. It was not the first time I had been kissed. Several of the suitors who appeared after I inherited Papa's money had presumed. . . . Well, let us be honest. I had encouraged them to kiss me. I was immensely curious about the process. In all cases it proved to be a deadly bore. It occurred to me, very soon after Emerson began kissing me, that previous experience in this field is not always a dependable guide.

At some point I must have closed my eyes, although I was not aware of doing so. I kept them closed after he raised his head. Thus I did not see him go. He was, I think, somewhat stupefied himself, or he would have waited for me to begin the divertissement he had suggested. The first intimation of his departure I received was a shot that struck the entrance above my head and sprayed my upturned face with little stinging pellets of stone.

I rolled over, snatched up a handful of pebbles, and pitched them down the path. They made considerable racket, but to my straining ears, Emerson's progress along the path made even more noise. I began throwing out everything I could lay my hands on. Boxes, books, bottles, and Emerson's boots went tumbling down, followed by tins of peas and peaches, the mirror, and someone's shaving mug. What Lucas thought of this performance I cannot imagine; he must have concluded that we had lost our wits. Such a cacophony of different sounds was never heard. The mirror made a particularly effective crash.

The action accomplished what we had hoped. Lucas was nervous; he let off a perfect fusillade of shots. None of them came anywhere near the mouth of the tomb, so I concluded he was shooting at the mirror, the tins, and the boots. A period of silence ensued. I had meant to count the shots, and had forgotten to do so. It would not have been much use in any case, since I had not the slightest idea of how many bullets the gun held. I could only hope that the cessation of shooting meant that he had emptied the weapon and was now reloading, or refilling, or whatever the term is; and that Emerson had succeeded in descending the cliff unharmed.

He had! Shouts, thuds, the sounds of a furious struggle told me that so far our plan had miraculously succeeded. I leaped to my feet and ran to join the fray, hoping to get in a blow or two on my own account. I had an urge to pound something, preferably Lucas, with my clenched fists.

As I neared the scene of battle I found Emerson engaged, or so it appeared, with two adversaries. The agitation of long white skirts identified one of them as the missing Abdullah.

In the struggle Emerson was flung to the ground. Stepping back, Lucas lifted the rifle to his shoulder and aimed at Emerson's defenseless breast.

I was several yards away, too far to do anything except shout, which of course I did. The sensation was nightmarish; I felt as if I were on a treadmill that ran backward as fast as I ran forward, so that I made no progress at all. I screamed again and ran faster, knowing I would be too late. . . .

And then Abdullah sprang forward and wrenched the weapon from Lucas's hands. The villain's finger had been on the trigger; the bullet exploded harmlessly into the air.

I did not pause to speculate on Abdullah's change of heart; I flew straight at Lucas. I shudder to think what damage I might have inflicted if Emerson had not anticipated me. Rising, he seized the wretch by the throat and shook him till he hung limp.

"Calm yourself," he gasped, fending me off with his elbow. "We can't murder the rascal until he has told us what we want to know." Then, turning to his erstwhile foreman, he said, "You will have to decide whose side you are on, Abdullah; vacillation is bad for the character. I am willing to forget your recent indiscretions in return for cooperation."

"But I did not know," Abdullah muttered, holding the rifle as if it were burning his fingers. "He say, he want only his woman; she is his. What is a woman, to make such trouble for us?"

"A true Moslem philosophy," said Emerson drily. "As you see, Abdullah, he lied. He was ready to kill—and you, I think, would have been among the victims. He could not leave witnesses against him. Now . . ."

He was still holding Lucas, whose face had turned an unbecoming shade of lavender. He gave him an extra shake for good measure.

"Now, your lordship, speak up. Where have they gone? I beg, don't tell me you don't know; for the expectation of that information is the only thing that keeps me from throttling you here and now."

His tone was almost genial; his lips were curved in a slight smile. But Lucas was not deceived.

"Very well," he muttered. "The royal tomb. I told him to take her there—"

"If you are lying . . ." Emerson squeezed.

Lucas gurgled horribly. When he had gotten his breath back, he gasped,

"No, no, it is the truth! And now you will let me go? I can do you no more harm. . . ."

"You insult my intelligence," Emerson said, and flung him down on the ground. With one foot planted in the middle of Lucas's back, he turned to me. "You must sacrifice another petticoat, Peabody. Only be quick; we have lost too much time already."

We left Lucas bound hand and foot where he had fallen—not with my petticoat, for of course I was not wearing one. Using Abdullah's knife, which he politely offered me, I ripped up the full skirts of my dressing gown, slit them fore and aft, and bound

261

them to my nether limbs. It was wonderful what a feeling of freedom this brought! I swore I would have trousers made as soon as possible.

Abdullah remained to guard Lucas. Emerson seemed to have regained all his former confidence in his foreman; he explained that Abdullah had not been fighting him, but had been trying to separate the two Englishmen. I suppose the Egyptian's attitude was understandable, considering his sex and his nationality.

If it had not been for the gnawing anxiety that drove us, I would have found the moonlight hike a thrilling experience. With what ease did I glide across the sand in my makeshift trousers! How lovely the contrast of shadow and silver light among the tumbled rocks of the wadi! There was food for meditation, too, in the events of the evening; our brilliant triumph just when disaster seemed imminent was a subject for modest congratulation. Hope began to raise a cautious head. Surely, if the mummified villain had carried Evelyn so far, her immediate demise was not meditated. We might yet be in time to save her.

The pace Emerson set left me no breath for conversation; and I do not think I would have spoken if it had. Let my reader not suppose that I had forgotten the effrontery—the bold action—in short, the kiss. I could not decide whether to bury the subject forever in icy silence, or to annihilate Emerson—at a more appropriate time, naturally—with a well-chosen, scathing comment. I occupied myself, when I was not picturing Evelyn in a variety of unpleasant positions, by composing scathing comments.

With such thoughts to distract me, the journey was accomplished in less time than I had expected, but it was a tiring, uncomfortable walk—or run—and I was breathless by the time we reached that part of the narrow canyon in which the royal tomb was located.

Emerson spoke then for the first time. It was only a curt order for silence and caution. We crept up to the entrance on all fours.

The precaution was not necessary. Expecting Lucas's triumph, the foolish Mummy had not kept guard at the entrance. When I peered into the opening I saw a tiny pinprick of light, far down in the black depths.

Now that we were almost at our goal, feverish impatience replaced the exhilaration that had carried me to the spot. I was on fire to rush in. I feared, not only for Evelyn, but for Walter; either he had lost himself in the desert, or he had met some disastrous fate, for if he had succeeded in wresting Evelyn from her necromantic admirer we would have met him returning. Emerson's anxiety was as great as mine, but he held me back with an arm of iron when I would have rushed impetuously into the tomb. He did not speak; he merely shook his head and pantomimed a slow, exaggeratedly careful stride. So, like stage conspirators, we edged around the fallen rocks still remaining from the avalanche, and set off down the long, steep corridor.

It was impossible to move in utter silence, the path was too encumbered underfoot. Fortunately there were other things in the tomb that made noise. I say 'fortunately,' but I am a liar; I would rather have taken the chance of being overheard than walk through a curtain of bats. The tomb was full of them, and night had roused them to their nocturnal life.

The light grew stronger as we advanced, and before long I could hear a voice rambling on in a soliloquy or monologue, which was a great help in covering the small sounds we inadvertently made. The voice was a man's, and the tones were oddly familiar; but it was not Walter's voice. As we advanced I began to distinguish words; the words, and the smug, self-satisfied tones filled me with amazement. Who could it be who was chatting so unconcernedly in a tomb in the Egyptian desert?

Emerson was in the lead; he stopped me, at the entrance to the side chamber from which the light proceeded. We crouched there, listening; and gradually realization dawned. What a fool I had been. The plot now seemed so obvious I felt a child ought to have detected it.

". . . and so you see, my heart, that cousin Luigi and I are a pair of clever fellows, eh? You say 'luck,' that I won your heart; but no, it was no luck, it was my charm, my handsome face—and that the fool old grandfather not let you see men, any men. When we run away, then Luigi comes to the old grandfather. If grandfather not be good fellow and make Luigi rich, then Luigi make new will himself! Luigi can write like anyone; he writes many fine checks at the university before they catch him and tell him, go home. Luigi is smart fellow, almost as smart as me. When bad old grandfather make new will, hide it in box and send away, then Luigi come to me with new plan. I search your room in Cairo, dressed up like old Egyptian fellow; but the box is not there. We must make another plan. Was I not fine mummy? I am fine actor; I make you all much afraid. And it is I who tell Luigi of this young fool—I was Arab in museum that day, when you meet Master Walter; you look at him as you look once at me, and I know. . . ."

An indignant exclamation from Evelyn interrupted this long-drawn-out piece of braggadocio. The relief of hearing her voice, weak as it was, almost made me collapse.

"If he had not been wounded, and drugged as well, you would never have overcome him," she cried. "What have you done to him? He lies so still. . . . Please let me see how he is injured. Unless —oh, heaven!—he is not—he cannot be—"

Emerson's shoulder, pressed against mine, jerked convulsively, but he did not move.

"No, no," Evelyn's tormentor replied, in a horrid parody of sympathy. "The brave young hero is not dead. But why you sorry? Soon you both be dead. You die together, like Aida and Radames in the beautiful opera of Signor Verdi. I thank my genius compatriot for this idea—so romantic. Together, in the tomb, in the

264

arms of each other." His voice changed; he sounded like a sulky boy as he added, "Luigi say, kill you. Me, to kill? Always the bad job for me; Luigi too much gentleman to make hands dirty. So, I leave you here. I am gentleman too; I do not kill woman. At least I not do it often. Not woman who once I held in my—"

This was too much for Emerson, who was quivering like a boiler about to blow up. With a roar, he erupted into the lighted chamber. I need not say that I was close on his heels.

The first thing I saw was Evelyn's pallid face, streaked with dust and tears, her eyes fairly bulging out of her head as she saw me. The first sound I heard was her cry of "Amelia!" as she collapsed in a swoon of relief and joy.

The poor child was huddled on the littered floor, her hands bound behind her, her pretty hair all tangled and dusty. I lifted her up, and watched complacently as Emerson finished choking Alberto. Yes; the Mummy, the confederate of Lucas-Luigi, the abductor of Evelyn, was none other than her erstwhile lover, whose relationship to her scheming cousin had been made plain by his own boasts. I think that of the two he was the worst; I didn't feel the slightest inclination to interfere as his face turned purple and his flailing hands dropped limply.

Emerson dropped him with a thud and turned to his brother. Walter was lying in the opposite corner, bound hand and foot; he was unconscious, and a darkening bruise on his brow showed how the villain had struck him down. Evelyn came back to consciousness in time to hear Emerson proclaim, in ringing tones, "He is alive! He is not seriously injured!" Whereupon she fainted again, and I had quite a time bringing her around.

The journey back was long and arduous, but it did not seem so to us; our hearts were overflowing with happiness, increased by the knowledge that we had left Alberto bound and gagged in the tomb where he had intended to entomb Evelyn and Walter. The last thing I remember seeing as we left was the mummy costume lying limp and harmless on the floor. It seemed absurd when I looked at it closely that it could have frightened anyone. The head mask was made in a separate piece, the joint being covered by strips of bandaging. And the suit itself buttoned neatly up the front.

II

Two years have passed since the events of which I have written —two years full of thrilling events, both personal and historic. Emerson's fears for the gallant Gordon were, alas, justified; he was horribly murdered in January, before the expeditionary force arrived. But the cause for which he died was not lost; the mad Mahdi himself died the same year, and our forces are beating back the insurgents. My friend Maspero has left the Antiquities Department, which is now under the charge of M. Grebaut, whom Emerson detests even more than he did Maspero. As for Emerson himself . . .

I sit, writing this, on the ledge above the familiar and beloved plain of Amarna; and when I lift my eyes from the page I see the busy groups of workmen scattered about like black ants on the pale sand, as they bring the ruins of Khuenaten's city back to the light of day. My self-appointed Critic has left me in order to supervise the clearing of what appears to have been a sculptor's workshop; several splendid busts have already been found. Emerson pushes himself unnecessarily, for Abdullah is an excellent foreman, reliable and skilled. As Emerson says, there is nothing like a spot of blackmail to make a man perform to the best of his ability. Abdullah never refers to the events of that winter two years ago.

They are surprisingly clear and present to my mind, as if they had happened only yesterday. I never had such a good time in all my life. Oh, certainly, at the time there were moments of extreme discomfort; but the adventure, the danger, the exhilaration of doubt and peril are in retrospect something I rather regret having lost.

We had to interrupt the excavations for a few weeks. To Emerson's deep disgust, it was necessary to carry our captives to Cairo and explain to the authorities there what had happened. I had suggested leaving Alberto in the tomb; it seemed a fitting punishment. But I was dissuaded by Evelyn's horrified protests.

So, at sunrise, we returned to the dahabeeyah, and Emerson made a fine speech to the assembled crew, who squatted on the deck staring at him with round black eyes while he explained that the Mummy had been a hoax, the curse imaginary, and that an ordinary human being had been behind the whole thing. He produced his downcast, shivering captive at the appropriate moment, and I think the sight of an Englishman, one of the Master Race, in bonds and held up to scorn as a common criminal did as much as anything to win their wholehearted allegiance. Lucas's crew gave us no difficulty; their loyalty had been won with money, and as soon as the source of funds dried up, their devotion withered. An expedition set out immediately for the camp and brought back a very thirsty Alberto, together with our luggage and equipment. I myself supervised the removal of poor Michael, on a litter. We set sail at once for Cairo.

It was an enjoyable trip. With the great sail furled and lowered onto blocks on the deck, we let the current bear us downstream. There were occasional misadventures—grounding on sandbars, an encounter with another dahabeeyah that lost the latter its bowsprit and won us the collective curses of the exuberant American passengers; but these are only the normal accidents of Nile travel. In every other way matters could not have been more satisfactory. Michael began to make a good recovery, which relieved my worst fears. The crew outdid itself to please us. The cook produced magnificent meals, we were waited upon like princes, and Reis Hassan obeyed my slightest command. The full moon shone down upon us, the river rolled sweetly by. . . . And Emerson said not a word.

I had waited for him to make some reference, if not an apology, for his outrageous behavior in—for his daring to—for, in short, the kiss. Not only did he remain silent, but he avoided me with a consistency that was little short of marvelous. In such close quarters we ought to have been much together; but whenever I entered the saloon it seemed that Emerson was just leaving, and when I strolled on the deck, admiring the silvery ripples of moonlight on the water, Emerson vanished below. Walter was of no use. He spent all his time with Evelyn. They did not talk, they just sat holding hands and staring stupidly into one another's eyes. Walter was a sensible chap; Evelyn's fortune would not keep him from happiness. Was it possible that Emerson . . . ?

After two days I decided I could wait no longer. I hope I number patience among my virtues, but shilly-shallying, when nothing is to be gained by delay, is not a virtue. So I cornered Emerson on deck one night, literally backing him into a corner. He stood pressed up against the rail that enclosed the upper deck as I advanced upon him, and from the look on his face you would have thought I were a crocodile intent on devouring him, boots, bones, and all.

We had dined formally; I was wearing my crimson gown and I had taken some pains with my hair. I thought, when I looked at myself in the mirror that evening, that I did look well; perhaps Evelyn's flattery had not all been false. As I approached Emerson I was pleasantly aware of the rustle of my full skirts and the movement of the ruffles at my throat.

"No," I said, as Emerson made a sideways movement, like a crab. "Don't try to run away, Emerson, it won't do you a particle of good, for I mean to have my say if I have to shout it after you as we run about the boat. Sit or stand, don't mind me. I shall stand. I think better on my feet."

Emerson squared his shoulders.

"I shall stand. I feel safer on my feet. Proceed, then, Peabody; I know better than to interfere with you when you are in this mood."

"I mean to make you a business proposition," I said. "It is simply this. I have some means; I am not rich, like Evelyn, but I have more than I need, and no dependents. I had meant to leave my money to the British Museum. Now it seems to me that I may as well employ it for an equally useful purpose while I live, and enjoy myself in the bargain, thus killing two birds with one stone. Miss Amelia B. Edwards has formed a society for the exploration of Egyptian antiquities; I shall do the same. I wish to hire you as my archaeological expert. There is only one condition. . . ."

I had to stop for breath. This was more difficult than I had anticipated.

"Yes?" said Emerson in a strange voice. "What condition?"

I drew a deep breath.

"I insist upon being allowed to participate in the excavations. After all, why should men have all the fun?"

"Fun?" Emerson repeated. "To be burned by the sun, rubbed raw by sand, live on rations no self-respecting beggar would eat; to be bitten by snakes and mashed by falling rocks? Your definition of pleasure, Peabody, is extremely peculiar."

"Peculiar or not, it *is* my idea of pleasure. Why, why else do you lead this life if you don't enjoy it? Don't talk of duty to me; you men always have some high-sounding excuse for indulging yourselves. You go gallivanting over the earth, climbing mountains, looking for the sources of the Nile; and expect women to sit dully at home embroidering. I embroider very badly. I think I would excavate rather well. If you like, I will list my qualifications—"

"No," said Emerson, in a strangled voice. "I am only too well aware of your qualifications."

And he caught me in an embrace that bruised my ribs.

"Stop it," I said, pushing at him. "That was not at all what I had in mind. Stop it, Emerson, you are confusing me. I don't want—"

"Don't you?" said Emerson, taking my chin in his hand and turning my face toward his.

"Yes!" I cried, and flung my arms around his neck.

A good while later, Emerson remarked,

"You realize, Peabody, that I accept your offer of marriage because it is the only practical way of getting at your money? You couldn't join me in an excavation unless we were married; every European in Egypt, from Baring to Maspero, would be outraged, and Mme. Maspero would force her husband to cancel my concession."

"I fully understand that," I said. "Now if you will stop squeezing me quite so hard. . . . I cannot breathe."

"Breathing is unnecessary," said Emerson.

After another interval, it was my turn to comment.

"And you," I said, "understand that *I* accept *your* proposal of marriage because it is the only way in which I can gain my ends. It is so unfair—another example of how women are discriminated against. What a pity I was not born a hundred years from now! Then I would not have to marry a loud, arrogant, rude man in order to be allowed to excavate."

Emerson squeezed my ribs again and I had to stop for lack of breath.

"I have found the perfect way of silencing you," he said.

But then the laughter fled from his face and his eyes took on an expression that made me feel very odd—as if my interior organs had dissolved into a shapeless, sticky mass.

"Peabody, you may as well hear the truth. I am mad about you!

Since the day you walked into my tomb and started ordering us all about, I have known you were the only woman for me. Why do you suppose I have sulked and avoided you since we left Amarna? I was contemplating a life without you—a bleak, gray existence, without your voice scolding me and your big bright eyes scowling at me, and your magnificent figure—has no one told you about your figure, Peabody?—striding up and down prying into all sorts of places where you had no business to be. . . . I knew I couldn't endure it! If you hadn't spoken tonight, I should have borrowed Alberto's mummy costume and carried you off into the desert! There, I have said it. You have stripped away my defenses. Are you satisfied with your victory?"

I did not reply in words, but I think my answer was satisfactory. When Emerson had regained his breath he let out a great hearty laugh.

"Archaeology is a fascinating pursuit, but, after all, one cannot work day and night. . . . Peabody, my darling Peabody—what a perfectly splendid time we are going to have!"

Emerson was right—as he usually is. We *have* had a splendid time. We mean to work at Gizeh next year. There is a good deal to be done here yet, but for certain practical reasons we prefer to be nearer Cairo. I understand that Petrie wants to work here, and he is one of the few excavators to whom Emerson would consider yielding. Not that the two of them get along; when we met Mr. Petrie in London last year, he and Emerson started out mutually abusing the Antiquities Department and ended up abusing one another over pottery fragments. Petrie is a nice-looking young fellow, but he really has no idea of what to do with pottery.

The practical reasons that demand we work near Cairo are the same reasons that keep me here, in my chair, instead of being down below supervising the workers as I usually do. Emerson is being overly cautious; I feel perfectly well. They say that for a woman of my age to have her first child is not always easy, and Emerson is in a perfect jitter of apprehension about the whole thing, but I have no qualms whatever. I do not intend that anything shall go amiss. I planned it carefully, not wanting to interrupt the winter excavation season. I can fit the child in quite nicely between seasons, and be back in Cairo ready for work in November.

We are now awaiting news from Evelyn of the birth of her second child, which is due at any moment. She is already the mother of a fair-haired male child, quite a charming infant, with a propensity for rooting in mud puddles which I am sure he inherited from his archaeological relatives. I am his godmother, so perhaps I am biased about his beauty, intelligence, and charm. But I think I am not.

Walter is not with us this season; he is studying hieroglyphics in England, and promises to be one of the finest scholars of our time. His library at Ellesmere Castle is filled with books and manuscripts, and when we join the younger Emersons there for the summer and early fall each year, he and Emerson spend hours arguing over translations.

Lucas? His present whereabouts are unknown to us. Without the money to support his title he could not live respectably in England. I wanted to prosecute the rascal as he deserved; but Baring dissuaded me. He was very helpful to us when we reached Cairo with our boatload of criminals; and he was present on the momentous occasion when Evelyn opened her boxes and found, among the diaries and books, an envelope containing her grandfather's last, holograph will. This was the final proof of Lucas's villainy; but, as Baring pointed out, a trial would bring unwished-for notoriety on all of us, particularly Evelyn, and Lucas was no longer a danger. He lives precariously, I believe, somewhere on the continent, and if he does not soon drink himself to death, some outraged husband or father will certainly shoot him.

I see Alberto whenever we pass through Cairo. I make a point of doing so. As I warned him once, Egyptian prisons are particularly uncomfortable, and the life does not seem to agree with him at all.

Michael has just rung the bell for lunch, and I see Emerson coming toward me. I have a bone to pick with him; I do not believe he is correct in his identification of one of the sculptured busts as the head of the heretic pharaoh. It seems to me to be a representation of young Tutankhamon, Khuenaten's son-in-law.

I must add one more thing. Often I find myself remembering that blustery day in Rome, when I went to the rescue of a young English girl who had fainted in the Forum. Little did I realize how strangely our destinies would be intertwined; that that act of simple charity would reward me beyond my wildest dreams, winning for me a friend and sister, a life of busy, fascinating work, and. . . .

Evelyn was right. With the right person, under the right circumstances—it is perfectly splendid! ,

Michael B - Egyptian Christian - short, dark _friendly_

Reis Hassan - Capt. of boat. Egyptian

Maspero — French director of antiquities

Brugsch - assistant   "

Walter Emerson

Alberto - Evelyn's former lover

Lucas Hayes - Evelyn's cousin